Nitro Wild

The adventures of a modern man cast onto an alternate earth of early 19th century technology, slavery, and competing colonial empires.

David C. Brown

International Standard Book Nr: 978-0-9831907-9-0
Library of Congress Control Nr:
1 2 3 4 5 6 7 8 9 0
BISAC codes: FICO40000 & FICO28010

Cover Design: David C. Brown
Editing: Molly S. Brown
Cover: Mark R. Hayes
www.DavidCBrownAuthor.com

Previously Published Works:
Concrete Girl
Serendipity Hollow
Gap Hollow
Sandlick Hollow
The Trashman's Daughter
Donnelly's War
Boilermaker
Caroom Raid

♠ Scott Depot, WV ♠

Chapter 1

Rex Knight's large mare required little guidance. Both had traveled this section of the trail along the Southern River dozens of times. The river flowed west out of the mountains that had blocked the western expansion of the Prussian territories. It terminated at River Point on the Erie River, a large south flowing river that originated in the northern ice fields and ended at Port Delta on the ocean.

The Southern River bisected the Wapiti homeland, allowing easy access to the Erie valley and the ocean. A mixed blessing since the waterway also provided an expedient route for marauders to raid and plunder Wapiti villages.

The war-ravaged terrain that the trail passed through was now quiet, the fighting had moved down the Erie valley with the onset of winter. The peacefulness had Rex mulling over what this world lacked compared to Earth. The list was sizeable. On this bitter cold late afternoon, with a dusting of snow already falling, he decided electricity.

Wood fires had lost their charm. There was no gas-powered chainsaw to cut the logs. To the person who has to cut, drag, and split the logs by hand, a wood fire represented hard work. Yes, he missed the convenience of heat pumps and gas furnaces that electricity made possible.

That modern world had vanished, gone without a moment's warning. It was the strangest thing. On that fateful day, he had been surveying, staking out the driveway to reach a new house site on a ridge overlooking Charleston. The complication was laying out the new drive to bypass a large sandstone boulder the property owner wanted left undisturbed. He was beside the rock when the cold blackness struck.

The boulder was still there when he regained consciousness. It looked the same. The topography of the ridge and valley looked the same. Only the city had vanished. Now, a forest of massive old oak and chestnut trees blanketed the ridge and river valley. He had no idea on what had occurred. Judging by the scorched twisted remains of his Topcon total station, that he had survived was the wonder. Later he had learned the inhabitants called the Earth like planet Erden.

Rex, endeavoring to understand how he had ended up in the alien world, had wondered if time travel might account for his experience after learning that the outpouring of melt water from glaciers fed the mighty Erie River. Similar conditions had occurred in the beginning of Earth's Holocene geological epoch. However, this world's stage of development, guns, colonial empires and steam engines, didn't resemble Earth's at the end of the last ice age. Then flint spear points and caves with wood fires were the advance technology.

The Wapiti language could support either explanation. It was a lingua franca of English and German, languages from Earth, and the indigenous Clovis language. Regardless, the presence of the non-human Ichneumons convinced Rex that he was in an alternate universe, not back in an earlier Earth period. The Wapiti language meant other Earthlings in the past had been teleported and survived.

The mare stopped, snapping his thoughts back to the present. He looked about, realizing his awareness had plummeted. If he wanted to remain alive in this harsh frontier world, he'd best not let woolgathering become a habit. Off to his right was Matt Brewer's burned-out horse stables and smithy, a victim of an Ichneumon raiding party out of Delta. The ruins meant the crossroad was near.

He would leave the Prussians at that intersection, his obligations to the Wapiti council concluded. While the officers continued east, he would turn south and cross the frozen river to check on his partner, Amy Caroom.

The prior evening the Wapiti Chiefs Council had convened an assembly at the River Point fort. The Wapiti people were an amalgamation of the aboriginal tribes, fugitives from the London uprising, Prussian adventurers, and escaped slaves. Even a few Ichneumons lived there. They considered the land west of the mountains to the Erie River their land.

The meeting was to decide whether to meet the Prussian Empire demand that they relinquish control of the former Ichneumon stronghold at River Point. The council members had been hesitant. Every Wapiti knew the world straddling empire had conducted a brutal colonization in the land east of the mountains a century earlier.

The invaders had enslaved the indigenous people and swept away their culture. The Wapiti had avoided a similar fate because the rugged mountainous terrain had frustrated the colonial migration and allowed them time to develop a defense. A low intensity war had simmered for years between the Wapiti and brigands seeking slaves for the eastern plantations. The defeat of the warlord, James Donnelly ended that. Now a new enemy threatened that made the Prussians seem almost benign.

The Ichneumon Empire that ruled the southern continent had spread north and entered the Erie River about fifty years ago. The invaders had constructed a series of forts to support their traders. The locals called the Ichneumons 'blue bloods', not because they were upper-class aristocrats, but because their blood was blue like a crustacean's.

For years, the Ichneumon traders' main interest was buying furs and the popular stimulant, winter-sole nuts. Than two years ago, without warning, their army had raided the Southern River valley. They murdered hundreds of Wapiti, and enslaved many young men and women for use in their revolting religious practice that required living sacrifices.

The Wapiti warriors had, after the initial surprise, recovered and defeated the raiders, seized the small Ichneumon fort at River Point, and captured Emperor Ratakonda's heir, Prince Cherukuru. The emperor had paid a large ransom for the prince's release.

Rex had later been shocked to learn the extent of Ratakonda's distain for him over his involvement in the affair. The Ichneumon emperor had posted throughout the Erie River, a 50,000 D-Mark bounty for Rex, dead or alive. In hindsight, he should have just shot the prince.

The steamboat owners, such as Rex, had contacts-spies at every port. He learned Ratakonda had ordered the reinforcement of his river garrisons. His informants told him another Ichneumon invasion of the Wapiti homeland was certain in the spring. That the action might precipitate a wider war with the Prussian Empire did not appear to concern the emperor.

Matt and Colonel Fritz Caprivi, both friends of Rex, joined him at the trail intersection. The Prussian colonels who had negotiated with the council would continue on to Salt Furnace, the Wapiti capital. From there, they would cross the mountains to New Hamburg and catch one of those new steamships starting to displace the clipper ships that had dominated the oceanic trade.

Rex didn't envy them, crossing the mountains in winter was hazardous, but the winter ocean crossing to Prussia was the dangerous business. The new ocean going paddle wheelers had a distressing tendency to vanish without a trace, between exploding boilers, collisions with icebergs, and violent storms.

"We need to keep moving, Fredrick," Fritz said to Colonel Leibinger who had followed him into the intersection with Larry Hopkins.

"When you two get back, tell the emperor that they need to strike first," Matt said to the colonels, renewing last night's squabble.

An older man of mixed Clovis and Prussian ancestry, Matt considered himself, as did most of the residents along the Southern River, a Wapiti. He was the former commander of the fort. The old warrior had a full-untrimmed gray beard, long hair, a barrel chest, and massive arms. His occupation before the invasion had been raising and trading horses. During the winter months, he supplemented his income by trapping bears, foxes, and minks for their pelts. Rex figured his voluble dogmatic friend would return to that trade.

"I believe in leaving military strategy to the general staff," Leibinger said, in no mood for advice from the shaggy frontier hunter.

Colonel Leibinger, a first cousin of the Prussian emperor, had been on a fact-finding tour of the Erie valley and territories. Tall and slim, the aristocrat was a handsome urbane thirty year old who appeared ill at ease in the rough frontier. Rex could sympathize, who likes fleas and reeking outhouses.

"Well that's fine, if it includes throwing those cerulean devils out of the fort at Hickory Ridge, otherwise the Erie River will remain closed to non-Ichneumon traffic," Matt said, ignoring the colonel's standoffish response. "Tell the emperor that, along with keeping your promise to have the ban on gun sales voided."

"I agree with the colonel," Rex injected. The colonel was a confidant of the emperor and he needed to leave with a good opinion of the Wapiti, not irritated by his friend's unsolicited and unappreciated advice. "Besides, the fort is no longer our responsibility."

Leibinger nodded in agreement. Matt, not agreeing, shook his head, and said no more. His concern was understandable. The subject on everyone's mind, except perhaps the colonel's, was the looming Ichneumon threat. Come spring, when the river ice cleared, the war would resume.

The colonels departed with their entourage. Their mission was to appraise the Prussian General Staff in Berlin of the negotiated terms.

"Is Larry coming right back after delivering the Prussians?" Rex asked. With the intersection to themselves, they had decided to have a brief visit before parting.

"I figure our young friend will manage a delay in Roanoke for a few days," Matt said. "Remember, Jenny Jarrell, is a student at the university."

"That's right; she's there at the medical school. Well, I wish him luck getting past those Jesuit proctors guarding the female students. At least with the rivers frozen we should have a bit of peace until spring."

"Ice won't stop those bastards trying to collect the reward."

Rex agreed, but figured Amy was safe in Smithtown.

"Has your lovely witch made any progress on that clean-burning gunpowder?"

"Please, don't even tease about witches. I don't want some zealous Jesuit seizing her for questioning."

He knew his friend meant no harm, still on Erden, best be cautious.

Amy Caroom was her name, comely of countenance, striking of person and of manner poised and intelligent. Rex loved the managing woman. Whether she did him, he wasn't certain, but took solace in the fact she had invited him to share her bed.

"She's optimistic she can make a better gunpowder, but needs ether to finish whatever she was trying."

"Ether," Matt started asking as three Prussian cavalrymen galloped into the intersection. Instead, he said to the officer, a friend, "I'd thought you would have stayed in your cozy fort."

"Are they already gone?" Captain Beck asked, looking about.

They both nodded. The captain commanded the respect of the two men for the enlighten way he treated the men under his command and the Wapiti. Vexed at having missed the colonels, he explained.

"Two of those new guards are missing. Ten arrived with the colonels, eight answered roll call."

"Other than the colonels, everyone else was a Wapiti warrior," Matt said. "I know all of them, there was no Prussian trooper or guard."

"Well, hell, I was hoping it was a misunderstanding and the soldiers thought they were to return with the colonels," Captain

Beck said looking perplexed. "They must have found a bottle or a whore."

With that, the big Prussian officer, with his escort following, rode back towards the fort at River Point. The wind and snow flurries had started again.

"See you in the spring," Matt said and headed up the north trail toward his farm.

Rex, alert for sounds of cracking, walked his horse, Zack, on to the river ice. They needed to cross the frozen Southern River to reach Smithtown where his crew was assembling the heavy lathe and milling machine stolen from Purnell's Orleans Boatyard. After that, he'd head to the cabin and Amy. The bullet changed his plans.

Amy Caroom was running late. She wanted to complete the experiment before Rex got home, but had run short of sulfuric acid. The ratio of sulfuric and nitric acids was critical, so she needed more sulfuric acid, which required a trip to the foundry. She had intended a quick trip, it was a half kilometer away, but the men assembling the milling machine had several questions for her.

The foray for the acid had delayed her an hour, but now the mixture was correct. Were those gunshots? Amy glanced towards Hokee, Rex's domesticated wolf. The sleek gray animal curled up on the floor by the fireplace was alert, looking towards the door. It was an awkward moment for an interruption. She had just poured the glycerin into her precious 500 ml glass beaker, but hadn't added it to the acid. If she had, then the safe option would have been to complete the experiment.

Two more distance gunshots, and a moment later the foundry bell started ringing, that decided the matter for her. She put down the beaker and grabbed her heavy fur parka and revolver. By then Hokee was at the door, growling, as she opened it.

Lance Corporal Stosh and Senior Gunner Lucjan had long discussed deserting the army and joining the western gold rush. Their unit's assignment to River Point had pleased them. It offered them a realistic chance of accomplishing that goal. They could stowaway on one of the river boats headed to Westport, located at the confluence of the Erie and Great Western River. There, they could join the migration headed up the Great Western to the gold fields and make their fortune.

However, in Roanoke, they learned the war between the empires had closed traffic on the Erie along with tales of a ten-thousand D-Mark reward for the head of a woman rumored to live near River Point.

"It's real," the gunner said to his doubtful partner, "That rich railroad owner, Purnell, posted the reward for his escaped slave. Everyone is talking about it. Len Ruffner, who operated the trading post at Narrows, is his agent. Bring him her head and he'll pay the reward."

"The guy must be nuts to pay that for a dead slave," the corporal said. "Besides how would this agent know it was the right woman?"

"It's real and Ruffner knows the woman according to Louis."

"Which Louis?"

"The bartender at the Yard, you know him."

Stosh did know the man. He was a loan shark from Berlin that had hired them to help him collect past due payments, until the Berlin police forced him to flee. With that quality endorsement, they had then asked around various Roanoke watering holes about Purnell and Ruffner. The responses satisfied them the reward offer was real by the time their unit embarked for River Point and they knew the woman's name, Caroom.

At River Point, they had met Rex Knight, the woman's man, husband, guard. They weren't clear on the relationship. What the aspiring bounty hunters were clear on, after listening to local talk, they might not live to enjoy their reward with her man alive.

Careful thought wasn't a strong element in those two as they zeroed in on a solution to an avenging spouse. Just bushwhack her man first, they decided. Lucjan was the superior marksman of the two. He would wait and ambush Knight at the river crossing to Smithtown while his partner crossed the river and collected the head.

"Will the snow interfere?" A worried Stosh asked.

They were on the riverbank looking across the frozen ice. Beating the meeting attendees to the intersection and the trip to Narrows had required horses, which neither of them owned. They borrowed two horses from the fort's stable, but that had created a new problem.

"What if Knight slips by in a heavy snow squall? You don't see him."

"I'm not worried about that. A dozen horses, I'll hear them," Lucjan said, looking about. "What I don't see is a good place to hide my horse. If they hear or spot it, they will wonder whose it is."

"Good point, I'll take it with me across the river and hitch it to a tree. You can follow the tracks in the snow to find it."

"That'll work. Is your bayonet razor sharp? Remember, cutting off a head, even a woman's, is not easy."

"Yeah, I know. I have an axe if needed. Remember, I was there on the Volga with Colonel Peiper."

"Oh man that wall of heads was gruesome. You were involved. What were there, a thousand?"

"I never counted them, but there were a lot. The general raised a royal stink over it, abuse of prisoners or some such nonsense. I never could figure why the uproar, for they were just Mongols," Stosh said shaking his head at the foolishness of the general staff. He added, "Don't miss that Wapiti bastard. I don't want him surprising me."

Stosh didn't trust ice on a river. The currents could form thin spots. Listening for sounds of cracking, he crossed the river, taking both horses. The blowing snow would later help obscure their tracks, but he worried it might obscured his partner's vision as he looked back across the wide frozen river.

After a short distance from where he'd tied off Lucjan's horse to a small hickory tree, he detected a faint whiff of wood smoke. Caroom's place was near. A few minutes later, the orange glow from several windows openings materialized out of the darkness. A rudimentary three-room wooden cabin loomed in front of him and he pulled his bayonet free. Then several gunshots from the river rang out, causing him to pause.

Some of the reports were from a high-powered rifle, and some sounded like shots from a revolver. Did Lucjan miss with his first shot? Then two more rapid gunshots and a nearby bell started ringing. So much for stealth, he rushed the cabin door. To his surprised the door opened just as he reared back to kick it. Instead of a stout door, his kick connected with a gray wolf leaping at him. It had been beside the woman who had opened the door. The lucky kick knocked the wolf to the side and he pivot to deal the stunned animal a lethal slash.

"No," the woman screamed.

The shot had come from the north river bank near the trail intersection. Rex, laying exposed in the middle of the river, was about a hundred meters from either shore. The pockets of snow swirling about the surface made visibility poor and offered him some protection, if he stayed down.

The bullet had hit the leather rein Rex had been holding to lead the horse across the frozen river, nicking his right thumb. The sudden snap of the rein had confused the big mare. The horse had stopped beside him, puzzled.

Another bullet hit in front of Rex and ricocheted between him and Zack, spraying them with ice particles, causing the horse to neigh and move off a couple of steps.

The whitish smoke from the black gunpowder used on Erden normally marked the location of a sniper, but not in a snowstorm. Still Rex thought he'd detected an instant before the boom of the shoot, a hint of a red flash from a small evergreen on the riverbank. He emptied his revolver at the location of the flash. The distance was too far for a revolver to be accurate, but the shower of slugs would occupy the sniper for a moment, and one could always hope for a lucky hit.

Another bullet zinged by his ear as he reloaded the revolver while laying as flat as possible. Two rapid shotgun blasts and Matt's holler stopped Rex from fleeing on Zack, the thin ice be damn. Instead, he jogged back to the riverbank with the horse following.

"Man, you're a lousy shot," Matt said. "I feared you'd hit me instead of him." He pointed at the man, in a white Wehrmacht winter uniform, lying dead behind the small scrub pine.

"Who is the bastard," Rex said, rolling the dead man over for a better look. The sniper's fatal wound, a ripped opening in the skull, was from a shotgun loaded with heavy lead shot fired at close quarter. Neither man recognized the solider.

"Must be the missing guard Beck was looking for."

"Why would he be gunning for you?" His friend asked, gathering up the man's rifle and petting Zack's muzzle. The horse had nudged in for a look.

"Beck said there were two missing. . ." Rex said looking across the frozen river. Always in the back of his mind was the awareness that a day of reckoning would come with Amy's father, Benjamin Purnell. He had thought they were safe for the moment in the Wapiti territory and the threat would come with the spring thaw. When the Ichneumon war would flare up and the assassins would renew their hunt.

"I'm going to check on her."

Rex's crew had constructed the building toward which they were galloping. Amy and he called it home. The walls were of rough-cut lumber, the floor of red oak planks smoothed with a hand planer, and a shake roof. A large stone fireplace formed one wall of the structure and its fires kept the cold at bay from frigid air that leaked through the clay caulked wall and floor joints every time the wind blew.

Hearing a gunshot from the direction of the cabin, he urged Zack forward. A minute later he could see the cabin door was open, allowing the glow from the interior lanterns to spill out and illuminate Amy kneeling over a body.

"Are you hurt," he shouted while leaping from the horse. He noticed Hokee a few meters away from her. The dazed wolf had a bloody head wound.

Matt arrived a moment later, dismounted and went to check the soldier's condition as Rex pulled Amy into his arms. After a pause to collect herself, she told them about opening the door to run to the foundry, and instead, encountered a Prussian soldier who attacked her.

"Hokee saved me. Then I couldn't react fast enough to save him," Amy said, stepping away and kneeling to comfort the collapsed wolf.

"Whoever he was, he's dead," Matt said and then gathered up Hokee while Rex helped Amy to her feet.

Under her guidance, he carried the wounded animal into the cabin while Rex addressed the several men from the foundry who had rushed over to learn what had occurred. He put the men to work rounding up the horses and putting them in the stable by the foundry, other than Matt's horse, which remained by the dead soldier.

The clean whitish light that greeted them on entering the humble adobe was thanks to Amy, who liked lots of light. When she discovered incandescent gas mantle lamps in the Delta market, she had to have them.

"The blade hit the skull bone," Matt said. The bright light had allowed him to make a careful examination of Hokee's wound. "A few cementers back and the blow might have severed the spine."

"Will he recover?" She asked while adjusting the unconscious wolf's body to lay on its favorite spot near the fireplace after Matt completed stitching together the cut.

The old horse trader, who all acknowledged had a healing touch with animals, was optimistic the wolf would recover.

"But animals are their own worst enemy with wounds," he cautioned. "Don't let him dig at the wound."

"Matt, it's been a long day for you, but you need to take those two bodies to Captain Beck and explain what happen. The foundry crew is waiting to help. I need to stay here."

The hunter nodded in understanding as they both glanced toward Amy kneeing by the wolf.

"Matt, thanks for everything. Tell the captain I had no choice," she said looking up from smoothing Hokee's fur.

Chapter 2

Rex hung up Amy's parka and his heavy coat on hooks near the fireplace where the melting snow wouldn't drip on the wolf. After everyone had left, she broke the silence.

"I reuse to live in fear, wondering if every stranger is an assassin." She stood up and added, "We are going to end this murderous business."

He was all for that, but to date a realistic solution had eluded him. "Short of killing your father, what are you thinking?"

"What happen to your hand?"

"Something snagged it. It's nothing."

"That's what those first gunshots were about." She studied him for a moment before adding. "There was another soldier, assassin, who tried to kill you, wasn't there? It wasn't just me." He shook his head.

"I'm not sure. They may have feared I'd find them before they could collect the reward."

"He could have been after the emperor's reward. Damn, why didn't you kill that monster when you had a chance?"

She had decided that tonight's attempt on his life was due to his rough treatment of the Ichneumon prince. He didn't agree, but didn't argue.

"Ratakonda would have welcomed being rid of that moron as his successor," Amy added. "Now to save face, he's obligated to support the prince's vendetta."

"He's alive because I needed the bastard alive to rescue those Wapiti slaves at Bone Valley," Rex said sharper than intended, "Plus the council wanted that ransom, two-million in gold."

"Two-million. . . I didn't know," Amy said. She then hugged him, adding, "Well, what's another assassin after us. We'll just have to be extra careful until the Prussians have kicked those creatures out of the valley and I kill Purnell."

Amy's father had hung her mother and sister and she intended, justified in Rex's opinion, lethal vengeance. Tonight's attempt on her life proved her father hadn't mellowed. Despite her defiant words, she sounded troubled. He kissed her and then, instead of voicing his opinion that the sniper team was after the reward on her, changed the subject.

"What were you working on?" Not dinner he hoped.

"Nitroleum," Amy said, giving his hand a quick check before returning to the heavy wooden workbench he had made. Seeing his puzzled look, she added.

"I don't want any more moments like this evening. To survive, we're going to need something to convince the Prussians we're more valuable to them, than my treacherous father is. Something like this," she said, picking up a clear glass beaker full of a colorless oily liquid that she poured into a four-liter earthenware jar, while stirring the mixture.

Rex was startled to realize her beaker looked identical to the ones he had used in the WVU chemistry lab. What did that signify? And what was the colorless oily liquid? Lamp fuel, kerosene, had a straw color.

The earthenware jar that received her beaker's liquid sat inside the large iron cauldron used for making soap. Whatever mystery his sweetheart was formulating, the process required cooling. This evening, the soap kettle served as a container for the ice water packed around the earthenware jar. Behind her on the floor was one of those large stoneware crocks used for making sauerkraut. It was half-full of more water and ice.

The sharp acid smell he'd noticed on entering the cabin appeared to come from the dark liquid she was stirring. Unlike some of her concoctions that fumed and bubbled, the liquid appeared to be a benign dark oily liquid.

Amy stopped stirring and watched the liquid for a moment. Satisfied, she laid her long handle wooden spoon across the earthen jar, and then hugged him as he came over for a better look. Her head fit comfortably under his chin and as they embraced, he enjoyed her clean smell.

Rex was a head taller than most men, which made Amy tall for a female. Her mother had been a native from one of the Gulf islands and she shared the race's characteristic angular cheek structure, high forehead, and dark hair. She had dark brown eyes, instead of the more typical green eyes of the Wapitis, and a light olive skin tone. Whatever her ancestry, Rex thought her a beautiful woman with an attractive lithe physique.

"Are the Prussians now our protectors?"

He shrugged. "Well, at least they have charge of River Point." Glad she seemed calmer now, he added, "So what are you making?"

She stepped away from the hug and pointed at the kettle. "It needs to set for a bit, and then I'll need your help to pour it in the crock."

"Okay, but what is it?" Rex asked. She tended to tune out people around her when concentrating on a problem.

"Here, set this on the table," she said, handing him the glass beaker, while focused on the dark acid smelling water. She then picked up her wood spoon and gently swirl the liquid for another minute. It was looking more like oil.

Rex sniffed the residue in the glass jar. The liquid had no noticeable odor and he placed the jar on the table.

"Use that ladle to start transferring the oil in the jar to that," Amy said, using her wooden spoon to point at the sauerkraut crock half-full of ice and water. "I'll stir as you pour. Be careful. Don't splash or spill the liquid."

Whatever the yellowish oil was, it sank, instead of floating as Rex had expected. Amy slowly stirred the icy mixture as he added the oil to the crock. She told him to put the lid on the two-liter earthenware jar, once he'd removed all the oil, she would clean it later.

"So what are you making?" Rex asked again, getting worried.

"It should be explosive, but I'm not sure how powerful," she said while stirring the mixture.

Rex again inspected the clear oily liquid in the glass he had set on the table.

"Is this glycerin?" he asked, rubbing a little of the oil between his fingers. She nodded.

"Was that nitric acid you were mixing the glycerin in?" he asked, now concerned.

"It was more sulfuric acid than nitric, why do you ask?" Amy asked still focused on the slow stirring.

Oh Lord, Rex thought, she has gone and made nitroglycerine. On Earth, most everyone knew nitro was a dangerous and treacherous explosive, but here it appeared to be a laboratory curiosity. If he admits knowing anything about it, she'll want to know how he knows. But could he afford not to say something of the danger. Nitroglycerine is shock sensitive and doesn't behave like black powder. He racked his memory on what he had read and learned in the U. S. Army.

Pure nitroglycerine was stable, but if it is sour and impure, it had the distressing habit, like poor quality guncotton, to spontaneous decomposition. And with the crude chemicals that Amy had to work with, how could it be pure?

"Is it safe?" he asked, stalling, not sure what to reveal.

Rex Knight's experience from the Afghan War had helped him survive in those initial days after being mysteriously teleported from a peaceful Charleston to a semi-lawless frontier of an alternate world of Civil War era technology, slavery, and competing colonial empires. He soon realized that a person without resources could be in trouble.

Punch mining was a side business of a few Wapiti farmers who had exposed minable coal seams on their land. The growing steamboat traffic on the massive Erie River that split the continent had created an increase demand for coal. Rex knew the industry from Earth and he started a local brokering business to sell the farmers' coal.

The other brokering opportunity Rex got involved in was the valuable winter-sloe nuts that many Wapiti gathered in the fall. They made Rex aware of Chief Cinnabar, a vile warlord who had a fort up remote Panther Creek. The thug operated cruel slave camps that provided the labor to collect and process the nuts. If Cinnabar hadn't started raiding Wapiti villages for slaves and killing coal miners, he might have never been aware of him. But the madman did.

Rex and the Wapitis raided Cinnabar's fort and arrested him. During the raid, he met Purnell's chemist, Amy Caroom, the lady making nitroglycerine in their kitchen.

"It's an experiment," Amy said. "I'm not sure what to expect, that why I made a small amount." She had stopped stirring and started decanting off the water with a ladle to reach the oily liquid at the bottom.

Rex made a decision as he watched Amy pour the last of the yellowish oil in two glass pickle jars. Her small amount had made about a liter of the oily material. It might seem a modest amount, but it was enough nitroglycerine to blow them, Hokee, and the cabin to pieces.

"Sweetheart, put a tiny drop of your oil on the anvil." He picked up the heavy iron maul used to split firewood. A puzzled Amy complied with his request.

"Now step into the kitchen and don't drop that container, he cautioned, "There may be a loud bang."

He swung the iron maul, hitting the drop. It detonated with a sharp bang and enough force to cause the heavy hammer to fly up, nearly jerking it from his grip. Hokee even opened his eyes for a moment. A startled Amy placed the jar on the kitchen table.

"How did you know it would do that?" She asked, walking over to the checked the anvil surface for damage. "It hardly marred the anvil."

"Gunpowder does the same thing," Rex said. "I thought it would be a quick check to see if your oil was explosive. It's shock sensitive. If a tiny drop did that, don't let that jar fall."

Amy looked toward the table, and satisfied the container was in no danger of being disturbed, asked.

"Is it stable? Will it spontaneously explode?"

"It sure the hell could. It's like guncotton. The unreacted acid can generate unstable compounds," he said, his voice rising. "You ought to not make any more."

Silence greeted Rex's outburst. Then Amy, sounding tense, asked, "How do you know all that?"

Rats, now she's wondering how a fisherman could be aware of guncotton's nasty behavior. His concern for Amy's safety had caused him to forget he shouldn't know about things not yet known here.

A loquacious Wapiti warrior, Scott Belcher, without realizing it, had made him aware that the Royal Prussian Church was a danger. The church considered anyone claiming to be from another world crazy or a devil and a threat to their dogma. The church calls such unfortunate souls false prophets and pays a handsome reward for their capture. Then after interrogation, the church burns them. Rex figured that explained why the Jesuits were often the source of new scientific discoveries and devices in the Prussian Empire.

Rex didn't want to attract the interest of a zealous Jesuit. To explain his presence, he had been vague at first, until Scott asked him if he was a cod fisherman. The question had puzzled him until the warrior explained that he reminded him of the heretics, the large blond haired nomads that the Royal Prussian Church often sent missionaries to save. Most of the nomads were hardworking cod fishermen, but some became vicious marauders, pirates. They lived on the edge of the northern ice fields, the most remote and uncivilized area on Erden.

What the fish looked like, or how one caught them, Rex hadn't a clue, still a fisherman he became. To explain being in the Wapiti homeland, he claimed his mother had been a Wapiti sold as a slave to Greek traders who later sold her to his father, a cod fisherman. He told Scott that he was searching for his mother's family.

Rex reckoned few people believed his tale since he was a head taller than most Wapiti and had a light complexion and blond hair compared to the Wapiti's darker coloration and dark brown hair. Most Wapiti had probably figured he was a deserter hiding from the Prussian army.

What was that name she had used for nitroglycerine?

"Whale hunters use, ah, nitroleum to make their harpoon points explode," Rex said. *Lord, where had that thought originate?* "It's considered very dangerous."

"You're telling me cod fishermen make and use nitroleum?" A very skeptical Amy asked.

"Well, no not them, the Greeks. They're the whale hunters. Their crews told us about the exploding oil," Rex said, hedging.

"Such astuteness, to understand how to nitrate organics long before the professors at Heidelberg University," Amy said. "I don't for a moment believe your nonsense about genius Greek whale hunters."

Rex wasn't sure if he should attempt to convince her, or ignore her challenge, when she added,

"I always did think the Prussian army knew more about explosives than those professors."

Amy kissed him. "Relax sweetheart, your secret is safe."

What secret of his was safe? Did she think he was a deserter from a secret Prussian Army research center?

"How'd you learn to make nitroleum?" He asked to get her off his history.

"At Heidelberg University," Amy said. "I worked in the lab where Professor Vielle was trying to make a smokeless gunpowder. He was nitrating different organic compounds and discovered picric acid."

"Did he ever try nitrating toluene?" Rex asked, remembering too late to quite displaying his knowledge of chemistry.

"Professor Vielle talked about it and thought it might yield an explosive," Amy said. "But, my father ordered me home to Orleans before those nitrating experiments started. Later I learned there had been a dreadful explosion in Professor Vielle's lab, killing him, Professor Kopp, and three students. No one knew what the group had been working on at the time."

"Maybe nitroleum," he asked while thinking it was fortunate the bastard had order her home, otherwise she might have been blown up with the lab.

"Or he was nitrating toluene. No one from Kopp's group survived. The explosion destroyed Vielle's notes and laboratory in the east wing of Heidelberg University's main chemistry building."

"That's why you need to be careful. Some chemicals are prone to exothermic reactions."

Amy was studying him again. He must watch what he says around her. Having nitroglycerine concocted in their kitchen must have distressed him more that he realized. He considered telling her the truth, but feared she might think him insane. Better, she thought him a deserter.

"That's why I used the ice water baths," she said and walked over to check on the wolf. After another worried glance toward the container of yellowish oil, she asked, smiling.

"Did those Greek whale hunters happen to say how they made their harpoon oil stable?"

Emperor Wolfgang Schnabel needed an heir. Should he die before accomplishing that happy event, Duke Rudolf Habsburg would be his successor. The empire didn't need that buffoon in charge, which meant he needed to find a wife. He'd been considering General Guderian's niece, Franciscka Weidman. They rubbed well together, she had the proper breeding, and he knew she was an outspoken opponent of slavery. He'd talk to her father.

The slavery issue threatened the stability of the Prussian empire. Schnabel now realized he had not handled a contentious matter well. Trying to do right, he had created what the cotton plantation owners considered an existential threat to their way of life.

Cotton growing in the Prussian territories started soon after the land's discovery over two centuries ago. The innumerable hectares of fertile soil, along with the favorable weather that existed in Myrtle and Guderian territories had attracted an influx of Prussians seeking land and opportunities. Their invasion overwhelmed the indigenous Clovis tribes. The cotton growers enslaved the survivors to provide labor for the explosion of plantations dedicated to growing cotton for the flourishing Hamburg and Berlin mills.

The snag for the cotton agribusiness was its profitability dependence on cheap and plentiful labor, slaves. The native Clovis population, devastated by war, smallpox, and other eastern diseases, was insufficient to meet labor needs. The plantation owners then hired frontier warlords to raid farms and Wapiti settlements on the western slopes of the mountains for slaves. Capturing Wapiti and Clovis slaves in the western wilderness proved to be a hazardous business and the warlords couldn't supply the number of slaves needed. The cotton growers turned to foreign slavers.

Zamia had the needed slaves, but they were located across an ocean and expensive. As a result, slaves of any ancestry became scarce and expensive as the cotton business grew in the territories. To guarantee a steady source of laborers, the larger Myrtle plantation owners began in the last century, the heartless business of breeding people to be slaves. The myopic fools had given little, if any thought to the dismal results to expect from the rampant consanguineous fornication occurring in those horror pens. Nothing good could result from an operation that forced fathers, mothers, sons, daughters, and siblings to breed indiscriminately.

Wolfgang's other irritation was the church and Jesuits unwillingness to condemn slavery outright. It perplexed him. Bishop von Bingen's failure even to censure those plantation owners with breeding pens exasperated him. The church's attitude reflected the continued obstinate indifference of the Prussian landed gentry to the threat slavery posed to the empire. Couldn't the upper class, his peers, see the iniquity in a culture that considered some people little better than subhuman savages?

Emperor Wolfgang Schnabel had heard all the arguments the proponents of slavery claimed to justify treating the Zamians and Cloves people like livestock. He thought their assertions disingenuous. The alleged uncivilized behavior of the Zamians and Clovis he believed reflected a difference in beliefs, not a lack of humanity.

Did the advocates of slavery comprehend that a slave economy survival depended on strict segregation laws, curfews, travel restrictions, enforced illiteracy, and heartless overseers and that the result would be an inhospitable society of prisoners and guards. That was not the vision Emperor Schnabel had for the Prussian Empire.

Pay the workers, he had told the plantation owners that visited him in Berlin, let the labor market determine whether a man chose to pick cotton or work at another occupation. The audiences ignored his message. Weary of trying to persuade the plantation owners to his view, he decided to try Duke Soltzendorff's suggestion. He issued a decree outlawing slavery in the Prussian empire.

The cotton growers ignored the decree. Two years later, most of the territories' plantations still ran slave breeding pens, traded, and used slaves. Their attitude he now understood. His antislavery decree would end their century old way of life. Regardless slavery was going to end.

Emperor Schnabel was well aware that an emperor who allowed his subjects to ignore imperial decrees risked having his reign ended tragically. One good from the slavery fiasco, he had come to realize the empire's bureaus were awash with incompetent, even corrupt, administrators. A problem he intended to address along with the plantation owners defiance. He'd start with a visit to the Prussian General Staff office and told his adjunct to have the yellow carriage brought around.

Chapter 3

The emperor's visit to the army headquarters changed many lives, including Victor Ludendorff's, a new mechanical engineer from Plön Academy. He had received an offer from the Berlin Baltic Railroad, on graduation, for a position supervising the locomotive maintenance shop. He wasn't quite ready to settle and wanted a bit of adventure first. Having taken the army officer-training course and the summer of basic combat training, Victor had satisfied all the requirements to be an army lieutenant. On graduation, he accepted the commission and signed on for three years active duty. His father had been proud of his choice.

The army assigned Victor, along with an eight-man squad from the 88th Mountaineer Brigade, to Port Augusta Customs, a branch of the Imperial Revenue Service. The assignment had pleased him. The ocean voyage to reach Augusta hadn't. After pausing to enjoy the feel of solid ground, Victor sent Feldwebel Prittwitz and his squad to locate the barrack and horses assigned to them. The men had brought their saddles, clothing, boots, and personal items along with their weapons from Prussia, but no horses. While the feldwebel was accomplishing that, Victor reported to his new commander, Lieutenant Colonel Jagger.

Augusta was the location of the Myrtle Territory government and a port with a bustling market and dock area. Available for export was a cornucopia of pecans, peanuts, corn, beans, rice, tobacco, white clay, turpentine, cotton, and lumber. The all-important export business required the plantation owners spent time in town. As a result, many of them had built second mansions in the city, which their families used during visits and the winter social season. Those lavish parties, dances, and dinners accounted for Augusta's reputation as a place for a young never married army officer to find a beautiful, wealthy bride. Victor intended to attend every social event he could wrangle an invitation for in order to check out the women.

The Port Augusta customs unit was located in a three-story red brick building at the rear of the old coastal defense fort overlooking the harbor. A flabby senior feldwebel, his nametag said Ehrisman, had greeted Victor in the front room. After telling him which office to enter, had followed him into the room. It was Jagger's office.

"I'll be damn, Berlin did sent someone," the colonel said, returning Victor's salute.

Colonel Jagger sorted through a crumpled pile of dispatches on his wooden desk, pausing to take a puff from a small black cigar perched on the edge of the desk.

"His orders are in the left bottom draw," Ehrisman said.

The colonel nodded, put the cigar back on the desk's edge and rummaged through the desk draw. Numerous burn markers on the desk's edge testified to past neglected cigars. Victor's new commander was a florid middle-aged flabby man. Neither man inspired confidence.

"Here's the dispatch," the colonel said, then taking a moment to find a pair of grimy reading glasses, he read a moment before adding, "Lieutenant Victor Ludendorff that is you, right?"

Victor snapped out, "Yes sir."

"Your assignment is to enforce the emperor's ban on slavery in Myrtle Territory."

He must have miss heard the colonel. Feldwebel Ehrisman laughed.

"I was under the impression the local sheriffs enforced those laws," Victor said. He knew nothing about Myrtle, cotton plantations, or slaves.

"Obviously, Emperor Schnabel is not satisfied with the sheriffs' performance and sent a lieutenant to remind them of their duty to destroy a hundred year old way of life."

Julian Penton, Count Harlem Penton's spinster sister and the brains behind the Highland Plantation's success, didn't agree with her brother. He believed the emperor's decree was just a rash gesture to placate his vocal liberal friends among the Berlin aristocrats.

"It has been two years," Harlem said. "The foolishness has been forgotten, as I said at the time."

Julian's brother had just celebrated his forty-fifth birthday. A large muscular man of Prussian ancestry, Harlem was the fourth generation of Pentons to be master of the vast Highland Plantation of three thousand hectares and over a thousand slaves. He was a widower, his wife dying during childbirth. Her brother, despite his noble birth, was a manager who enjoyed overseeing the plantation's day-to-day operations and enforcing her instructions to the foremen. He also liked hunting, whiskey, and Zamian wenches.

"Maybe so," Julian said, "But I want to invite the owners of Myrtle Territory's twenty largest plantations for a weekend of festivities and horseracing."

"Racing, now that's a capital idea," her brother said. "I'll enter my new stallion, Diamond, against Duke Soltzendorff's nag. Make some serious money, great idea sister."

"I'm thinking in two weeks, well before spring planting starts," Julian said. Harlem nodded in agreement. "And don't let the betting get out of hand. I don't want the duke upset or any duels."

Julian didn't bother explaining to her brother that she wasn't interested in parties. The carnival atmosphere would provide cover for the organizational meetings she planned to form a new cotton grower association and a secret militia. The goal was to counter the growing abolitionist movement in the coastal areas of Guderian and Myrtle territories. She hoped Harlem's oldest daughter, Susan, an attorney in Augusta with the Myrtle Cotton Bank would help. Lately the girl had been showing a certain sympathy for the enemy.

The prior October, Benjamin Purnell had asked Julian to consider such an assembly. He had promised to attend and outline the steps he thought the plantation owners should take to form an alliance with the Ichneumon Empire, where slavery was legal.

Unfortunately, the Prussians had arrested Benjamin in Orleans and shipped him to Berlin. He was no longer available to help her.

Julian's contacts in the Port Augusta garrison and governor office didn't know why, but Benjamin was involved in many deals and there was no telling which one might have attracted the emperor's ire. Her only exposure was those false navy orders ending the Zamia blockade and Benjamin hadn't been involved with that, only Susan and Archduke Habsburg. If those orders were a problem, the authorities would have already arrested her. She decided to proceed with forming the growers association and a secret militia.

After the fort handover, Matt Brewer had a successful month of trapping. To obtain top price, he had hauled the mountain lion skin, three bear hides, fifteen mink, and forty fox pelts to Roanoke. While there, as was the custom, he had checked at the imperial post office for mail that needed delivered to Salt Furnace and River Point. There were a number of letters and packages for Amy. He delivered them on his return trip along with a hitchhiker, Kit Jacobs.

Kit was the oldest nephew of Bill Jacobs, owner of a large successful group of hardware and feed stores in the Guderian Territory. Matt had first met the enterprising merchant two years ago in Roanoke during Rex's second rifle-buying trip for the Wapiti. The businessman had asked him to allow his nephew to accompany him on the return trip to Smithtown. He agreed to the request, knowing Amy and Rex would be glad to see young Jacobs who had gone with them on the harrowing Delta trip.

Counterfeit money explained the reason Rex had invited Kit to accompany him on that Delta trip. Along the Erie River, Prussian currency, both paper and coins enjoyed wide acceptance in the lawless frontier. Even the Ichneumons used it. However, the currency tended to be scarce or bogus, resulting in the need during larger commercial transactions, like the annual Wapiti nut crop, to use gold coins and silver bars. The problem was fake coins and bars.

Rex, not trusting the Atlantic Tobacco Trust, had wanted someone that knew ways to test gold and silver for purity. Kit Jacobs was that man and he had verify the nut crop payment was gold and not brass or gold plated lead. Later during the escape from the Ichneumon navy, he never flinched from doing what Rex asked.

"I'm glad to see Hokee is up and about," Matt said, as the wolf licked his hand.

The knife slash the assassin had dealt the wolf had healed to a reddish fur-less scar across the forehead, which with the missing right ear, gave Hokee a fearsome look.

Rex, after greetings all around, wondered why Kit had made the difficult winter mountain crossing. It wasn't just to visit friends. Something important had happen for Bill Jacobs to send his favorite nephew across the mountains in the dead of winter. He hoped Bill was okay.

Amy invited their visitors to lunch. During their meal, Matt told them about the meeting planned at River Point in two days. The new Prussian commander, General Markel had requested Matt attend.

"The meeting concerns the general's plans for a spring offence against the Ichneumons," Matt said. "You know more about Hickory Ridge defenses, than I. Will you go with me?"

Rex was agreeable. He had high hope for the new Prussian commander at River Point, having seen him in action. He had been in Delta the very night Markel seized the Ichneumon fort. Then a colonel, the Prussian officer had taken advantage of the chaos following the explosion of the fort's magazine.

The blast had capped a dreadful day for Rex. The Ichneumon garrison commander at Port Delta had learned the man selling the Wapiti winter sole nut crop at the tobacco warehouse might be the man their emperor wanted. He had Rex arrested and thrown in the fort's dungeon to await interrogation.

The mutilated prisoners he encountered on the way to his cell left no doubt to the fate awaiting him. He managed to overpower a prison guard that same evening and obtain his key ring. Escaping the cellblock was one challenge, escaping the dungeon and fort alive was another. One fit man at night had a decent chance of slipping across the courtyard and overpowering a lone wall or gate guard, but not with thirty men and women, some severely crippled from the Ichneumon's policy of amputating a prisoner's foot or hand as punishment.

Rex's conscience hadn't allow him to abandon the desperate souls, and though a number of the prisoners did die in the final rush of the gate, most escaped. The act that still nagged his conscience was not trying harder to stop Chief Hopkin's older brother.

Bill had been an Ichneumon prisoner for two years, during which time the monsters had cut off his right foot and left hand. The crippled Wapiti warrior wanted revenge and had remained behind to detonate the fort's main powder magazine. Rex knew the pandemonium from the explosion would aid their prison break and had deferred to his decision. He wondered if General Markel knew the story.

Matt's other news was construction of a railroad through the mountains would soon be starting, though details were sparse.

"That's great," Rex said. "Al needs to do a right-a-way deal with them for the telegraph line."

Several of Rex's friends had invested in Al Leslie's wire company on his recommendation. He was confident a telegraph would be a smashing success in a world that sends news by pigeons and fast riders. Matt's news reminded him that he had been meaning to check on Al's progress. Kit shook his head.

"There's a problem, my uncle wanted you to be aware Herr Leslie lost control of the company."

Rex looked perplexed. "I knew he'd need more money to build it. He planned to sell more stock. He told us that the amount sold would depend on the right-a-way and copper wire costs. There was even a rumor that the railroad would provide the right a way, did that fall through?"

"That's not what happened," Kit said. "Over a year ago, Leslie sold bonds, three quarters of a million D-Marks worth."

"I didn't know that," Rex said, "Leslie never said a thing. I thought it was a stock company with no mortgage, debt free."

"Leslie never told anyone about the bond. Maybe he didn't think it was important."

Having met the man, Rex wasn't surprised. Leslie struck Rex as one of those brilliant introverted scientists with a one-tract mind. They tended to ignore other important items, such as how were they going to meet interest payment commitments.

"My uncle is very upset. Like you, he had told a number of friends the company was a good investment."

"So what happen?" Amy asked, getting up from the table to put her plate by the sink.

"Ten weeks ago, Leslie failed to make the 100,000 due at the end of the first year. Then he allowed the sixty-day grace period to pass without making the payment or even telling the stockholders. My uncle would have made the payment. The bondholder put the company in bankruptcy."

"That doesn't sound like the Al I worked with," Amy said, getting a knife from the wall peg. "That company was his life. Where does that leave us, Herr Simpson, and your uncle?"

Simpson, a Wapiti distiller and cooper, had a successful whiskey and barrel business. He'd also invested in Leslie's company.

"The Leslie Wire Company is bankrupt, the common stock worthless." Kit said. "It leaves us with nothing."

"Won't that depends on who owns Leslie's patents," Rex said. "Who is the bondholder?"

"BCCB," Kit said and seeing the puzzled looks added, "Berlin Commerce and Commodity Bank. It's not a large bank, but the Habsburg and Schnabel families control it. Arthur Kolmar runs the bank."

Rex had enough gold left from the successful Delta trip to make the missed payment and asked, "Would Herr Kolmar be satisfied with a late payment and some extra D-Marks for a late fee?"

"My grandfather, Felix Cohen, has extensive business with BCCB and deals with Herr Kolmar. He said the banker is a typical stiff-necked Junker and inflexible on loan terms."

Clearly amoral opportunists are as much of a plague on Erden as on Earth, Rex thought.

"What do you suggest?"

"Emperor Schnabel has a reputation for fairness," Kit said. "My grandfather might convince him to ask the BCCB to void the bankruptcy, if Leslie had a good reason. We need to find him and learn his side. Amy's correct his life was the telegraph. More worrisome, no one has heard from him since he left for Augusta over a month ago to make a loan pitch to Myrtle Cotton Bank. The bank's president answered my uncle's letter and said Al had never arrived for his appointment."

"Is Benjamin Purnell involved in any of this?" Rex asked.

"He has connections with the Myrtle bank, but not BCCB. After his arrest, I'm not sure what his status is."

Purnell's arrest was news to them. Amy wanted the details regarding her father's arrest. Kit told them about the emperor having Archduke Habsburg and Benjamin Purnell incarcerated in Berlin's central prison for their alleged involvement with bogus naval orders.

"Think they'll hang him," Amy asked, turning her attention back to opening the mail.

Rex hoped the Prussians already had. The elimination of Purnell and his bounty offer for Amy's head would remove one of their major worries. Her detached demeanor to the arrest news surprised him. It was not that of a person learning the Prussians had just thwarted her malicious nemesis. It reminded Rex that his partner remained an enigma.

"No idea," Kit said, "But did you know Purnell is the major stockholder in NH&R, the railroad from New Hamburg to Roanoke? It's the railroad the new spur to River Point has to connect to in order to reach the coast."

Rex nodded. He knew that from Chief Smith, head of the Wapiti Chief council, and his daughter, Tara. They were very interested in the new railroad being build.

"There's a rumor the emperor asked Duke Soltzendorff to buy the railroad, but Purnell refused to sell," Kit said. "His arrest might be the emperor's method of putting him in a mood to sell."

Amy just shook her head in disgust. "The emperor is a fool. He should execute the traitor, not bargain with him."

No one commented and after a pause, Kit added.

"Uncle now fears the worst, and has hired a Berlin investigator. One thing he did learn from Duke Soltzendorff was Leslie had approached him about buying more shares."

"Hard to get excited about that," Rex said. "It would diluted our holdings. Is the duke part of the Habsburg family that owns BCCB, the bondholder?"

"No, but Duke Soltzendorff and Herr Kolmar are partners in various commercial properties in Berlin," Kit said.

Amy and Rex exchanged a glance. She appeared to be thinking, like him, a forced bankruptcy could be a cheap way to pick up a company. Well, Leslie had been foolish, likely the duke underhanded, but Rex wouldn't starve if he did lose his 25,000 D-Marks. It was a timely reminder to be cautious on this alien world. Railroads and telegraph investments were a bit rich for a man of his means.

He needed a coffee refill and started to ask Amy for the pot, but didn't. He remembered that Kit had gotten the last cup. She was busy reading and sorting the mail Matt had brought, so he got up to find the grinder.

"Don't, your coffee is like tea, I'll make it."

"Has your uncle sent anyone to Augusta to look for Leslie?" Rex asked, handing the bean grinder to Matt.

"I offered to go, but he said no," Kit said. "He's worried Soltzendorff may have some involvement in Leslie's disappearance. The duke has many connections in Myrtle Territory and he may not want the bond paid. Asking questions might be dangerous."

"Has your uncle read the bond covenants?" Amy asked, reaching for the last letter. "The patents may not be pledged as collateral."

"That's a good idea to check the contract with BCCB," Kit said. "Never know what's in the fine print. I'll do that as soon as I get back in Roanoke. My uncle wanted to know if you had any suggestions or would consider going to Augusta and inquire?"

"I can't at the moment," Rex said.

Amy's safety in the event of a sudden Ichneumon raid before the Prussians reinforced River Point worried him. Learning what the general wanted with Matt would give him insight to the Prussian plans. Also, she was pushing him to complete the lathe installation.

Slater Sawmill had ordered two of her steam engines and the boring of the fifty-centimeter diameter steam cylinders depended on the lathe. His crew would have the machine shop completed within the next couple of weeks. If what the Prussians planed didn't involve him, he could make a Myrtle trip after the shop was running. Besides, that absent-minded scientist might surface in the meantime.

"Look," a beaming Amy said, holding up the last letter, "Deutsche Battery received an order for four thousand batteries."

"Congratulations," Rex said. Her success made him think of Nikola Tesla, a brilliant inventor on Earth in the late nineteen century who died destitute though others made billions off his work. He needed to help her avoid Tesla's outcome and added, "You'll be a rich woman one day."

Matt and Kit looked bemused and a delighted Amy explained.

"Thanks to Tara, I patented my new high current copper-zinc design. Then she helped me negotiated a royalty deal with the Prussian chemical company, Deutsche, to manufacture it. This letter is proof people are buying my batteries."

Tara Smith was an attorney representing the chiefs' council, and in Rex's opinion, its brains. She had taken on the Guderian Territory Bar Association and won the right to practice law in all the Prussian courts. She had even met Emperor Schnabel in Berlin to present the Wapiti's request for their own territory under Prussian rule.

"Well I don't know anything about currents and all that, but I'm happy for your success," Matt said while grinding coffee to make another pot.

"Wasn't Leslie buying them for the telegraph?" Kit asked.

"Yes, but the telegraph will need batteries, regardless of who builds the wire," Amy said. "We still need to find the numbskull and salvage our investment."

"There's another matter your uncle may be able to assist us with," Rex said. "I'm sure Matt told you about the attempt on our lives." Kit nodded.

"Someone convinced those two soldiers that there was a person in the territories who could pay the bounty. If Purnell is in prison, who would he use as his agent in the territories?"

"He is one of the main stockholders in the NH&R railroad," Kit said, "So maybe the head of the railroad police or the manager."

"Maybe, but there're other stockholders involve in the railroad that might ask embarrassing questions. I was just thinking about Donnelly's partner, Ruffner. Do you think Purnell might trust him? His place is in Narrows, not far from Roanoke. Rumor said he was involved in the Jarrell sisters kidnapping and their sale to that apple plantation."

"Ruffner . . ., I'd forgotten him. I'll bet he's the agent, assuming one exists," Amy said. "Wu and Ruffner came to Orleans on several occasions to see my father. The man was always polite to me, but he's a slaver and he would have the advantage of knowing he was paying for the right head."

"I should have hunted him down after Donnelly's fort fell. Matt, you're turning that coffee into dust."

"Don't be yelling at Matt," Amy said. "He's a better coffee maker than you." That earned a rare smile from the bristly hunter as he completed pouring boiling water in the contraption Amy called a coffee pot and placed it on the fireplace grate.

"There's a better way. We're all busy. Those Clovis ice bear hunters are in the village. They're returning to their mountain homes from the annual ice field hunt, and stopped to have the foundry repair their bear traps. I'll ask them to deliver a letter to Ruffner."

"You think a letter will stop him?"

"Unlike most of those psychopaths working for my father, I had the opinion Ruffner was rational. I think a letter telling him that you, Rex Knight, will guarantee he'll lose his head, if I lose mine, will give him pause. Or maybe he'll rat out who ever Purnell is using."

"It can't hurt, but the guards will stay."

"Is the coffee done?" She asked while pulling a fresh sheet of letter paper from her desk drawer.

Chapter 4

General Markel got up from Matt Brewer's old desk in the commander's office at the River Point fort and stepped around to greet them. The Prussian officer was a clean-shaven, muscular man with dark thick hair, cut short, and wearing the gray-green Wehrmacht combat uniform sans rank. Rex would guess their ages were similar, though the new commander wasn't quite as tall as he was. The man's greetings were perfunctory. *A serious man with much on his mind*, Rex thought.

Besides Chief Smith, Jeremy Slater, and Matt Brewer, the other person present was a Colonel Palitzsch, a thin man, half dozen years older than General Markel was. The Prussian colonel had dark mean eyes, though he smiled and spoke pleasant enough during the handshakes. Rex wondered if he was bitter that a much younger man out ranked him.

"Herr Knight, I understand a couple of our deserters tried to kill you," the general said. Rex nodded. "Well, I'm glad they didn't succeed and are no longer a concern. They're just one more item Purnell needs to answer for. Anyway that's old business, would you answer some questions about the layout of the fort?"

"Sure, and call me Rex. We've all been there," he said indicating his three friends with a hand gesture.

Rex had no illusion that the general's concern for him and Amy extended much beyond the loss of a source for useful information on the Ichneumon defenses. Still he rather liked the

Prussian and told him about his meeting with General Mehta and his impression of the Hickory Ridge defenses.

"You're of the opinion that the rear wall is the weakest point of the fort?" Colonel Palitzsch asked. Rex nodded. "The ten or twelve meter high stone wall that you describe would be a formable obstacle. Without heavy cannons to breach the wall, an assault could become a killing field."

"I don't disagree," Rex said, thinking the colonel had stated the obvious. He better understood why the younger officer was in command.

"Jeremy, you have delivered firewood through the rear southeast service entrance. I recall there's a fortified stone room built over the entrance. Is there a second gate behind that at the main fort wall?"

"A barbican?" the general interrupted.

Rex nodded and continued, "It was dark when I was there and I couldn't tell if there was a portcullis."

"Yes," Jeremy said. "There's a heavy iron grate built into a slot in the ceiling of the entrance through the main fort wall."

The Slaters ran a successful sawed timber business thirty kilometers down the Erie from Hickory Ridge. The Ichneumons had made an enemy of Jeremy when they arrested his younger brother who had been an innocent passenger on the ill-fated Prussian warship sunk at Hickory Ridge. Instead of releasing him, the Ichneumons had enslaved the brother along with the surviving Prussian sailors. The unfortunates were on their way to Delta as slaves to help rebuild the fort when Rex's men and Captain Dalporto seized control of the Clovis Belle and rescued them.

"There's a wood gate there also, but it's never closed," Jeremy added.

"Sounds like storming the southeast gate could be difficult," the general said. The timberman nodded.

"Rex, you wouldn't have been able to see it," Jeremy said, "But where the east barbican wall ties into the main wall there was an earlier entrance. The barbican wall is thinner than the main wall. It's maybe a meter thick where as the main wall is much thicker."

"How thick is the main wall?" The general asked.

"Three to four meters in the rear, up to seven or eight meters on the sides facing the river," the lumberman said. There were moans in the room.

"There's a cove on the east side of the intersection of the barbican and main wall. The fill in of the old entrance was never completed. The Ichneumons sealed that part of the wall with about two meters of rock, leaving a space about a meter deep, several meters wide and high on the exterior of the main wall. If you could pack it full of gun powder, it might blow open the wall."

"Wouldn't the Ichneumons see us carrying kegs and get curious?" An older feldwebel asked.

The general shook his head, "It wouldn't matter. The gunpowder is not contained and would just flash off and wake the garrison."

"That's always that risk, it depends on the tamping," the colonel said.

"With what would you tamp it, snow?" The general asked.

"I don't know, you guys are the experts," Jeremy said, after a moment when he realized the colonel had nothing to add. "But you'd have time, for nothing ever happens behind the fort during winter, except for an occasional sled of fire wood during the day. At night, there's never activity, the guards are sleepy, and that east corner is dark, except during a full moon."

General Markel asked Rex his opinion of Jeremy's idea.

"The weakest section of the wall may be that plug," Rex said, "But, we all agree an untamped black powder charge won't breach it. Since there's no practical method to tamp the charge, we need another idea."

"What about a navel bombardment?" Matt asked.

"Our navy was severely mauled at Delta by the Ichneumon rifled cannons firing armor piercing shells," General Markel said. "The Ichneumons sank our newest battleship and several troop carriers, killing over a thousand of our men, plus many hundreds of prisoners. It was a disaster. The Rhine Mar was lucky to escape."

Verification of a Prussian defeat at Delta caused noticeable apprehension among the visitors. No one in the room commented until Rex asked.

"Why didn't the Prussians keep the Delta fort after the blast?"

"You knew about that?" the general asked.

"I was in Delta delivering the Wapiti winter-sloe crop to the tobacco warehouse," Rex said. "I saw the Prussians enter the fort that night. Ten days later when I returned, the Ichneumons were in charge. What happen?"

"Where were you returning from?" Colonel Palitzsch asked.

"Orleans," Rex answered. No need to hedge, it was common knowledge among the Wapiti. The general appeared surprised and asked about Rex's business.

"Brokering coal is my main business, though I also haul items. I was in Orleans to pick up some machinery for Caroom Industries. So why did the Prussians give up Delta?"

"It's not a secret," General Merkel said and told them about the false orders, the gullible Admiral Wilhelm, and the naval disaster that followed.

Matt and the Chief Smith appeared as surprised as Rex that such a stratagem could be successful with all the imperial codes in use. However, the treachery was a painful subject for the general and Rex instead asked.

"Then you expect the Ichneumon navy to attack River Point as soon as the river ice clears?"

"If I was in their position, I would," the general said. "Those exploding shells would rip these stonewalls apart."

The colonel appeared about to comment when the general added.

"Colonel Palitzsch, we're pressed for time, I would like you and Chief Smith to go meet that Wapiti chief, Chief Chin, from Johnsontown. Find out what the pest wants while I finish with these gentlemen. He's at the main gate."

The colonel wasn't pleased, but said, "Yes sir."

Chief Chin, the treacherous Ichneumon stooge, would also be unhappy when he saw Chief Smith with the Prussian colonel.

"What about using those two siege cannons the Ichneumons abandoned down the river to ambush the warship?" Matt asked.

During last year's Ichneumons attack to recapture River Point, the Ichneumon commander, General Meringa had off loaded two massive cannons four kilometers down river from the confluence of the Southern and Erie Rivers. His plan was to place the siege cannons on the ridge across the Southern River from River Point and bombard the fort. The Wapitis struck before the cannons could be place. After Meringa's defeat, the heavy iron cannons were spiked and left in the forest.

Rex wondered what the general would think, if he knew Amy had her eye on those two cannons. She'd talked about buying them as scrap to machine into steam cylinders.

"Those old guns throw a heavy iron ball, but as I'm sure you folks know they're awkward to load and aim. On a moving target, the gunner might only get one shot off."

"I saw the warship, Helot. It has heavy armor plates," Rex said. "Solid shot is not apt to penetrate those hull and gun-turret plates, but the ball could cause havoc in the upper decks and paddle wheels."

"I doubt the Helot could get past Panther Creek, even if the spring high water allowed it to clear the sandbars. It's under powered and would have difficulties handling the higher currents," the general said.

"Not the Saukko," Rex said. "It is a powerful sidewheeler and would have no problem reaching River Point."

"That's why I wanted to strike first with a ground assault on Hickory Ridge before the Ichneumon reinforcements arrive," General Merkel said. "But the lack of cannons to breach the fort's rear wall makes that iffy."

Prussian troops had experience in winter fighting, unlike the Ichneumons, and Rex thought they should take advantage of that skill.

The general realized his cup was empty and said. "Guard, find out where the coffee is."

Rex wouldn't mind a refill of the garrison's hot black coffee. Unlike that tarry liquid, his sweetheart calls coffee, the Prussians had good coffee.

"I have an idea," he said, thinking of Amy's yellow oil. It might be the answer to breaching the fort wall. That drop on the anvil sure indicated it was powerful. He told the general about nitroleum.

"The ground's frozen and digging a tunnel to mine the wall couldn't be done without discovery by the Ichneumon garrison,"

"You're thinking of black powder. I'm talking about a new powerful explosive Amy knows how to make. It can be effective just placed against a wall."

Amy's oil was nitroglycerin and that was the key ingredient in dynamite. Thanks to the US Army, he knew how to use it as a breaching charge to penetrate bunkers and walls.

"I've heard those rear walls are four to five meters of solid rock," Markel said. "The charge would just blow outward if it wasn't contained." The officer was doubtful, but Rex sensed he was also intrigued.

"Make a section of wall and I'll demonstrate," Rex said.

"How, there's no cut stone available," the general said, than after a pause, added, "Would ice blocks work?"

"If the blocks had a few days to freeze into a solid mass, it would sure provide a demo of nitroleum's power."

"The ice is a meter thick along the shores. The men could cut it into blocks and make a wall, say five meters thick and seven meters high. If her explosive, untamped, can breach that, it might work. Would a fifteen meter section be long enough for a test?"

Rex nodded and after agreeing to a date for the test, left to find Captain Beck, a cup of coffee, and to read the latest Roanoke newspaper the general had loaned him.

On the paper's second page was Dean Kristol's announcement that the Jesuits and Roanoke University were sending all the senior medical students to the Berlin Royal Medical Center, along with the top student from each of the undergraduate classes. The students would attend lectures on new developments in the Prussian pharmaceutical industry and pioneering surgical methods, such as the safe use of ether and chloroform as an anesthetic.

Reading on Rex learned Indira Hopkins and her best friend, Jenny Jarrell, had won two of the three open slots available to undergraduates for the Berlin trip. He wondered if the dean was aware of the mayhem that seemed to follow those girls. He hoped the Berlin school kept fire extinguishers handy with those two girls in attendance. He needed to tell Amy and to send them congratulations.

The first person Rex met on Erden was Indira Hopkins, then thirteen years old. Slavers had caught her along with three other Wapiti teenagers. She was the sole captive still alive when Rex encountered the slaver on the forest trail. Indira, a rope around her neck, was struggling to keep pace with the horse. Rex had realized if the girl fell, and the rider didn't stop, the rope would have dragged and strangled the girl.

Rex, not sure that day where he was or what he had encountered, hesitated. The slaver didn't, but his bullet missed and Rex's didn't. Indira and he became friends. He learned the skinny little girl was fearless when they teamed up to free her sister and other slaves. She also later vouched for his character and that helped smooth his introduction into and acceptance by the Wapiti society.

Indira was in the Roanoke University's medical program by default. In a different time and world, she would have pursued a career in law enforcement or the military. She hadn't because the Prussian empire limited females in those professions to clerical positions. Much of Prussian society still frown on women being physicians, but in the territories and frontier areas, all doctors, even a Wapiti female, were accepted and compensated well.

Jenny Jarrell, her beautiful friend, had been attempting to persuade her to apply for acceptance in Jesuit's medical program. Indira had hesitated, knowing Jenny had a scholarly side and was a poor judge of what normal people might find difficult to comprehend. Then Larry Hopkin had told her mother about Jenny's effort.

"Don't tell me that you rejected the Jesuit offer," her mother said.

"I'm not sure I can stand to be around sick smelly people all the time," Indira answered. She wasn't about to admit to her mother that she feared not being smart enough to pass the courses, which everyone knew were demanding.

"You prefer goats and changing diapers in the day care, or skinning swamp rats?" Her mother asked. "How do you plan to support a family?"

"I'm a good hunter. I shot that panther killing our goats," Indira said, searching for a better reason. "There's money in trapping. I sold that panther hide for four hundred D-Marks."

"There's more money in hoeing tobacco, than trapping. You want to be a field laborer?" Her mother asked, knowing her daughter hated hoeing.

"You know doctors make good money. Look how well Freda is doing. Now, help me with the dishes." They had been eating breakfast.

"Freda's beautiful. Who would want a doctor that looked like me?" Indira asked while starting to dry the iron skillet. "The animals don't care what I look like."

"Bah, you don't fool me, daughter. That's an honorable scar. Anyone that didn't like you because of the scar isn't worth knowing," her mother said. She studied Indira for a moment and apparently decided her daughter agreed. "Indira, I want you to get serious, there is no future in trapping and hunting. Take advantage of the opportunity."

During the last raid up the Hopkin River by Warlord Donnelly's marauders and the Ichneumons, Indira had tried to defend the nursey and suffered a sword slash across her face. The raiders had enslaved and hauled her and her mother to Donnelly's stockade at Hinton. As a result, the cut wasn't treated and she now had a fearsome scar. In the last year, Indira had grown fourteen centimeters in a final spur as she approached her fifteenth birthday. By Wapiti standards, Indira knew she had been no beauty before the scar, but now she towered over all the other women. She felt like one of those Clovis totem poles.

Indira's friend, Jenny, had all the attributes that made many Wapiti women famous for their comeliness, a lithe physique, smooth blemish free skin with a slightly mocha tone, dark brown, nearly raven hair, bright green eyes, sharply defined facial structure, straight white teeth, interesting lips, small straight nose, and a high forehead. And if that wasn't enough blessings, Indira thought, Jenny was smart and an extrovert.

Indira enrolled in the medical program. Happily, she discovered the course work wasn't overly difficult, even interesting. At the conclusion of the first semester, her grades topped all the other freshmen, an alarming omen for the future of medical care in the territories she thought. Then a miracle, the school decided to include the top freshman in the Berlin excursion.

Jenny's grades had always been top of her class, so she had the sophomore undergraduate slot. They would share a bed on the Aruba steamboat that the university hired to carry the Roanoke students to the Baltic port. From there, they would travel by railroad to Berlin. Indira was thrilled over the opportunity.

It was a tossup over who was happier over Colonel Palitzsch's new orders assigning him to Berlin. General Merkel had never seemed to trust or care for him, still the general had wished him well on his new assignment. Just escaping the hardscrabble life of frontier duty would have been enough to bring a smile, but the Prussian General Staff position would allow him time to manage his investment, the Berlin gentlemen's club, Spirits.

Palitzsch's operation was an elegant fashionable bordello with an evil secret. The club had a private floor that catered to wealthy deprave men that found sexual release in abusing, even murdering their partner. The club used slaves to supply the victims, young girls and boys that authorities wouldn't miss or could trace. The club was a lucrative investment, but it was also a dangerous occupation in that exposure of his involvement with slaves and snuff sex would send him to the gallows.

The Wapiti success in throwing the warlords and slavers out of their territory had complicated the club's ability to supply the clientele's favorite victim. The several moneyed perverts, who were willing to pay the astronomical fees, preferred female Wapiti teenagers. He believed they'd pay upwards of eight-ten thousand D-Marks per girl.

Len Ruffner, who operated a trading post at Narrows, a small remote village on the southeast border of the Wapiti territory, had been in the past a dependable source of Clovis and Wapiti slaves. However, Hedrick, the club's manager had sent word to him at River Point that the trader hadn't bid on Spirits' last request for girl slaves.

The colonel decided to take a side trip to Narrows, before embarking for Berlin. He wanted to learn why no bid and to negotiate an order for two Wapiti teenage female slaves. Unfortunately, Ruffner who in the past was always ready to do a deal, no matter how vile or illegal, wasn't interested.

"Tell your aristocratic perverts that they need to settle for Zamian girls."

They had been in Len's private upstairs office with his prized large glass window, rumored to be the largest one west of the mountains. Both were drinking Simpson aged corn whiskey, and watching the frozen Southern River below, between comments.

"I'm aware the Wapiti warriors have shut down the slave trade in their territory," the colonel said. "I heard all about it at River Point. I even heard your name mentioned as the person behind that attempt to collect Purnell's reward on the Caroom woman."

The colonel was surprised his news merited only a shrug from the slaver. He would have thought learning his name was being linked with the attempted murder of Rex Knight's woman would have alarmed him. During their last dealings, Ruffner had expressed his fear of retribution from Knight for his involvement with Donnelly.

"I don't know where those buffoons got the idea I was holding Purnell's gold. I haven't had and want nothing to do with that or your business."

"Is the reward for that bitch's head ten thousand?" He asked, trying to spark the slaver's interest.

"As I said, I don't know. I'd say it is nonsense, bar talk. If Purnell wanted her dead, he'd spend the money to hire a professional assassin."

"That's what I'd do, but then the other rumor at River Point was the Ichneumon emperor has a fifty thousand D-Mark reward out for Rex Knight's head. Maybe rewards work better in the territories."

"For sure that bastard did humiliate Ratakonda's nephew, but the amount sounds ridiculous."

"I think we'd all agree he could afford it. And the Ichneumons have a history of using rewards along the Erie to apprehend wanted criminals."

"Well, I hope they're successful, Knight is a first rate ass who helped stir up the Wapiti tribes and wreck Donnelly's and my business."

"I'm trying to help your business," the colonel said. "Look, I agree the Zamian girls are fine looking, but some customers have peculiar taste."

"That's a polite way to put it."

"It's a shame you can't find a few. My customers will pay serious money for a couple of young Wapiti girls. I figure ten thousand."

"It's also a sure way to get hung," Len said, "By the way I just recently acquired four prime ice bear pelts, if you're still wanting one. Let's go below and check on dinner."

Chapter 5

Julian Penton's newest irritation was learning a Zamia family of four had escaped last night from the Opossum Creek slave pens. She heard Max, her nephew, in the hall outside her office.

"Max, have you discovered how a prime breeding pair escaped?" Julian yelled, and after a moment to allow the handsome fool to enter, added. "You said that new, and I'll add, damn expensive iron wire fence was escape proof."

"Not if some parsimonious shrew insists on reusing ancient locks a child could open, all to save a pfennig," Max said, entering the office. He slammed the office door shut, adding, "You know I warned what could happen."

"Where were the gate guards, drunk, off bothering the women?" She asked, unimpressed by Max's effort to avoid responsibility. "What about the slink, wasn't it on patrol?"

Slinks terrified most people, including Julian. The flightless birds are Erden's version of an ostrich, except larger and with a powerful hook beak for tearing prey apart. Terror birds were ferocious hunters, smart, and trainable, though the aggressive creatures were dangerously unpredictable. The nasty creatures occasionally turned on their trainer with lethal results. Still, a few reckless people, for example, her brother Harlem and his enforcer, Grover, liked to use them for guard duty and hunting escapees.

Seeing Max's hesitation, knowing his slothfulness, she asked. "Have you even been to Opossum creek this morning to check, or as usual are you just serving up hearsay?"

"Grover is on it," Max said. "He'll have them by midday. With their two young children, they can't out run the slink."

What a useless bit of baggage, Julian thought. *The slink has more brains than those two. Harlem needs to get his son out of management, send him to Augusta and Berlin to entertain the bureaucrats.*

"Duke Soltzendorff and Keith Woodman are scheduled to arrive today," Julian said. "Those Zamians were to show them we're dealing with the inbreeding problem."

The duke was a Prussian aristocrat, and rumored a confidant of the emperor. The noble, among his vast holdings, owned several smaller Myrtle cotton plantations that, between them, used over a thousand slaves. He was an important customer for the excess juvenile slaves produced at the Opossum Creek operation. Julian wanted to assure him that the number of culls in that last batch of slaves was a fluke and that they would reimburse him.

On the other matter, she figured they could count on Soltzendorff to share their hatred of the abolitionist moment. Herr Woodman, the other expected visitor, was Myrtle Cotton Bank's president. He was a fussy weak man. Still she figured the banker understood the importance of slavery to the territory's economy and would support her idea.

"What difference does that make?" Max asked, helping himself to a cup of her Ichneumon coffee. "Every plantation has run away workers. Give the slackers a good whipping and put them back to work."

"Yeah, that's what we've been doing and each year more try to escape. I suppose you've already forgotten your father's promise to hang every runaway. He'll want to make an example of that family when Grover brings them back."

"Are you serious?" Max asked. "The place needs new blood. That young Zamia male has to be worth 20,000 D-Marks. Maybe we could just hang one of the kids. Would that satisfy father's new law?"

"Go ask him, he's in the kitchen."

Duke Soltzendorff arrived an hour after lunch at the Penton Plantation. He was traveling in his attractive black four-in-hand carriage, the type of coach Julian wanted someday. The winter roads had muddied the wheels, horses, and splattered the coach's sides, still it was a handsome outfit.

Harlem had left earlier to check on Grover's efforts to capture the runaways, so she handled greeting their royal visitor.

"Harlem is in the field and I expect him soon," she said while wondering why the Duke's party included a middle age Ichneumon.

"Harj Bhojwani works for the Atlantic Tobacco Trust," the duke said. He then pointed to a tall gangly Prussian unfolding himself out of the second black carriage pulled up beside the first coach. It was loaded with the duke's luggage and servants.

"That's Al Leslie. He's a business man that wanted to see the Highland Plantation before returning to Berlin."

A command from Julian had the driveway a hive of activity as the Highland servants rushed to join in helping with the luggage. The stable foreman then directed the coaches and teams to the main stable where another crew of grooms would unharness, rub-down, and feed the horses.

The tobacco man expressed his appreciation for their warm welcome. Unlike the duke's hug and messy kisses on each cheek, Harj just shook her hand, the accepted method of greeting in the territories, and the one she much preferred. The businessman just nodded.

Julian was tempted to forget manners and ask the duke why he brought an Ichneumon to their meeting, but Soltzendorff's interest was already distracted. He was looking over the maids. Satisfying her curiosity about the Ichneumon would have to wait.

The aristocrat was a well-put together man in Julian's opinion. He was about the age and size of her brother, but where Harlem had a rough sloppy appearance, the duke had a refined trim air. Duke Soltzendorff was clean-shaven unlike most of the plantation owners who seemed to think a scraggly beard made them look virile. The tasteful black suit, cape, and knee boots with the snow-white dress shirt completed the duke's elegant ensemble. It's a shame he's a psychopath, she thought as she instructed the maids waiting at the mansion's entrance to show their guests to their rooms.

A muddy Harlem returned a couple of hours later and told Julian that Grover was still searching for the missing slaves.

"Why do you figure that Ichneumon is here?" Harlem asked handing the butler his wet hat and coat.

Her brother didn't appear concerned the runaways were still uncounted for, which surprised her. His normal policy was never to leave the hunt until after the apprehension of the escapee.

"Soltzendorff wouldn't say," Julian said. "You know how the misogynic bastard is about women. He wanted you present before he discussed business."

"I'd better get cleaned up first."

"You're be fine, just kick off those muddy boots," Julian said, pointed to a pair of clean knee boots by the door.

Her brother appeared ready to argue and she added, "I just had the rugs cleaned, put those on, I don't want the duke to think we're a couple of bumpkins. Another minute won't matter, I've been listening to the duke relate the latest mindless gossip in Port Augusta and Berlin for an hour."

Clean boots on, her brother said, "Let's get some answers."

Julian had long ago seized her grandmother's elegant music salon for her office. It was a cozy room with large windows facing the southwest to provided warmth and light on winter days in the high ceiling room. Two trusted clerks shared the large room with her along with dozens of wooden file cabinets and shelves of books, ledgers, and maps. She instructed her staff to take a long break, and then settled her visitors around the massive polished oak conference table that dominated the room's center. A servant served small cakes, coffee, tea, and whiskey while the men exchanged greetings and lit their noxious cigars.

After the unobtrusive servant left, closing the door behind him, Harlem, spewing smoke, asked the duke the purpose of his visit while nodding towards Harj Bhojwani. The Prussian businessman was over studying the large topographic map of Myrtle Territory mounted the wall.

"It's no secret Schnabel is not the leader his father was. But since the armistice in the east, our emperor's behavior has been unpredictable," Duke Soltzendorff said. Her brother shrugged his shoulder and Julian thought so what's new, all emperors act odd at times.

"He had his uncle arrested, Archduke Habsburg."

Julian gasped, "Arrested . . .?" Was she in danger of arrest? The Duke's news had her brother's attention and he asked his guest for an explanation.

"The return of two Prussian fleets to the Baltic port because of false naval orders and the abandonment of Port Delta's fort, enraged the emperor," the duke said. "Then the archduke couldn't explain the source of his funds he used to pay off his gambling debts."

"Two fleets. . ." Julian asked. She exchanged a worried look with her brother. "Who abandoned the Delta fort, the Ichneumons?" She asked.

Duke Soltzendorff nodded to Harj to explain. The Ichneumon told the Pentons about the sabotage of the fort's main magazine.

"In the confusion following the explosion, the Prussians seized the fort," Harj said. "A few days later, new navy orders arrived ordering the entire Prussian fleet to abandon the Erie River, the fort at Delta, and return to the Baltic. General Paget had arrived by that time with reinforcements and the Ichneumon army reoccupied the fort."

Both Pentons were shaking their heads in amazement at the tale. "The Prussians aren't that foolish," she said.

"But they were," the duke said. "That idiot, Admiral Wilhelm never questioned the dispatch. He's now under arrest."

Julian didn't know rather to feel relief or not on the news that the Archduke's arrest was for an unrelated matter and not the bogus navy order lifting the Zamian blockade. That had been her idea, though Harlem's daughter, Susan, had supplied the wording and Duke Soltzendorff had handled the dealings with the archduke. The duke was studying them both. Wondering the same thing, who was behind the Delta orders and praying not one of them.

"How did such a thing happen?" Julian asked. She noticed the question had the businessman's interest.

"Rumor is an Ichneumon agent, Sanita Chopra, paid a disgruntled army major, John Lyon, at the General Staff Berlin headquarters to issue those bogus navy orders," the duke said.

Could those Delta orders explain Benjamin's arrest? Julian asked the duke, "Are we in the clear?"

The duke shook his head, nodding toward the businessman.

"That bastard needs to have . . .," Harlem said and realized Al Leslie was listening. "Al, excuse us for yakking about our cotton troubles. Julian find Max, he needs to show Al the operation."

Locating Max required a few minutes. During the wait, Harlem and the duke gave Al advice on how to convince Herr Woodman to approve his loan at the Myrtle Cotton Bank. While they discussed strategies for obtaining a bank loan, Harj Bhojwani walked over to examine the topo map that had the Prussian's interest.

"The archduke's replacement as head of the empire's spies is Joe Hansen," the duke said after Al and Max had left. "Hansen doesn't believe the major's account. He suspects Purnell and the cotton growers were behind the bogus orders. That they had some deal with the archduke and Ichneumons."

"How's that possible? I thought the Habsburg family, the archduke, controlled the emperor," Julian said.

"The old emperor, yes, he listened to them, but his son doesn't," the duke said. "Fortunately for us, the emperor hasn't allowed Hansen to use torture."

"Emperor Schnabel, the weakling who outlawed slavery and public whippings, would stoop to torture," Harlem said. "I think not. Purnell and the archduke need not worry. They just need to keep quiet, let their attorneys do their job."

"You might be right if the emperor hadn't tried to recover the fort by racing the battleship Schlesien and a battalion of marines back to Delta," the duke said. "The Ichneumons were ready and sank the battleship at great loss of life. The emperor can't allow that act to go unpunished. Someone will hang over those Delta orders."

"That rumor was true? I thought the ship was unsinkable. Are we at war with the Ichneumons?" Harlem asked, looking at Harj.

"That's not clear," the duke said. "Where we're not at war is in the east. The Mongol armistice seems to be holding and the emperor is considering whether to pull troops from the east and send them here."

"You mean to the Erie, Port Delta?" Julian asked.

"No, he wouldn't try to take Delta until the two new battleships being built at Baltic are ready."

"Are you guys going to invade us?" Harlem asked Harj, joking. The Ichneumon shook his head and appeared amused.

"The Ichneumons aren't our problem, Harlem," the duke said. He appeared as irritated by her brother's levity, as she was. "He intends to use the troops to enforce his antislavery decree. What I think will happen is the emperor will boost the army garrisons in the territories by several brigades, replace your sheriffs, and outlaw the guardian posses. Then he'll free the slaves."

"He can't be serious," Harlem said, jumping up. "God, that's madness. It'd be anarchy. The slaves would murder our families."

"We need slaves to survive," Julian said. The thought of those animals running free chilled her. "They need us. They'll revert to their savage ways without our firm hand to guide them. Why would he do this, it'll start an insurrection."

"The emperor is serious," the duke said. He seemed amused by their fear and added. "Be seated Harlem, relax, we'll nip it in the bud.

"There's already a lieutenant running around making a list of slave breeding operations," the Ichneumon said. "You do appreciate those operations will be what emperor closes first as he frees the slaves."

"Harj, quit alarming our friends," the duke said. "Tell them the Ichneumons' plans."

"It's no secret the Ichneumon army will seize River Point as soon as the river is ice free in the spring. Other than reclaiming the emperor's property from those Wapiti savages, there are no plans to attack Prussian territories. But Emperor Ratakonda doesn't want a large Prussian army on his east flank either. He'd prefer the territories to be independent. I'm to ask if we can help the plantation growers maintain their way of life and avoid being under the thumb of the Prussian army."

"You tell me to be serious, duke," Harlem said, "When your guest, a tobacco seed salesman, a peon, suddenly claims to speak for Ratakonda." Unlike the red-faced duke, Harj appeared unoffended.

"Your obtuseness distresses me," the duke said. "Would you expect the man to introduce himself as an Ichneumons agent, while in a Prussian territory?" Her brother looked disconcerted, and after a moment, Harj continued.

"Herr Woodman is expected today. He'll answer any concerns you harbor as to my authority."

Before Harlem could respond, Grover Zagat opened the office door and tracked manure and mud onto the rug.

"Master Penton, come look. I have them," Grover said.

"The runaways," her brother asked, getting up.

The rawboned, stubble faced, unkempt middle-aged man, smiling, nodded. Her brother followed the slave hunter out of the office. The duke asked her about the runaways and Julian explained as they followed Harlem out to see what all the excitement was. She hoped Grover's body odor didn't reach the duke's delicate nostrils.

"I'm looking for a young female slave," the duke said, while standing on the front verandah. "If you decide to break up the family, I'll pay well for the daughter."

The duke had a reputation for rough sex, but surely, he didn't want the six year old for that. The scene that greeted her was ugly. She wasn't as hardened against feeling compassion for those animals, as she wished. The runaways, bloody, abused, and in chains, were on their knees in the driveway surrounded by a dozen gun bearing scruffy guardians. The runaways' six-year-old daughter, tied up like a bedroll with only her head showing, watched helpless from the packhorse as her parents begged for their life.

A small bloody, fly covered, forearm and hand dangled off the horn of the packhorse's saddle where Grover had lashed the girl. She later learned from Max that the slink had killed the boy and Grover had let the bird eat him as its reward for finding the runaways. He then explained Grover had saved the forearm and hand, just in case her brother needed proof no one had escaped.

The afternoon strategy meeting at the Highland plantation was a cheerless gathering. Harlem had hung the two adult runaways and sold the girl to the duke. Keith Woodman, President of the Myrtle Cotton Bank, who had arrived during the hanging, suffered a shock. Julian had served him several stout whiskeys to settle his nerves while wondering what her niece saw in the wimp.

Al Leslie had been outraged at the treatment of the captured runaways. He'd told the duke he was leaving for Augusta and was withdrawing the loan request. His conscience wouldn't allow him to enter a business dealing with such savages. He even refused the whiskey and stormed out as the duke rose to address the group.

"Pay him no mind, he's a weak man. Proper discipline is critical when dealing with slaves. Do we all agree that without slaves our plantations can't prosper?" Duke Soltzendorff asked.

Everyone at the table, Harlem, Julian, Harj, and Woodman nodded, pretending they hadn't just witness a guest cursing their society. Julian, for a moment, wondered if the businessman's response to the hanging was a portent, before deciding he was another weak ineffectual man whose opinion was of no import.

"I believe Emperor Schnabel is now serious about ending slavery," the duke said. "Our neighbor, Herr Rupprecht told me about that Prussian lieutenant that Harj cited. A few soldiers paid his plantation a recent visit. The officer wanted to know if his field hands were slaves or freemen. He told him they were indentured laborers. Contrary to what he expected, the lieutenant seemed satisfied with his nonsensical answer. What our friend didn't appreciate was the lieutenant had accomplished his mission, locating slave operations."

"He should have tarred and feathered him," Harlem, with a loud slap on the table for emphasis, snarled. He then added, "If that's the emperor's idea of getting serious about ending slavery, making lists, we have nothing to worry about."

"What will our friend do when a captain, backed up with a battle-hardened company of a couple hundred troopers from the Fourth Brigade, asks that question?" The duke asked. After giving the mute Harlem a disgusted look, he added.

"I see two choices: The territory declares independence and asks the Ichneumons for help before the emperor can replace the sheriffs with loyal troops. Or we replace our current emperor with someone who understands our needs."

Harj had another assignment that Emperor Ratakonda had given him, but decided this gang of halfwits couldn't help him on that matter, so he didn't mention it. The meeting ended and the guests retired to their rooms to dress for dinner.

Chapter 6

A sensible woman, Amy was hesitant on learning Rex's plans to demonstrate her explosive oil. "You told me it was too dangerous to handle, and now you want a couple of hundred kilograms."

"Maybe more," Rex said, figuring she wouldn't resist an opportunity to test her idea. "I want to test a breaching charge against the wall the Prussians are building."

That had his sweetheart's interest. She asked what he meant and he explained the limitations of the current explosives.

"If your explosive is successful, then General Markel will need enough to breach Hickory Ridge's rear wall."

"Will the Prussian commander attack the fort?"

"He will if he's convinced your explosive can blow a hole in the fort's wall."

"If the Ichneumons lose Hickory Ridge, wouldn't that stop them from attacking River Point and hunting us?"

"That's my hope and why we need to help the general."

She looked tired sitting by the kitchen table and Rex wondered if she wasn't feeling well.

After a moment she said, "Nitric acid will be the limiting factor. So what I have at the foundry is it, maybe enough for several hundred kilograms. There is plenty of the sulfuric, but glycerin is in short supply. Could Markel and the Prussians find me several barrels of glycerin?"

"I'll find out. Did Kit get off okay for Roanoke?" Amy nodded. Hungry, he asked, "Ready to eat those ducks you roasted?"

Rex's job was to carve the bird's breast meat into thin slices. Potatoes, cabbage, goat milk, and bread rounded out their evening meal.

"You must have been famished. Weren't you nauseous this morning?" He asked while using the heel from her delicious loaf sour dough bread to soak up the drippings on the platter. Normally a light eater, she had ate most of the breast meat.

"Some of the mornings have been a bit rough, but my appetite is good," She said smiling.

Sorting through the remains of the demolished birds, he salvaged a wing and part of a leg.

"You still look hungry. Want this?" He held up the wing. She shook her head and he wolfed the wing. "Wait, we missed this." He held up one of backbones with a few shreds of meat still attached. In a playful mood, he added, "I'll trade it for your piece of apple pie."

"Silly, you wouldn't want your daughter to go without her fruit."

"Our daughter . . ., sweetheart, are you expecting?" A beaming Amy nodded.

"Our baby is a girl."

Rex wasn't sure what to make of her amazing bit of certainty in this medically primitive world.

"Not that I care whether it's a girl or a boy, ah . . ., how do you know?"

"I'm a witch, we have girls," she said, amused at his startled look.

She delivered that astonishing fact in the same tone of voice he would have expected her to use when commenting on the time of day. His skepticism must have shown for she added.

"My mother, grandmother, and great grandmother only had girls. So if you want sons, I'm the wrong woman for you."

Is she serious? God, just when you think you understand a woman, they surprise you. He'd never paid any attention to how Wapitis went about getting married. Was there a license? Regardless, he'd do what was right. Still he couldn't resist teasing her a bit.

"But I am curious, what happens if you have a boy, are you no longer considered a witch?"

"The sun rising in the west is more likely."

"Daughters are fine and you're the woman I want. Shouldn't we get married?"

Amy had become the best friend he had ever had. He wanted her as his wife. One could never be certain, but he believed given a chance to return to Earth, he wouldn't go unless she could accompany him. Not that he had any expectation of that miracle happening.

"Forget the kitchen, husband. Let's go to bed and get warm. We'll worry about the general in the morning and marriage in the spring."

Glycerin was more available than Amy had thought. Rex learned local moonshiners collecting the mother-liquor from the soap makers and recovered the glycerin, which they added to their raw whiskey to sweeten and reduce the harshness. Tony Cenci, a convenient local bootlegger, had several barrels of glycerin, which Rex thought was a good indication of the quality of his corn whiskey. He sold two of the barrels to Amy, and the garrison at River Point donated two barrels.

Rex's concern was losing Amy. If there weren't a pending Ichneumon attack to block, he would have never suggested using her nitroglycerine to make dynamite. Thanks to him, Amy, the ever-vigilant entrepreneur for new opportunities had realized her curious yellow oil might have enormous commercial possibilities if there was a safe way to use it.

If she was carrying their child, he didn't want her stirring batches of nitroglycerine. On second thought, he didn't want her messing with explosives, even if she wasn't pregnant. None of his arguments, including concern for her, or their unborn baby, deterred her from wanting to make the new explosive.

"I'll go to General Markel," Rex said, trying one more time to persuade her. "Ask him for a half-dozen Prussian soldiers for you to train on how to make your oil. While you do that, I'll build a pole barn away from Smithtown to house the process."

"You're a dear to be concerned, but it not that dangerous of a process with proper temperature control. Your idea of mixing the nitroleum in the dry clay powder seems more dangerous," Amy said. She followed that with a kiss, a hug, and a compromise.

"We'll do it your way after the first batch. I don't want the army to have the knowledge until after you demonstrate dynamite works, and I have filed a patent application in Berlin."

"Didn't you tell me a number of Heidelberg professors were working on the nitrification of these organics?" Rex asked. She nodded. "Surely one of them survived the process and has already applied for a patent." She brushed off his sarcasm.

"Let them. That's not what we need to patent," Amy said. "It's your idea for making it safe to handle, that dynamite material. Enough nitroleum needs made to mix up a batch to demonstrate its power. Tara is ready to file the patent application after there's proof it works." After a pause, smiling, she added, "However, I did prepare one for making nitroleum, on the off chance that none of those professors had survived."

Everyone was still alive, and Rex had what he hoped was the equivalent of fifty kilograms of straight sixty percent gelatin dynamite. Amy, bundled up in a tan colored fur hoodie, heavy fur lined trousers, and knee boots, was talking with Chief Smith as they waited for General Markel and his staff to arrive at the ice wall. Colonel Fritz Caprivi, Captain Beck, and Matt Brewer were studying the six burlap bags that Rex and Herr Crouch had stacked at the base of the test wall.

The Prussian soldiers had made a neat, smooth, solid wall about six meters high and four meters thick and just a bit longer than it was high. The zero weather had refrozen the blocks together and created a huge brick of ice that looked very solid to Rex. The six watermelon-size burlap bags stacked against the wall looked inconsequential. It would offer a good test of the dynamite's breaching potential.

The general arrived on a horse with four mounted guards. After greetings and various salutes, the Prussian commander dismounted, while the guards remained alert and mounted. The general walked over to Rex and handed him a brass tube with a clockwork attached.

"That's going to breach the wall?" General Markel asked, nodding towards the bags.

"We'll know shortly. Is this the Ichneumon naval mine detonator that Amy ordered?" Rex asked, flipping the device over to better study its fabrication. It looked like no detonator he'd ever seen in the US Army. “She said it was a more powerful detonator than any the Prussians have.”

“She’s right, so try not to drop it,” the general said. “And keep in mind the delay period is only an estimate, so don’t dally after you attach the cap and cock the striker.”

Amy had told Rex that the Ichneumon detonators used a booster charge of picric acid and as a result, was more powerful than the Prussian detonators. She also cautioned they were dangerous due to unstable compounds formed during the corrosion of the metal shell holding the picric acid. If his wife thought Ichneumon detonators dangerous, Rex wanted nothing to do with them and the Prussian ones didn’t sound much safer.

“Looks like oily dirt,” General Markel said, wiping his finger. Unimpressed, he had poked the dynamite exposed by the hole Rex had cut in the burlap bag. The detonator needed direct contact with the explosive.

“Here let me have that. I’m familiar with them. You gentlemen, and lady, wait over by those trees while I insert and activate the detonator,” Herr Crouch said. He pointed down the riverbank to a grove of sycamores about two hundred meters away.

The unshaven, crotchety, Prussian artilleryman knew ordnances of all types and a relieved Rex handed over the brass contraption. The group then scattered among the sycamores that Crouch had suggested they take shelter in from flying debris. Rex and Amy shared a large tree trunk and waited for the explosion.

He felt the rolling ground shock just before the boom and knew they had been successful. The wall blew apart in a cloud of dirty snow and ice. The noise and falling debris reminded him of Afghanistan.

All the Prussian officers, including the lieutenants and several senior feldwebels, were present in General Markel's crowed office when Captain Beck, Rex, Tom Jarrell, and Larry Hopkins entered. The successful demonstration of the dynamite had the men in an upbeat mood.

Matt Brewer was missing. He was off tracking a female wolf hoping to find her den and then capture and domesticate her puppies. Matt thought breeding domesticated wolfs and foxes for guard animals could be a good business. Rex agreed, since Erden didn't appear to have dogs.

"Gentleman, welcome," General Markel said. "We've been discussing how to successfully storm Hickory Ridge without cannons. The consensus is we have to breach the fort's wall for our assault to have a chance of success. So, Rex, you and Tom have been there, are you confident your magic explosive will breach the wall? We all agree it sure did a number on the ice wall."

If the explosive was US Army's 60-percent gelatin dynamite or TNT, Rex had every confident that he could breach the wall that sealed the old gate, but the nitroglycerine used to make the dynamite was homemade and of uncertain strength. Still the general was right. It had demolished the wall.

"I have approximately a thousand kilograms of the dynamite. If the charge could be tamped, then yes it would breach any wall I have seen at Hickory Ridge, otherwise the old gate plug is our best chance of a breach."

"Is that enough?" The general asked. "The danger is the surviving troops in barbican. They could recover and cut off reinforcements from reaching the wall breach. Then the Ichneumons would be in a position to trap the initial assault force that enters through the breach in the main fort."

"Would the barbican be that hard to take?" a feldwebel asked.

"I wouldn't think that rear gate enclosure is any tougher than our test wall, and six bags of the dynamite demolished it," Rex said. "The dropping of the portcullis at the main wall entrance is my concern."

"Do both breaches, the notch in the main wall, and the barbican, then we can bypass the portcullis if it drops," General Markel said. "The surprise and panic would be great. We'd be in the fort before the Ichneumons knew what had happen."

"What are you thinking? Ten bags on the gate and forty bags on the wall?" Feldwebel Crouch asked. The old grumbler had become a believer in the power of dynamite.

Rex figured the feldwebel was thinking of those same size bags used at the ice wall.

"Something along those lines, but how do you cause a simultaneous detonation in both charges?" Rex asked.

If he had some electric blasting caps and cast primers, he thought. *But he did, he realized. With a shunt, a couple hundred meters of insulated copper wire, and a strong battery, he could fabricate one.*

"Use trip wire snap primers," Crouch said, interrupting Rex's chain of thought.

Seeing puzzle looks in the room, the cantankerous artilleryman added, "They look like those ones used in landmines, except with a longer wire. Get fifty or hundred meters away, pull the wire, the blast shouldn't kill you."

"The person might want to watch out for falling debris," Rex said.

"Well, feldwebel figure something out," General Markel said to Crouch. "I'm attacking as soon as the reinforcements arrive. Rex, I want the explosives transferred to River Point."

The Ichneumon warship, Saukko, had just returned from Westport and docked at Delta. General Paget sent word to the captain to meet him at the green canvas tent that served as the command center for the fort's garrison. The tent was one of many in a vast field of cut stone rubble. Two magazine explosions and the Prussian fleet's bombardment had devastated the fort, but hadn't broken the Ichneumon grip on Port Delta and the entrance to the Erie River.

"Burgdorf told me Rex Knight and the Wapiti convoy went up the Great Western River to avoid being trapped at Hickory Ridge," Captain Chetan said, explaining why the Saukko had failed to catch the Wapiti convoy.

"He also told me the Wapiti had your son and daughter in chains."

"Did you check with Colonel Savarin?" General Paget asked. He couldn't decide if Captain Chetan was a fool or simply unlucky. "His job is guarding the river's entry."

"I did, that's how I met Burgdorf. He was there telling the colonel about his escape and the Wapiti plans. The problem was no one at Westport reported seeing Wapiti steamboats and barges on either river."

General Paget found that claim hard to believe. His skepticism must have shown.

"I wasn't sure if the Wapiti boats even existed until Burgdorf," the captain said. "His story made sense, if the savages had heard about Hickory Ridge blocking the Erie. I went up the Great Western to check. I stopped at several river camps and finally located a couple of Ichneumon traders. I didn't trust anyone else. They hadn't seen any steamboats go upriver and I decided the Wapiti had duped Burgdorf. By the time I got back to Westport, the Erie had iced over up river and I heard General Mehta had let the Wapiti by Hickory Ridge."

"He did, the old fool traded passage for my children's release. Where's Burgdorf now?"

"He's in the Saukko's brig."

"Have him bought here," General Paget said. "It's not yet widely known, but the Prussian prisoners seized the Clovis Belle below Hickory Ridge."

"How is that possible . . . Where is it, at Westport?" Captain Chetan asked.

"At River Point, they bluffed their way back by the fort by claiming you told them to pursue the Wapiti convoy. By the time the watch asked General Mehta and he ordered the boat sunk, it was out of range."

The captain liked the Hickory Ridge commander and felt bad for him. Emperor Ratakonda would demand Mehta's head for failing to stop the Wapiti convoy and allowing the prisoners to escape.

"General Emwazi is expected on the next supply ship. He was to be the Delta commander, but I need him at Hickory Ridge. I want the Saukko ready to take him there as soon as the river clears."

"I've heard the ice is gone from the upper Erie River by vernal equinox and navigable."

"You heard correct, so figure on being there in two months," General Paget said, finishing his now cold coffee and standing up. "Let's go see Captain Zarif. I'm sending him with the Kura to support you. I want to strike River Point before the Prussians can bolstered the fort's defenses. You're to tell Mehta he has been relieved of command and report to Delta. A harbor police boat will go with your convoy to transport him and the children back."

Friedrich Burgdorf, too late, realized Rex Knight had used him to mislead the Ichneumons pursuing their convoy. Like a fool, he had gone to the Westport garrison, instead of hightailing up the great Western River to the gold field. Wanting revenge, he had told the Ichneumon commander about the Wapiti convoy plan to hide up the Great Western River. His reward for the information was jail.

The summons from General Paget meant he would soon know his fate. Four grim marines escorted him to a large tent in the middle of the rubble field that used to be the largest fort on the Erie River. The three gallows with Zamians twisting in the wind added to his sense of doom.

"Friedrich, I heard you had a rather dismaying adventure," General Paget said. "Have a seat. Would you care for a coffee, something stronger?" He declined the drink offer.

The general hadn't changed much. He still had that surface amiability that hid his mercilessness. Burgdorf had first met the general when he was a young captain. He had been traveling with the Ichneumon trader, Manuel Prado, on one of the trader's winter sloe nut buying expeditions in Wapiti land. Likely, the captain had been spying. Burgdorf had been one of the trader's guards.

"Captain Chetan thinks you're a saboteur, a Wapiti spy."

"I'm not. I told him what I heard," Burgdorf said. Begging was a wasted effort with Paget. "I now realize your old nemesis, Rex Knight, played me for a fool, just as he has other people. He allowed me to over hear their plans and then to escape."

"I believe you," Paget said. "Thanks for being polite and not naming me, but we both know I was also a victim of Herr

Knight's treachery. One of these days someone will collect the reward on the bastard."

"I'm thinking about trying," Burgdorf said. Hope of surviving the interview was stirring.

"Don't waste your time," the general said. "I have a better offer for a mercenary with your talents. I want you in Berlin to help Sanita Chopra on a state matter. I'll pay you twenty thousand D-Marks upfront, if he is successful because of your help, I'll add a hundred thousand bonus. Interested?"

Burgdorf didn't want a job. He wanted to travel up the Great Western River to the gold strike. He'd heard the law there was the gun, and that suited him just fine. Unfortunately, the Ichneumons had hauled him back to Delta as a suspected Wapiti spy for an interrogation. However, the general's remark about a hundred thousand D-Marks bonus had his interest and he did like Berlin's nightlife.

"What do I have to do?" He asked, knowing for that money, it would be something dangerous, even suicidal. Worse, once he knew what the general planned, he'd have to agree to help for the Ichneumons would never allow him to leave for fear he'd tell the Prussians.

"Help Chopra with a problem in Berlin," the general said.

Burgdorf knew the one answer that would allow him to see tomorrow, "Count me in."

"Excellent," the general said, "And I have the man to deliver you to Berlin, Levi Ottoman. His ocean-going side-wheeler with a load of Fenwick sulfur and acids is in port. The cargo is headed to Port Baltic and embarking tonight. The Prussian blockade of Delta is expected at any moment."

General Paget didn't inform Burgdorf that the large scarred ex-Prussian sailor would also remain in Berlin to aid Chopra. The time on the ocean would provide Levi an opportunity to satisfy their concerns about the mercenary's loyalties, before Chopra told him his part in the planned operation.

Chapter 7

The breaching charge preparation had proceeded without a hitch. Tony Cenci and his crew had helped Amy make another six-hundred liters of nitroleum, which consumed most of the nitric acid. As Amy's crew completed a batch of explosive oil, Rex's crew blended it into the dry marl-clay powder he had the boat-works forges producing from the local gray clay.

Safety had been Rex's concern. Tales about the ice wall destruction by a few bags of the oily dirt had swept the neighborhood, but he had also heard talk that magic had been involved. Any talk of magic had the potential of turning to talks of witches and his wife. To stop that nonsense and make the men cautious when working with the explosive, he arranged for a demonstration.

Tom Jarrell shot, from a safe distance, a small whiskey bottle of the chemical sitting on a wooden post. The resulting violent explosion and shredding of the post top had offered grim evidence for the need to handle the oily liquid with care as they transported and mixed it with clay.

The newly mixed dynamite went in double bags, an outer burlap bag with a waxed cotton inner bag. Beside the constant danger of explosion, the nitroleum was a poison and exposure to the skin gave some of the crewmembers severe headaches. The waxed cotton helped protect the burlap from becoming oily and dangerous.

"I don't know what inspired you folks to invent this dynamite, but I'm thankful you did," General Markel said. Rex and the general were watching the Prussian soldiers load the bags of explosives on small sleds.

"The hard part is ahead," Rex said, "But Amy and I appreciated your certification of the test results in the patent application. Did those heavy duty detonators arrive?"

"Not yet, Chief Smith assures me that the council's police superintendent, Larry Hopkins, will have them here in time."

"It was opportune that Larry was in New Hamburg seeing his girlfriend off," Rex said. "How serious was that encounter with the Ichneumons at Panther Creek?"

"It was damn serious for the Ichneumon squad, none of them survived, but I lost three good men. Captain Beck thinks their orders were to check on those siege cannons. I'm worried the patrol not returning will put Hickory Ridge on alert."

"Is there any truth in the rumor that fifty thousand troops are being sent to the territories?" Rex asked.

"Since the Wapiti Council and Governor Bullard know the plans, I see no need to keep it secret. I'm expecting the rest of the 88th Mountaineer Battalion to arrive any day, and the Fourth Brigade by spring. Berlin hasn't finalized the deployment orders, but with a peaceful eastern frontier, I expect one of the regiments will come to River Point. The other two regiments probably will go to Delta or Port Augusta to enforce the emperor's unpopular antislavery law."

"You're referring to the armistice with the Mongols?" Beck had told Rex the good news. The general nodded and Rex asked, "That's a couple of thousand soldiers, where will you billet them?"

"Why at Hickory Ridge."

General Markel's plan was to have soldiers transport the thousand kilograms of dynamite across the rugged terrain south of the river. Each man would carry a twenty-kilogram bag of the explosive. The trip was a three-day journey from the Prussian forward base near Panther Creek's confluence with the Erie to the attack's staging area at Slater's sawmill and cooperage operations, located an easy half-day trip south of Hickory Ridge.

Since General Markel planned to use a thousand troopers in the Hickory Ridge assault, finding fifty strong men to carry the additional weight wouldn't be a problem. The new worry, after the recent scrimmage, was the Ichneumon commander, General Mehta, sending patrols into the mountains behind Hickory Ridge. Discovery of the Prussian staging area would destroy the opportunity to surprise the Ichneumon garrison and endanger the precious dynamite.

Rudolf Habsburg's new assignment was to represent Emperor Schnabel on the Armistice and Trade Commission. He had been fortunate that the current Prussian emperor didn't believe in holding a father's sins against the son. The emperor had offered him an opportunity to salvage the Habsburg name and rank. If Rudolf kept the eastern border peaceful for three years, and an investigation showed his father's treachery had only involved the Zambian coastal blockade, the emperor would allow the former archduke to retire and reinstate the Habsburg family privileges.

A grateful Rudolf had accepted the emperor's offer and had worked hard to master the commission's business. He understood the emperor couldn't ignore his father's corruption and venal behavior. His fear was those miserable abolitionists had convinced the emperor that his father's honest effort to help the cotton growers' labor problem was treason. Surely, the emperor, who had known his father was a vain and foolish man, understood it was all an attempt by the archduke to satisfy creditors and gambling debts. Besides his father had sworn he was not involved with those reprehensible Delta orders that cost so many lives. Those orders had triggered the action that resulted in the loss of the battleship Schlesien and over a thousand Prussians.

Who wrote the orders was the mystery. Then new accusations had surfaced last week that his father was involve in the orders to abandon the strategic Delta fort. His father continued to deny any knowledge.

Rudolf believed they resulted from Ichneumon clandestine activities in Berlin. The admirals were no help. They would rather the emperor blame the navy order mess on treason than their incompetence. Anyone involved in that business was in danger of hanging. Rudolf prayed his father hadn't been that foolish.

Sanita Chopra, the bastard son of the Ichneumon emperor's curator of relics, along with being a contract assassin, on occasions, served the emperor as a high-ranking diplomatic courier. Emperor Ratakonda, in person, had briefed Chopra on the mission, and had entrusted a fifty-two million D-Marks horde of gold bullion bars to his care. It was an unheard of honor for a baseborn person such as himself and he intended to accomplish the mission or die trying.

The first part of the operation was just a money transfer. Chopra had made many such deliverers to the Myrtle Cotton Bank over the last ten years, only the amount involved made it noteworthy, one hundred and twenty of the bars, six-hundred kilograms of gold. He reckoned the emperor must have Harj Bhojwani, the agent who handled the empire's liaison with the cotton and tobacco plantation owners involved in something heavy.

The second part of Chopra's assignment required considerable travel and had to remain secret. The eighty remaining bars he would use to start a war, the main task that Emperor Ratakonda had assigned him.

To accomplish the second half of his mission, Chopra needed the help of the disgraced Archduke Habsburg's eldest son, Rudolf. The Prussian aristocrat was the one contact he had that could arrange a meeting with Prince Morihiro. The prince represented the tribal council that ran the Mongol Empire after the death of the prince's uncle, Khan Temujin. The complication for Chopra in any meeting with the barbarians was their murderous behavior towards Ichneumons who they considered non-human and often killed for no reason.

The Prussians and the Mongols meet every month on an island in the Volga River to discuss issues concerning the peace. The Prussian ban on the trade in slaves was a bitter point of contention during the prior day meeting of the Armistice and Trade Commission. Nothing had been resolved. Prince Morihiro had told the Prussians that several of the Mongol warlords wanted reimburse for seized slave shipments or they would no longer honor the armistice. The Prussian army officers on the commission were unconcerned about what a few barbarians thought and shrugged their collective shoulders.

The following day, Chopra had arrived at the Volga crossing along with news that the Prussian emperor had hung the Archduke. He found Rudolf at the Prussian fort on the west bank of the Volga. The aristocrat was staying in the private apartment the commission had built in the frontier garrison for the emperor's representative.

Rudolf, cursed Chopra when he saw who had entered his front room, "I'll kill you, you treacherous pimp," reaching for his revolver.

"I didn't know about the false Zambian orders," the agent said, lying, "Or your fathers involvement." He beat the drunk to the gun and set it on the hallway table out of reach of the stumbling man. Trying to calm Rudolf, he added, "Your father had nothing to do with those Delta orders. His involvement was with the naval order lifting the blockade. The Prussians investigators know that. Ask Joe Hansen, he knows I paid Major Lyons to issue those orders."

Rudolf, drunk and too mad to listen, charged Chopra who, with little effort, sent the big Prussian sprawling into the wall. The man laid there bemoaning the emperor's injustice and Ichneumon treachery.

"If you're done feeling sorry for yourself, we need to talk," Chopra said.

Straightening up the chair, he picked up Rudolf's coat, and checked the rest of the apartment for other occupants. There were none, but he discovered an open, half-empty liter bottle of vodka on the small marble table by the rear door. He corked that and sniffed the decanter of brown liquid beside it. That turned out to contain one of those shitty berry wines that the Mongols like and he thought undrinkable. He poured a glass for the duke who accepted the glass after regaining his feet.

"Is it poisoned?"

"At least it won't addle your brains. Emperor Ratakonda wants to help the Habsburgs take control of the Prussian Empire."

That sobered Rudolf. He recognized they were about to discuss treason and had looked around to verify no one was near enough to hear.

"The Schnabel line is weak," the Ichneumon added. "They will weaken the empire if allowed to continue. The next thing you know, those evil Mongols will be in Berlin, hell on the Baltic shore, if someone doesn't take charge. It's common knowledge the territories are in turmoil over the emperor's ban on slavery. The cotton growers hate him."

"That's a sour point with the Mongols," Rudolf said in a weak voice after draining the glass of wine.

"Damn right it is," Chopra said. He wondered if Duke Soltzendorff was correct that Rudolf Habsburg had the drive to head a coup d'état.

"Slaves are an important business for them," Rudolf said in a stronger voice. "The prince was just complaining that Prussian soldiers seized several shipments of prime female slaves headed to Berlin. He wants the slave owners reimbursed for their loss. Those savages are threatening an invasion of East Prussia to force the emperor to stop interfering in their rightful business."

"Who would blame them?" Chopra asked. He was elated to hear that. "The Mongols have sold and used slaves forever. Everyone did until your foolish emperor decided to interfere. That's why powerful men want you on the Prussian throne."

"Talk like that my friend will get us hung."

"If the opportunity came, would you be willing to serve?" Chopra asked. A dubious Rudolf nodded.

"Can you arrange a private meeting between Prince Morihiro and myself, preferably in the morning?"

The one advantage the Mongols had over the other empires was their vast number of people. A thousand mounted soldiers represented a meaningful portion of the Ichneumon army strength, for a Mongol prince, it was his entourage. Chopra's three attendants with their seven pack mules looked lost and terrorized in the milling swarm of fearsome mounted Mongol warriors surrounding the prince on his white horse.

Prince Morihiro was older than Chopra had expected, around sixty, but still quite agile for his age. The prince, wearing a fine white fur parka made from an ice bear, dismounted from his horse with no difficulty. He then waited as Chopra dismounted and join him by a large gold colored tent. A crew of Zamian slaves had erected it earlier.

"Thank you your majesty for meeting with this humble servant," Chopra said while kowtowing.

"I'm honored the mighty Ichneumon emperor thought the Mongols worthy of his attention," the prince said and gestured for Chopra to enter the tent while adding, "You speak our language well."

The interior of the tent was a wonder in rich colors. Green and red curtains lined the tent walls, a purple drape screened off the back third of the tent. Thick, bright colored carpets covered the ground, two iron stoves heated the room, and a large round table made from a smooth dark wood graced the center of the tent. Four unpadded straight back wood chairs were place around the table.

Two beautiful Mongol women in green silk kebayas stood by a small table on which several white porcelain cups and small covered dishes sat. A large sterling silver moka type coffee maker was hissing on the rear stove. The women served the prince and Chopra coffee and disappeared behind the purple curtain.

He was tempted to ask how many guards lurked behind the curtain, ready, at a word from the prince, to rush out and slay him. Or perhaps those beautify women served as guards too. He'd heard some Mongol women were talented and fearless warriors, trained in secret hand combat that could render a foe helpless or dead in a blink of the eye.

"The tall one, my niece, is fluent in all languages," the prince said. "The Prussian interpreters are all spies for Schnabel, so I use her, but now we don't need one. We're all busy, so let's try to avoid the usual diplomatic feigning and ambiguousness. What is Ratakonda after?"

"He wants the Mongol army to invade East Prussia."

"That's getting right to the point," the prince said and laughed. "Is the Erie campaign not going well?"

Chopra started to deny the Erie war was in trouble, before remembering Prince Morihiro's request for no evasiveness.

"At the moment, it's more frozen, until the spring thaw clears the river. My emperor's concern is reinforcements. The Prussians are going to ship fifty thousand soldiers into the territories to block our advance up the Erie and to intimidate the restless plantation owners."

"Your hope is the Prussians won't send those reinforcements if we attack them?"

"Yes. The other goal is generating turmoil in Berlin. The emperor's war with the Ichneumons is not popular, nor is his stand on slavery. Our friend will spread the news that the Mongols attacked in retaliation over Schnabel blocking their slave trade. His mischief will reinforce the concerns among key Prussian aristocrats that the man's obsession over slavery is endangering the Prussian Empire."

"Habsburg's father, the archduke is in prison, why would the emperor not arrest the son?"

"Why indeed, Ratakonda would have hanged all the male Habsburgs," Chopra said. "You should be aware the archduke was hung." Prince Morihiro looked surprised.

"How is our friend bearing up?"

"He's grieving his loss," Chopra said. "He'll soon be worrying that Emperor Schnabel might decide to hang him too."

"He should be," the Mongol prince said, sipping his coffee.

"Fortunate for Rudolf, but it's an example of what ails Berlin. Schnabel is soft, irresolute, and the nobles fear his dithering threatens their empire."

"Seems to me that Prussia has the irresolute weak leader that Ratakonda wants. Why chance changing it?"

"Having one we own is even better."

"If the man stays bought," the prince cautioned and then said. "Our last incursion across the Volga cost a hundred thousand Mongol lives. The tribal council chiefs lost a number of their sons, and though they're mad over Schnabel's anti slave stance, I'm not confident they'd support another war."

"Would eighteen million D-Marks in gold help your effort to persuade the council?" Chopra asked. A smiling Prince Morihiro nodded.

With a command, the Ichneumon soldiers with the pack mules carried the bullion into the tent and stacked it on the floor. The agent suspected gold wasn't the prince's principal motivation for agreeing to violate the armistice. The more of those chiefs and their sons the Prussian army cut down in battles, the clearer the prince's path to having the grand council name him the new Mongol emperor.

To cover the expected bribes and expenses that Rudolf would need in Berlin to promote Duke Soltzendorff's coup d'état, Chopra held back couple a million D-Marks. That wouldn't be enough. He needed to meet with Benjamin Purnell who controlled those special funds that Ratakonda had deposited in various Prussia and territorial banks. The Berlin coup organizers would need a good deal of gold, perhaps as much as ten million D-Marks.

Chapter 8

Two weeks before, Lieutenant Victor Ludendorff and his men had visited the Rupprecht Plantation about seventy kilometers inland from Port Augusta. The bucolic land they rode through had a flourishing appearance, fences, barns, and corrals in good repair, many plowed fields awaiting the spring planting, and herds of fine looking horses, sheep, and goats. The presence of armed men among the field workers reminded Victor that the bountiful land's prosperity depended on the wretched institution of slavery. The very evil the Berlin General Staff had assigned Victor to help end.

Two undersheriffs from Augusta had tagged along with Victor's cavalry squad during their first inspection of the Rupprecht Plantation. The owner and a dozen armed mounted men called Guardians had met them at the property's entrance. As the colonel had told Victor to cxpcct, the owner denied owning slaves and claimed the workers were indentured laborers. The presence of Herr Rupprecht's intimidating thugs ensured the few laborers even willing to acknowledge Victor's questions, stayed on message. To a man, they denied being slaves. It had been a fiasco.

Victor's report on the inspection had alarmed Colonel Jagger.

"Lieutenant Ludendorff, we have to obey Berlin orders," the colonel said, "But I don't want to start an insurrection. Until

Berlin gets serious and sends a brigade to enforce the emperor's decree, I don't want you bothering people for having slaves."

"What should I do? Ignore the order?" Victor had asked, hoping for new orders.

"Go through the motions, start an inventory of where the slave breeding operations are located," the colonel said, "An unobtrusive reconnaissance. I don't want anyone tarred and feather."

For once, he had been in complete agreement with his commander, comprehending who would be the one tarred and feathered.

Victor's social life had not blossomed in Augusta. Prussian army officers were suddenly out of favor among the landed gentry and invitations to dances and dinners evaporated. Stymied in gaining access to Augusta's élite social life, he spent his evenings exploring the waterfront and markets where young Prussian officers with D-Marks to spend were welcomed. A week ago, a young attractive Zamian girl had, uninvited, joined him at his table in the Smokey Jug bar where he was waiting for his friend, another bored lieutenant. A prostitute looking for a customer he had thought.

"Are you involved with finding slave breeding sites?" The woman asked, out of the clear, with no greeting. She acted nervous, making a quick glance about the smoke darken low ceiling room. Victor also looked. No one appeared to be paying attention. Her question had him curious, and he decided to play along.

"Yes, why do you ask?" Victor asked and added, "What is your name?"

"Uma, that's not important," the Zamian said. "What is important is finding out what Penton Plantation needed a hundred rolls of iron prison wire for."

"What kind of wire is that?"

"Expensive, the fencing is two-meter high chain link. Each roll contains fifty meters of fence. It has to be for a slave-breeding pen. You need to get that operation on the army's list."

"I'll do that," he said, perplexed over how she knew about the army's plans to inventory all the slave camps. Her owner he wondered. Judging from her appearance, her owner was at least a caring master, for Uma wore a clean gray dress and matching gray slacks with glossy black knee boots. The outfit reminded him of the Royal Prussian Church school uniforms. The thin black woman had all her teeth, clear dark eyes and no visible tattoos or scars.

Who's your master?"

"I'm not at liberty to say," she said. "But, it's good information, check it out." She then hurried off as the artillery lieutenant hailed him. Uma was out of the bar when his friend asked him whom the pretty girl was. Victor decided to protect her and told him she was selling jewelry.

"Told her no thanks, I didn't have anyone to buy jewelry for," Victor said, "Tell me about the test firing today." He ordered a bottle of wine as his friend told about the new 320 mm rifled cannon the Prussian navy was installing for coastal defense.

Colonel Jagger had thought the large prison wire order merited checking out. As a result, Victor, Feldwebel Prittwitz, and six troopers were on a brush-covered ridge swatting midges while looking down on Opossum Creek valley. A gleaming chain link fence formed a rectangular shaped enclosure, well over a kilometer long and maybe half that distance wide. The well-built pen was located along the bottom of the gently sloped valley. The fencing had to cost a fortune. The consensus among the Prussians was no one would spent that kind of money to fence in farm animals. The facility had to be a prison, or a slave-breeding pen.

A small creek ran along one side of the fenced area. Rows of long narrow one-story sheds with gravel lanes between them covered the enclosed north side of the valley. On the south side of the creek, outside the enclosure, were dozens of plowed garden plots ready for spring plantings. Without the fence, Victor would have thought from the layout of the facility that it was a huge hog or turkey farm.

Victor was considering whether to ride into the valley and verify the Opossum Creek facility was a large slave breeding operation, when a group of hard looking armed men rode up. The rawboned, stubble faced, unkempt middle-aged man nodded to him.

"What are you doing boy, trespassing on Penton land?" The band's leader asked, as the eight riders with him formed a line to the upper side of the Prussian troopers clustered around Victor.

"Not that army business is any of your business, we're making an inventory of plantations using slave labor," Victor said. "And who are you to question the emperor's men?"

Victor had sensed the thug's hostility and didn't like the way the riders had arranged themselves. It suggested an ambush and he wasn't sure what to do. The colonel didn't want him starting any confrontation with the guardians and plantation owners.

"I'm Herr Penton's overseer, Grover Zagat; now leave before I have to run you off, boy." The clicks of cocking hammers caused both Victor and Grover to look.

"Herr Zagat, if you and your men want to see the sunset, tell your men to throw down their weapons." Feldwebel Prittwitz said. He gave Victor a disappointed look and added, "And that revolver you're holding."

Victor then saw Grover had been holding a cocked revolver down by his right leg. The realization the bastard had intended to threaten him, even shoot him, and he hadn't even realized the danger, embarrassed him. Thankfully, his feldwebel and men knew when to act, however Grover was frozen and hadn't yet ordered his men to disarm. Prittwitz had Grover covered and the troopers had his thugs covered, so any order other than to disarm would result in a slaughter.

Since Victor was in command, he needed to break the standoff before Grover did something stupid and that might require killing the man. Forcing his feldwebel to make the next move would be a craven dereliction of duty. He drew his revolver as he nudged his horse forward to close the distance separating them.

"Drop your revolver and tell your men to," Victor said, aiming the revolver at the posse's leader. The man didn't appear impressed or fearful.

"Get that gun out of my face, before I smack you," Grover snarled. Victor cocked the hammer.

"We're here on the emperor's orders and will tolerate no interference," he said, whishing he was elsewhere. If the old bastard didn't back down, Victor would have to carry through on his implied threat to shoot him, or lose control of the confrontation along with his men's respect. The man's smirk and raising his revolver broke Victor's vacillation and he shot Grover's arm holding the gun.

"Feldwebel, kill any man who hasn't dropped his weapon."

Grover was still in the saddle cursing and trying to stop the blood running down his arm. The man's revolver was on the ground, but Victor, being inexperienced in violent encounters, wondered if the colonel would think he overreacted, if he shot the bastard again.

"Do what the ass wants," Grover managed to said, "And then help me."

Corporal Hyman and another trooper dismounted and collected the posse's weapons, a collection of Krupp rolling block rifles, muzzle loaded double barrel shotguns, and few old cap and ball revolvers. The thugs were no stranger to violence, for they quickly had a makeshift tourniquet on their leader's arm.

"You'd better ride hard for Augusta, sonny, for come night it'll not be safe around here," Grover said. With that parting remark the disarmed posse thundered down the trail they had arrived on.

After a quiet moment, Victor said, "Well, after all that, let's go inspect the facility in the valley."

The four older men who were the guards did not challenge or try to stop their inspection. After inspecting the Opossum Creek buildings, none of the men thought the place was anything other than an extensive slave breeding operation. Victor counted forty-two adult women in the slave pens. Their skin tone ranged from black to olive and appeared to be a blend of Clovis and Zamian ancestry. Other than a dozen or so young very pregnant women, the rest were elderly. Too old to be of use in the fields, Victor reckoned, though still useful to care for the young. One building had an area set aside for a nursey that held eight babies.

If it hadn't been for the obvious intelligence and fear that he saw in the eyes of a few of the women, he'd have thought he was interviewing zombies. The prevalent latrine odor and swarms of flies amplified his opinion that the forlorn camp was an abomination, and the society that benefited from it no better.

The children, too active to get an accurate count, numbered around sixty, none was older than four or five. Unlike the mute adults, they were noisy and flocked to the fence to inspect the armed riders in strange uniforms and with the large Imperial Iron Cross flag.

A few of them had birth defects or they had suffered past injuries. Most startling were the two young kids with one eye. Where the other eye should be, smooth skin covered the eye socket with not a trace of an eyelash or eyebrow. Several others had hands with only two long fingers and a thumb. Victor wondered if the well water was bad. He wished he had thought to bring hard candies to hand out to them.

The kids' chatter and crowding against the fence appeared to irritate the youngest and only clean-shaven guard. He yelled at the children to fall in. The Prussians were stunned at the results of his command. Within seconds, the children had lined up in the center of the yard in four rows by age, the youngest in front. The yard was silent. The adults, a bit slower, silently shuffled into a line behind the kids. It was eerier. It was amazing to Victor.

"How do you get children to behave so well," he asked the guard.

"The troublesome ones we give to Snapper," the guard answered, nodding toward a high fenced corral that held a terror bird, a slink.

"You're kidding," Victor asked, realizing that maybe the man wasn't. "You feed them to that bird?"

The colonel had told Victor that slave operations usually kept one of the intimidating creatures. The large flightless bird, it was the size of a horse, had him checking his revolver was still in its holster and handy. The bird's baleful scrutiny made him leery.

A couple of the guards nodded and one of them said. "It's important those animals learn early to behave for their betters. It's for their own good."

Victor was at a loss on how to respond to such evil when a shout captured his attention. Apparently, the camp also served as a jail for the sheriff. A bewhiskered, tall, scrawny, middle-aged Prussian man was waving and shouting from inside the caged enclosure attached to the wooden barn.

"Help me," the tall scrawny man yelled. "I've been kidnapped."

The prisoner's shout caught the slink's attention. It dashed to side of the corral, hissing, and straining its razor sharp hook shaped beak to reach the man only an arm length away. The man was obviously use to the threating creature. He ignored it. The two troopers with Victor didn't and brought their rifles up.

"Wait, there's no danger," the older guard shouted.

"There is to that creature if it gets out," the feldwebel said. He told the troopers to keep their rifles on the slink.

“He’s a horse thief we’re holding for the sheriff.”

The guard’s comments riled the prisoner who renewed his pleading.

“Please, you have to listen. The duke had the Pentons kidnap me. He’s stealing my invention. You have to help. You’re Prussian soldiers, save me.”

The site inspection had proven an unnerving and disheartening experience, now this. After the earlier confrontation with Herr Penton’s overseer and thugs, Victor figured he was in enough trouble without getting involved in the sheriff’s business. He got the man’s name, Al Leslie, and promised to report his tale to authorities in Augusta.

Chapter 9

Benjamin Purnell hadn't known a good night's sleep since that morning a month ago when General Markel's soldiers had him dragged from his warm bed in Orleans and shipped him to Berlin for an interrogation. The eight days wearing a slave collar and chained to the Aruba's aft coalbunker was the most uncomfortable period. But the waiting in a damp dark stone cell off the room with the rack had his nerves on edge. That cruel machine would tear him apart. At best, he'd end a pathetic cripple.

Then two days, ago, the former Roanoke IRS manger and now, Purnell was shocked to learn, the head of the Prussian spy agency, Joe Hansen, visited him.

"Do I need to start with you on the rack or are you ready to answer my questions?" Joe asked through the cell door's barred window.

Of course, he had agreed to cooperate. After a bath and clean orange coveralls, one of the old prisoners serving as a trustee, had taken Purnell to a cell on the third floor of the building. The questioning started the next day in a small conference room and focused on Cinnabar's operation in Panther Creek.

"Why'd you send Amy Caroom to Cinnabar's settlement, if not to use her expertise in chemistry to get the cocaine conversion process back on track?" Joe Hansen had asked.

"She wanted to visit the upper Erie Valley and see the area, meet some of the natives," Benjamin said, prevaricating without shame. He hated that bitch.

"The girl wanted a vacation and I figured letting her travel with Herr Wright on a winter-sloe nut buying expedition would broaden her education," he had explained. Joe didn't need to know that Wright was to see that she didn't return.

"Her sworn deposition said you forced her to go the Cinnabar's place for the expressed purpose of fixing the cocaine conversion operation. The vats, mixers, grinders, and drying beds along with barrels of chemicals used to convert winter sloe nuts into cocaine paste found by the Wapiti supports her story."

"Cinnabar is a repulsive drunk that could scarcely organize his tribe's annual winter-sloe nut harvest. Herr Wright, who someone murdered, was there to buy those raw winter sloe nuts. The Wapiti bootleggers killed him to prevent him from discovering that equipment. They knew he'd tell the authorities. I figured they threatened the Caroom woman and terrified her into telling that nonsense."

So the interview had gone the first day, a he said, she said waste of time. Purnell worried Hansen would decide to start the rough stuff. The Cinnabar business a warmup, before the interrogation focused on the origin of those false navy orders that caused the abandonment of Delta. Then to his relief, a Prussian colonel had interrupted the interrogation on the second day and told Hansen that the emperor wanted Herr Purnell and him at the palace.

"I have to face the emperor in these vile yellow coveralls?" Purnell asked. An amused Joe just nodded.

The walk from the General Staff headquarters to the Imperial Palace was about two kilometer across a large plaza. Despite the freezing weather, Purnell noticed he wasn't the only one who had broken a sweat hurrying up the endless stairs to access the palace and trying to keep up with the colonel leading them.

Hansen was red faced and sweating profusely by the time they reached the palace south wing entrance at the top of the stairs. Purnell hadn't been much better and hoped he didn't start smelling off, his armpits were dripping.

The two guards at the side palace entrance appeared to be friends with Hansen. On seeing the spymaster's flush color and sweating, they teased him about needing less time at the desk and dinner table and more time in the field. He took the guards kidding in good sprites. The colonel didn't and silenced the guards with a look.

"The emperor is waiting," the annoyed colonel said.

The officer had then entered the palace and subjected them to another brisk walk down a long empty marble hallway. They passed several solid unmarked doors, before arriving at a door guarded by two Imperial guards. Emperor Schnabel, plus several very serious and alert guards waited for them in the palace conference room.

Purnell had met Emperor Schnabel's father during a fleet review in the Baltic. The man, tall, strong, and lucid, had conveyed a magnificent presence. He had looked and acted like an emperor. The old man even had a welcoming manner toward the businessmen seeking Prussian naval business. Purnell never sensed from the old emperor a hint of the disdain toward businessmen that was so prevalent among the navy officers and aristocrats that haunted the government bureaus and palace.

The current Prussian emperor, Wolfgang Schnabel, Purnell had heard, and could now verify, bored a striking resemblance to his father. He had never met the son before, but Harlem Penton, the cotton grower, and Necho Allen, a mine owner and his partner in the New Hamburg Roanoke Railroad had.

Necho didn't think the emperor was as sharp as his father was, but he was no fool. He thought Wolfgang had been ill advised by the Habsburgs and Duke Soltzendorff. He warned Purnell not to place much weight on Penton's opinion, who thought the man obtuse and liked to ridicule him.

The emperor was a young handsome man in his early thirties, and dressed in an unadorned grey green army officer's uniform. He had offered his hand in greeting, much like two businessmen meeting, and seemed not to notice the filthy coveralls or be the least tense. One would never suspect from the man's demeanor that, just two days ago, an assassin had ambushed him as he exited the palace. The Ichneumon had emptied his revolver at the emperor, managing only a slight wound to his leg. Two of his guards weren't so fortunate they died.

"Has Joe got you to confess yet?" The emperor had asked in a relaxed voice. "Or should I okay the rack?"

"Your majesty, I'm an innocent man," Purnell had answered, bowing. He hadn't known what to expect from this sudden summon to an audience with the Prussian emperor, but not taunts.

"I have difficulty accepting that claim, having read the depositions of Herr Wu and Fräulein Caroom," the emperor had responded in a harder voice, before concern for Joe diverted his attention.

"Are you okay Joe? Guard, pour him some cold water," the emperor said, handing across the desk to the guard the pitcher of ice water from the small table by his chair. "Colonel Essen, in the future, please keep in mind most men are not as fit as you."

"Yes your honor," the officer said, not appearing the least chasten by the emperor's remark.

Purnell, while careful not to appear pleased, agreed Hansen didn't look well. Dare he hope his nemesis would have a stroke? Then he realized that pitiless Colonel Essen would be in charge of his interrogation and hot pinchers and the rack might soon be in use.

"Joe, loosen your neck cloth, see if that helps," Purnell suggested. The emperor, appearing concerned, nodded in agreement.

After the guard removed the tight neck cloth and Joe was breathing again, Purnell addressed the emperor's remarks. "I was just explaining to Herr Hansen that those bundles of Wapiti falsehoods were obtained by torture."

"Herr Wu's possibly," the emperor said. "Not the Caroom woman's statements. A woman I trust, Franciscka Weidman, was there when that young lady made her statements concerning your orders that she fix Chief Cinnabar's cocaine paste operation."

"Amy Caroom is a smart beautiful woman who has thrown her lot in with the Wapiti. Last I heard she's living with one, and she has apparently decided to help spread their lies to cover the Wapiti bootleg cocaine operation."

"I can't believe you're still spouting that nonsense," Joe sputtered. "You belong on the rack."

The emperor added, "Her testimony must have you worried. I understand you put a ten thousand D-Mark reward on her head. Is the rumor correct that she is your daughter?"

"That claim is just another example of that witch's dishonesty. The woman stole my property and designs," Purnell said. "Go to Smithtown, you'll find all their equipment came from my machine shop. She's a thief, that's the reason for the reward, not her bootleg cocaine nonsense, which is a Wapiti fabrication."

"I doubt Balaji Ratakonda would react well to learning his principal agent in the Prussian territories ran a cocaine business on the side that cut into his business."

"I would suspect not," Purnell agreed. His partner, Allen, had the right of this emperor. The fools were the ones that thought Wolfgang Schnabel was a fool. "Thank goodness, I have no involvement in cocaine, bootleg or otherwise."

"Please, spare the emperor from your nonsense. It's well known you're in cahoots with the Ichneumons," Hansen managed to croak, though still an alarming red in the face.

"The damn nonsense being thrown around is this Ichneumon agent business. I repair and build steamboats and operate a railroad. Until the war, I did business with both Ichneumons and Prussian interests, now just Prussians." He sensed he might survive this audience with the emperor, and then the man changed the focus.

"A point I could never resolve was why an Ichneumon agent in Berlin would want orders sent to the Prussian fleet at Delta to abandon a fort that they didn't control. For your claim to be correct, Berlin wrote those counterfeit naval orders at least a week prior to the magazine exploding and General Markel seizing Delta. How's that possible?"

His armpits were dipping, the flaw in his scheme to help Ichneumons recover Delta laid exposed. The emperor expected an explanation, or a confession.

"I haven't seen these orders, so I don't know what they ordered. If I have to speculate, I'd say Chopra's purpose was clearing the fleet out of the bay so Ichneumon troop ships could enter and disembark reinforcements. That the Prussians had taken the stronghold wouldn't have entered his mind." From the looks of his tormentors, that explanation hadn't entered their mind. He added, "Besides, what sane Ichneumon would expect the Prussian army to just up and abandon the fort after seizing it."

Hansen, shaking his head, exchanged looks with the emperor, who after a moment softly said. "Isn't that the truth, who would have expected them to walk away?"

Purnell waited, believing he had said enough. The emperor tried another approach.

"My understanding is the Ichneumon emperor financed your railroad in Guderian Territory. Would he do that if you weren't a trusted agent?" the emperor asked.

"Well, I thought the fact that the Ichneumon Trade Bank financed the New Hamburg and Roanoke railroad was common knowledge," Purnell answered. He hoped the emperor thought the sweat beading on his forehead was from the colonel rushing them to the meeting. "There was no nefarious geopolitical reason. The bank liked the eight percent interest the NH&R railroad offered to pay on the debt."

"And what is the amount of the debt?" Joe had asked.

"The loan was for thirty-two million D-Marks." The emperor and Joe exchanged glances.

"What's the current balance on the loan and terms?" Joe asked after another glance at Schnabel.

Purnell had never dreamed a Prussian emperor would be interested in the practical details of finance. That revelation surprised and worried him.

"It's thirty-two million. The company is only paying the interest. The loan was set up for a balloon payment, due after twenty years."

"Those are amazing terms. I had no idea the Ichneumon Trade Bank was so generous with Ratakonda's money, and you being not even one of his trusted agents."

Purnell figured no comment was called for. After a moment the emperor added, "I want NH&R to build a rail line to River Point."

Hansen appeared as startled as he was at Schnabel's request.

"You are asking NH&R to construct a rail line to River Point?" Purnell asked. The emperor nodded. "Where would the financing come from?"

"That's your concern. I expect you and your partners to provide the financing," the emperor said. "Work your magic on the Ichneumon Trade Bank."

"But the war closed the trade bank, and we did consider such a route. It would cost fifty million to tunnel and cross those mountains," Purnell said. The idea was absurd. The time allowed, impossible. Besides, why would a Prussian emperor even care? He tried to think of other difficulties.

"How would the army know where the railroad needs land to transverse those mountains and rivers? What about the Wapiti farmers? And the right-of-away, who even owns the wilderness? It'd take years to build that three-hundred kilometer railroad spur."

"Forget years, I expect you to have that track completed before next winter. Military engineers have a route picked and assure me if a sufficient effort was mounted, it's feasible. The army will provide the necessary right-of-way."

His skepticism must have shown.

The emperor added, "The Wapiti Council wants to be named a Prussian Territory. I'm confident the farmers will not be a problem. The army will be reasonable and settle with everyone in due time. I want the rail line finished this construction season. Are you willing to guarantee the effort is successful?"

"What if I can't find a lender?"

"Perhaps you should consider it a gesture of goodwill to the empire. I would view the financing as your earnest atonement for your inadvertent participation in the Delta fiasco, but of course it's your call."

A somberness settled across the room, even the normally twitchy Hansen was still. The Emperor raised eyebrow emphasized that negotiations were over. It was decision time.

It was an unreasonable request. Neither Purnell, Allen, nor the railroad, between themselves, had fifty million D-Marks to spare, especially to build a rail track that would take years, if ever, to earn back the investment. The new Erie war would prevent the Ichneumon Trade Bank from financing the project. Then again, Purnell now comprehended, not agreeing to build and finance the Prussian spur was liable to prove lethal.

"Your majesty," Purnell said, "I'd be honored for an opportunity to demonstrate my loyalty."

"Excellent," the emperor said. "Joe, you'll be my liaison with Herr Purnell. Colonel Essen, you will provide his protection and transportation. And colonel, arrange for our guest to stay in a suite at the Royal Bismarck."

Was he free? He held up his arm to remind the emperor of the prisoner coveralls, not exactly a suitable outfit for the Bismarck.

"Oh, yes," the emperor said with a smile, then added, "Colonel, make arrangements for some decent clothes and a tailor. Herr Purnell, you have no time to waste, I want construction starting by the mid-March. Colonel, after he has a chance to freshen up and change outfits, I want you to introduce him to his new office and staff. Anyone have any questions?"

Purnell did, and he could sense Joe did too, but he wasn't about to chance a query that might derail his escape from the dungeon. He shook his head.

"Joe, another moment," the emperor said, standing up to signal the end of the current meeting.

Joe Hansen believed the emperor had made a mistake in trusting Benjamin Purnell. He was well aware that the Prussian aristocracy expected a commoner, such as him, to defer to their superior knowledge. That social taboo in particular applied to interactions with the Prussian emperor, who also happened to be Joe's direct boss. Still, the emperor had told Joe he didn't want a yes-man. After Herr Purnell, the guards, and Colonel Essen were gone and the room's door closed, Joe asked the emperor why.

"You ask why turn a treacherous and murderous psychopath loose," the emperor said. "Because he's the owner of a railroad that works, though I suspect his partner, Necho Allen played an important part."

"Allen's not much better, but at least he's not an Ichneumon agent," Joe said. "Why not use his expertise and hang Purnell?"

"Did no one ever tell you that you're not to question an emperor's decision?" A frowning Emperor Schnabel snapped.

Damn, he'd pissed off the emperor. Joe hesitated, not sure how to respond. The emperor appeared embarrassed, shook his head and added.

"Sorry Joe, you reminded me of the hell I'm catching for hanging Habsburg. When it becomes known I spared Purnell, who many think was also involved in the same crime, the criticism will be severe."

"I'll concede he made a good argument. Maybe the purpose was to clear the way for troop ships, but I still think his forgers were just very good and the effort was to prevent the Prussians from gaining control and ending slavery."

"He is a slippery fellow, but let's move on. My official goal is uncomplicated. It's to build the rail spur that General Markel needs to supply his Erie River campaign without paying for it. Purnell will pay for the project to keep his head."

"Then why not just seize his properties, such as NH&R railroad and his bank accounts to pay for the spur?"

"Joe, as the former head of the Guderian Territory IRS, you have to appreciate that felons like Purnell have most of their wealth in secret bank accounts and stashes under fake names." Joe shrugged.

"There's always hot pinchers."

"You're thinking torture would get those names? Maybe it would, certainly some of the accounts, but I have a bigger target than that, the Ichneumon slush funds."

"I never had any luck finding those rumored accounts," Joe said. "I figured the Ichneumon emperor used trusted couriers to transport the funds, someone like Sanita Chopra or the late Herr Wu. The Ichneumons would only send money when needed to pay the bribes and buy a territorial election. Without a doubt, the Ichneumons have a few accounts hidden throughout the territorial banks, but I figure they're small."

"I don't want guesses, Joe," the emperor said, relaxing a bit. "The cotton growers are in a rebellious mood. You need to determine if the Ichneumons have accumulated a substantial financial presence in the territorial banks, and if they have, why?"

Joe, though still skeptical about the existence of secret funds, asked. "I'm to force Purnell to spend enough money on the spur that he'll have no choice but to tap those funds?"

"Yes, that's what I want. If such funds exist, I want them spent on the railroad, not used to support an insurrection and a mercenary army in the territories. Do you remember Donnelly's Ichneumon force?"

"I do and I wondered at the time where James Donnelly managed, so quickly, to find over a hundred mercenaries to bolster the Hinton stockade defenses."

"I was also curious and asked Archduke Habsburg to look into it. My belief, worry, was and still is that Ratakonda is helping the slave owners assembling a private army of ex-Ichneumon soldiers in the territories. Armies are expensive and require payrolls. Someone is paying those soldiers, if they exist. He found nothing, but now I know Purnell and the Ichneumons had their hooks in him, so I want you to follow up."

"Do you have any sold information on numbers?" Joe asked. Emperor Schnabel shook his head. "Then I will push Purnell, tell him I want proof he's serious about honoring the deal. I want the rails and other big-ticket items ordered and proof of payment. Force the man to spend a lot of money early on, while I track its source. He'll need to be allowed freedom to travel."

The emperor shrugged.

"It'll work if he has no qualms about raiding the Ichneumon funds," Joe added. "Rogue territorial banks I can question using tax fraud and money laundering as the reason."

"Your men need to accomplish this without alerting anyone that the emperor has concerns about insurrections in the territories."

"If anyone asks, the purpose is to assure all taxes are being paid." Joe said. The emperor nodded.

"That should suffice, now go find the answers. I don't want this rot infecting the homeland and face a coup d'état. It's disconcerting enough that the Mongols are threatening to break the armistice. I don't have to tell you fighting two wars will stress the empire's resources."

Chapter 10

The Prussian solider guarding the door to General Markel's River Point office, opened it, and announced that Colonel Fritz Caprivi had entered the fort. The general, relieved, directed the guard to bring the colonel straight away to the office.

"How many men are with you?" General Markel asked, skipping pleasantries.

Caprivi, his most effective subordinate, had returned from Guderian Territory's main ocean port, New Hamburg. He had sent the colonel there to facilitate the 88th Mountaineer Battalion rapid transportation across the mountains. The unit was part of the powerful Fourth Brigade, renowned for driving the Mongol army back across the Volga River two years ago. The general needed the battalion for his pending attack on Hickory Ridge. Later the troopers would help staff the forts.

"I gather the pigeon didn't make it?" the colonel asked.

Concerned, the general shook his head.

"The Mongols are threatening to cross the Volga with a hundred thousand men. The emperor sent the Fourth Brigade back to the Volga front. Only two companies of the 88th Battalion came with me."

"Two wars, that's not good," the general said, shaking his head, and then asked, "So how many men are with you?"

"Three hundred, all with the new bolt action repeating rifles," Fritz said.

“Well that’s something. Those rifles do make a difference.”

“Also here is the dispatch bag from Berlin.”

The general accepted the bag from Fritz. While searching for his key, he told Fritz to get out of his wet coat and warm himself by the fire. The snow on his heavy coat was starting to melt and make a puddle.

“Well, a bit of good new, Captain Beck is now a major,” General Markel said. After reading a bit more, he said. “There will be no reinforcements until the east settles down. Our orders are to defend River Point.”

“The attack on Hickory Ridge is off?” Fritz asked.

“With the new men, we have about six hundred soldiers. I never have gotten a firm number on the size of the Ichneumon garrison. Depending on whom you talk with, it’s from two hundred to over a thousand.”

“We have that new explosive.” Fritz said.

“Yes we do, a thousand kilograms of dynamite. Feldwebel Crouch and our friend both believe it is enough to breach the wall.”

“We would have surprise, if we do it now. With the thaw four to six weeks away, the Ichneumons won’t be anticipating an attack before that occurs.”

“Also, I figure the Ichneumon command in Delta is aware of the possible renewal of hostilities with the Mongols and that Berlin is unlikely to dispatch new reinforcements to River Point. They’ll expect us to focus our limited forces on defending River Point. So, what would you suggest?” The general asked.

“I’d attack, now, before the river clears. If we had Hickory Ridge with its high cannons, we’d have a chance to sink the Helot, Saukko, and Kura, and block the river.”

"Well, the best defense is a good offence," the general said, repeating the aphorism beating into all young Prussian officers. "We'll attack."

Though neither man under estimated the difficulty of the task before them, both were delighted with the decision to attack first, not wait for the blow to fall on them.

The cargo of Zamian slaves General Emwazi had delivered was a welcomed boost to Delta's repair effort. The extra bodies would enabled General Paget to speed the rebuilding of the fort. Several more weeks of intense construction effort on the outer walls would be required for him to have confidence a surprise landing by Prussian marines wouldn't overwhelm his garrison.

His fear was a landing down river out of range of Delta's rifle cannons and the marines attacking the fort's rear. The Prussians had the resources to launch that sort of attack any time they recovered their nerve from the loss of the Schlesien. No battleships were required to ferry troops to an unopposed landing site.

Those new Prussian battleships under construct at Port Baltic might threaten Delta, but not until their completion and launch, which spies had assured him was at least a year away. And the fort defense now had two of the Ichneumon's new rifled cannons on line. In another year, he would have six. Their explosive shells could sink any enemy warship foolish enough to enter the Erie River.

The effort for accomplishing Emperor Ratakonda's first order, secure the entrance to the Erie River was making good progress. Now General Paget had the emperor's second order to achieve, seize River Point and block the Prussian army from occupying the upper Erie valley. He had the ancient, underpowered battleship, Helot, and two small, modern warships, the Kura, and the fast Saukko, all armed with the new rifle cannons, any one of them capable of blowing away the fort at River Point with a short bombardment.

However, until the river cleared above Westport, the Ichneumon warships couldn't reach River Point, and that thaw appeared in no rush to occur. A nagging concern to him was the state of Hickory Ridge defenses under General Mehta who had allowed the Wapiti convoy to slip past the fort. Paget decided not to wait on the thaw.

"General Emwazi, I'm going to give you a chance to shine. Instead of taking charge of Delta, I'm assigning you the Hickory Ridge command." He sent a guard to find the Saukko captain.

Emwazi was one of those wiry strong Ichneumons that reminded Paget of those Wapiti trappers he once dealt with in the Southern River. If not for his eyes with the Ichneumon iris vertical slit pupil, most people would think the young man was just another local mutt. The man had no royal connection. Like Paget he had make general through merit. In Emwazi's case, he had gained the emperor's favorable opinion by brutally putting down the miners' insurrection and reviving the production of gold.

"As you wish," the young general said, "But please allow me to help teach those Wapiti warriors manners."

Paget nodded, and then added, "We'll do that, but first I want Hickory Ridge secured. The Prussians understand the importance of Hickory Ridge in controlling the upper Erie valley. We all know River Point is a pimple compared to Hickory Ridge's commanding location and armament. I want a commander there that I can count on."

"What about Mehta?"

"Handle him as you see fit," Paget said. "I want you to travel overland and reach Hickory Ridge, not wait on the river ice. The few Prussian soldiers that escaped because of Mehta's incompetence belonged to the 88th Mountain battalion and a ground assault in winter by those troopers isn't unthinkable. Their Wapiti allies are equally unpredictable. The loss of Hickory Ridge due to a surprise attack would greatly complicate the campaign to prevent the Prussian occupation of the Erie valley."

"How many soldiers can I take?"

"Horses are the restraint. They're in short supply at Westport because of the gold strikes up the Great Western River. I figure the garrison can spare sufficient animals for a hundred men," Paget said.

"Okay to live off the land?"

"Sure," Paget answered as the Saukko captain entered the tent.

"New orders, I want you to haul the general and his men as far up the Erie, as conditions allow. He'll disembark at that point and ride ahead to reinforce Hickory Ridge. You follow with the Saukko, as the ice retreats, until you can reach River Point and eliminate the Prussian threat."

In the end, General Emwazi picked ninety soldiers and one hundred and twenty horses from the Westport garrison for the overland ride to Hickory Ridge. If horses hadn't been in short supply because of the gold strikes up the Great Western River, he'd taken two hundred men and three hundred horses.

The plan had been to move fast and forage off the land. By the second day, the soldiers realized the wilderness had little to offer in winter. The Clovis settlements they encountered had been abandon. Other than fodder for the horses, the men found few supplies among the cabins and tents. To express their displeasure, the Ichneumon soldiers burned the first settlement.

The following morning's rollcall revealed two soldiers missing. A camp search discovered their bodies behind the latrine in a small ravine with slit throats. The men wanted to hunt for the killers, but General Emwazi understood the message. He told the troopers that vengeance would wait, and ordered the next abandon Clovis village not looted. No soldiers turned up dead the following morning.

The expedition settled into one cold hungry day after another while crossing one snow-shrouded ridge after another with an occasional treacherous frozen river crossing adding to their misery. Falls on ice injured a number of horses and riders. Two horses and their riders broke through the river ice and drowned. The Ichneumon fort at Bone Valley was a welcoming sight.

Captain Kakani, the commander of the fort, was new to his command. General Paget had sent him to Bone Valley just before the river iced over. He was one of the few officers to survive the Delta disaster, though the explosion had left him with terrible scars. Emwazi and his soldiers' arrival and news cheered the captain and entire garrison.

"The threat of a Mongol invasion should help our campaign," Captain Kakani said, referring to the Ichneumon move to seize full control over the Erie River.

"You think the Ichneumon army needs help. Nephew, you need to be cautious with defeatist talk," General Emwazi said. The mild reprimand seemed to settle his nephew. "Your responsibility is protecting the saline works."

"This saline operation is a losing endeavor, a wasted effort. The men spend all their energy in obtaining firewood for the brine furnaces. We have to go twenty kilometers to find trees."

"I wondered what happen to the trees," the general said looking again at the frozen bare terrain. As far as one could see from the fort's ramparts, there were no trees on either side of the river. "Is there no coal?"

His nephew shook his head.

"Benjamin Purnell owns the saline works, so he'll have to decide whether it's worth continuing. What kind of trail runs from here to Hickory Ridge?"

"Better than what is between here and Westport," the captain said. "The lack of bridges over the frozen creeks will make a four day trip, a week trip. The Slater sawmill and dock are about half way."

The general asked if the Slaters were loyal.

"They deal with us, but I wouldn't trust them," the captain said. "There's a lot of them, all with rifles, and quick to take offence."

"I'll try to not antagonize them, for now," the general said. "I know you want action, nephew. You're going to get all you want this spring, after we kick the Prussians out of River Point. General Paget wants the Erie valley secured."

"Pacified?" Captain Kakani asked. The general couldn't tell if the news pleased his nephew, or not, due to the facial scars.

"Yes, the Clovis, Wapiti, and all the other denizens will kowtow to Ichneumon rule or die."

Colonel Palitzsch had left the territories with no promises of girls. Two weeks later, he encountered Duke Soltzendorff in the east hallway of the Berlin Imperial palace. The wealthy aristocrat had just returned from a tour of his plantations in Myrtle Territory.

"I saw your pal, Benjamin Purnell, at Myrtle Cotton Bank," the duke said. "He was transferring funds to build a new railroad, told me that you had been in Wapiti territory."

"I heard the railroad project will cost in the fifty million D-Mark range. Do you think Benjamin has that kind of money?"

"I don't know the details, but our friend pulled millions out of the bank. We both know cotton has been booming in the last couple of years and will as long as the emperor keeps starting new wars. Purnell was in a good mood when I saw him. He even told me the bank's solid and I should buy out Rupprecht. The old man wants to sell his ten percent interest. I'm thinking I might."

"Millions . . . I knew Purnell wasn't poor, but I would have thought that his main accounts were in Berlin," Colonel Palitzsch said. He wondered if his investigation into the bogus navy orders might offer an avenue to shake some of that money out of Purnell.

"Who knows what that gangster owns? Of more interest, does your club have any new girls?" The duke asked. The colonel shook his head.

"Not Wapiti ones."

Rex's idea had fascinated Amy. He had used one of her prototype batteries and a roll of insulated copper wire to demonstrate the effect of short-circuiting the current through a very thin iron wire. The iron shunt had glowed bright red before burning up.

"So, if we replace the percussion cap in the detonator with one of your shunts, the battery can explode the detonator?" Amy asked. Rex nodded. "If it works, and it should, I'm going to write a patent for you."

Rex had no idea who had invented the electric blasting cap on Earth, but figured the person would never learn they had stolen his idea on another world. His sweetheart, along with all her other talents, was a skilled worker with metal and within an hour had a device to test. Amy had fabricated the test-blasting cap from pieces out of a Prussian detonator. It was a brass cylinder, about the size of one of his mother's lipstick tubes, with two wires running out of one end.

A hole in a block of ice by the rear door was the test site. He placed the detonator in the hole so the ice could contain the metal fragments if the test was successful.

"Why'd you have me twist the wire ends together first?" Amy asked.

Rex, reminded that he was dealing with a genius who tended to notice things, considered her question. He didn't want to get side tracked into a discussion of static electricity and her inevitable questions of how he knew.

"It seemed the thing to do. Now separate the wire ends and touch them to your battery terminals," Rex said. A sharp bang from outside the rear door announced the test was successful. Amy was delighted and forgot her question.

Chapter 11

In a way, the weather had cooperated. The winter had turned ugly the prior three days with a bitter subzero wind and blinding snow squalls, though spring equinox was less than a week away. The sudden hard freeze had brought them a few extra days to mount the attack on the stronghold.

Jeremy Slater and several timbermen familiar with the country behind the Hickory Ridge fort had guided, without mishap, the small Prussian assault force to the fort's rear. Rex and Feldwebel Crouch's assignment was supervising the proper placement of the dynamite. They were about a hundred meters from the looming barbican guarding the rear gate into the fort waiting for the final word. The weather was perfect, no moon, windy, and snowing, nearly a whiteout. Behind them in the swirling snow waited twenty-five soldiers chosen for their strength. Each man had two twenty kilogram burlap waxed cotton liner bags stuffed with dynamite. Dawn was about four hours away.

The success of the assault depended on the crude dynamite breaching the fort's rock wall to allow the waiting three hundred Prussian soldiers to storm into the fort before the Ichneumon garrison could organize a resistance.

Thanks to the US Army, Rex understood the breaching effectiveness of an untamped charge depended on the explosive's velocity of detonation. He didn't have that value for their crude dynamite, but the earlier demonstration had convinced Rex, along with General Markel, it would be effective in punching a hole through the wall.

The assault would use two charges: a larger charge of thirty-four bags to blow out the old entrance plug in the rear wall, and a smaller charge of sixteen bags to take out the guards in the barbican. The testy master artillery feldwebel, Herr Crouch, assisted Rex.

"Simultaneous detonations would be best," Crouch said for the tenth time. "That's the way to maximize surprise and confusion in the fort garrison's response."

The artilleryman still wasn't convinced Rex knew what he was doing. How to achieve the desired simultaneous detonation was the issue they had argued. The short-delay detonators available from the Prussian army had an average pause after activation, of five-minutes before exploding. The delay period depended on the time required for acid from the broken glass capsule to eat through the copper or zinc wire holding back the spring-loaded striker.

"That five-minute delayed period claimed for those detonators is a joke," Rex said. "No telling when the damn things might go off."

With a bit of investigation, Rex had learned the actual delay period of those five-minute delayed detonators exploding was every bit as bad as he had feared. Detonation ranged from three to seven minutes. He wanted better control.

"Well at least they do go off," Crouch countered. He was examining the odd thumb size brass tube with wires sticking out of the top, as they waited for the troopers with the explosives to arrive.

The electric blasting cap Amy had made for Rex would provide the near instantaneous detonations of the two charges, because he would simply wait until one of Couch's three detonators exploded the main wall charge, before setting off the blasting cap in the barbican charge.

The insulated copper wire needed to connect the blasting cap to a battery only existed on this pre-electric world in a few labs. By good fortune, Amy had managed to obtain two 100-meter rolls of thin copper wire as part of her magnet and battery project. Since two wires were required to complete the circuit, Rex had enough wire to use one blasting cap, though the distance of 100-meters was iffy for safety.

Major Beck would assist Crouch in placing the thirty-four bag charge in the old gate plug while Rex with several troopers placed the sixteen-bag charge under the stairway to the barbican over the rear fort gate.

"After you active the charge detonator, meet me back here," Rex told Crouch, pointing to the large chestnut tree they had decided to use as their shelter. "Be careful those wires don't touch the battery."

The old feldwebel nodded and said. "What if you're not back when my charge goes off?"

"A minute's not going to matter. Just don't mess with those wires. I'll be back."

Satisfied with the charge placement, Rex told the soldiers to leave while he installed the blasting cap. The men needed no encouragement and they had just disappeared into the dark, when three Ichneumon cavalrymen materialized out of the snow.

The Ichneumons caught Rex in the act of rising from connecting the blasting cap. The sound of hoofs on the cobblestone drive had alerted him. In an instant, he realized making a dash for the woods would get him shot. Instead, he turned and beat loudly on the stairway door.

With three rifles pointed at him, the lead horseman, a captain, asked, “Who are you?”

“I’m a freezing timberman trying to wake these worthless guards and find out how much firewood they need in the morning.” Rex banged on the door again.

The burlap bags didn’t look out of place. If the cavalrymen even noticed them, they’d figure the bags contained grain. In the dark passageway, a rider on a horse wasn’t apt to notice the small wires. The greater risk was one of the horses stepping on and breaking the wire.

“What’s the racket about?” A dishevel older guard, holding a flaming torch, asked Rex. The sleepy guard had on his uniform trousers with the braces dangling down the pants, a woolen undershirt, and unlaced boots. Then he saw the horsemen and the captain.

“Sir, we weren’t notified to expect you.”

“Do the Prussians and their savages send you notice to expect them? You’re a sorry excuse of a guard. Open the gate. I have business with the general. And who is this?”

Since the guard hadn’t a clue, Rex volunteered, “Jeremy Slater sent me to find out if you needed firewood.”

“In the middle of the night,” The guard asked. Holding the torch, better to see Rex, he added. “I’ve never seen you before. Besides, you look like a damn Prussian.”

As the main gate clattered open, another guard, dressed in a proper uniform appeared at the door.

The cavalry captain said to the new guard. “Lock the timberman up until I have time to question him.”

The cavalrymen trotted into the fort while the two guards and Rex looked at each other and the gate rattled back closed.

"I hope you have a fire going, I'm cold," Rex said walking up to the guard.

He had to overwhelm the guards and escape before the Prussian assault and explosion of the main charge occurred, which could be any moment. Worse, from the prospect of his survival, he worried those hardnose soldiers, Couch and Major Beck, wouldn't hesitate, when that time came, to detonate the charge.

The clang of an iron door opening in one of the barbican's murder ports above the driveway warned Rex not to attack the guards. The three of them looked up and saw a sergeant pointing a rifle at them from the opening in the ceiling. He demanded to know what was going on.

"Slater wants to know if you need firewood today and your other item," Rex answered before the guard could. Jeremy had advised him the rear gate sergeant took his kickback in the form of corn whiskey.

"With this late storm, I want a double delivery, today."

"Okay, that what I needed to know. I'll have the wagons here by midmorning."

"Not so fast," the dressed guard said. "The captain said to hold him." He explained to the sergeant about the three cavalrymen who had just entered the fort.

"Well, hell," the sergeant grumbled, "I'll be down in a minute." He slammed the murder-hole door shut.

Rex struck with his boot knife. He left both guards holding their throats as he ran for the entrance. Two shots rang out just as the larger charge exploded.

"You cut it damn close, Sonny," Crouch said. The feldwebel was holding the battery and the wire ends.

"Talk about being hoisted with your own petard," Rex thought, as he flopped behind the tree and asked. "You were going to wait for me?"

The feldwebel looked at him for a moment with a slight smile and then touched the wire ends to the terminals. For a heartbeat, nothing happened, and then the barbican erupted. The next minute they spent attached to the backside of the large chestnut tree trunk as bucket size chunks of stone rained down around them.

Everything went as planned. Both dynamite charges had exploded with in a minute of each other, breaching the main wall and collapsing the barbican. The Prussian assault forces stormed through the breaches and in less than thirty minutes, the Prussians had control of the fort.

"The stoutest resistance was at the headquarters and magazine," General Markel told him. They were in the same room where last fall, Rex had negotiated the safe passage for the Wapiti convoy in exchange for General Paget's children.

"General Mehta tried to organize an Ichneumon counter charge to block the breach," the Prussian general said. "He died fighting I'm sad to report as I know he was a friend of yours."

"He had no future," Rex said. He had respected and trusted the Ichneumon general, but their values were too different to allow friendship. Mehta's silver teapot had survived the assault and sit unscathed on the table. He wondered who would get it.

"What is the butcher's bill?" Rex asked.

"Fritz is still sorting that out," General Markel said. "I know two lieutenants died taking the magazine. That was a near thing, a young Ichneumon boy tried to throw a torch into the black powder storage. Thanks to your directions we were able to reach the magazine before anyone could sabotage it."

"What happen to the kid?" Rex asked. The Paget children would have left for Delta before the river froze over.

"He was shot dead," General Markel said, while taking a seat behind Mehta's old desk and motioning for the waiting officers to enter.

As the Prussian officers made their reports, Rex realized there hadn't been much more than a hundred Ichneumon soldiers in the garrison. However, as he listened to the lieutenants and captains report, the Ichneumon soldiers had put up a stalwart defense despite the near total surprise of the attack. Prussian casualties numbered over a hundred.

Questioning of the prisoners revealed that several of the prisoners had expected an overland relief force, though none of them knew its actual size. Rumor had the expected reinforcements numbering in the hundreds. Nor did the prisoners know the expected arrival date. Rex's information about the three cavalrymen convinced General Markel the relief force was near and he dispatched a large patrol to locate and ambush the rumored Ichneumon relief force.

Rex had done his part. The rest was up to the Prussian army. He needed to escort Amy across the mountains to New Hamburg. She was to embark from there for Port Baltic. The voyage's purpose was for her to contract with a chemical company for the commercial manufacturing of their new explosive. He didn't tell the general that afterward, he would travel to Myrtle territory and look for his partner, Leslie.

The general wish them success and a safe trip. After a brief leave-taking, Rex, Larry Hopkins, and Tom Jarrell left the fort the following morning to start the grueling two-day walk to Panther Creek where the horses waited. The rear wall of the fort was still visible through the trees when Sam McCoy yelled for Rex. Sam had been the manager of Rex's Hickory Ridge coal yard until the war shut it down. He now ran a small firewood operation.

"Rex, where are you going? Are you going to open the coal yard?" Sam asked, while looking back the trail toward the fort, before adding, "Any Prussians with you?"

"We're headed to Panther Creek and on to River Point." Rex said. "Sam, good to see you survived. You still need to be careful, there's an Ichneumon force somewhere down the river. The fighting isn't over, but the Prussians are ready."

"I'm sure there is a lot of ugly fighting ahead, but I have a person that wants to go with you." Sam said. He pointed toward a group of pines about fifty meters off the path.

Rex could see Sam's tracks in the knee-deep snow from the trees to where they stood. He told Tom and Larry to wait, and walked back to the pines with Sam. A fearful Aziza, General Paget's daughter, wrapped in a heavy hood coat made from a bison hide, wool pants, and fur boots waited under the pines.

Chapter 12

Benjamin Purnell wasn't free, but at least so far, he'd avoided the disgraced Archduke Habsburg fate. The hanging of the archduke had surprise most Berliners and shocked Purnell. An emperor who would hang his uncle would have no qualm in hanging a businessman suspected of treason.

For once Purnell could not see a way clear. Colonel Essen and his alert guards rendered his hope of escaping from the Aruba to an Ichneumon controlled port as unlikely as finding the fifty-million needed to build the River Point spur. He had already decided to raid the slush funds that he had authority to access, despite knowing that act would enrage his Ichneumon collaborators.

One of those accounts was in Augusta at the Myrtle Cotton Bank. As a rule, its balance was in the neighborhood of five million D-Marks, but the amount could fluctuate wildly depending on what black operation Ratakonda had going in the territories. His own two accounts at the bank, the Pine Hill Plantation working account and his private Orleans Boatyard account, held around six million D-Marks. Another possible source of funds was the Southern Textile Trust special project account that held around two million D-Marks. Accessing that account would require his and Duke Soltzendorff's signature. He didn't want to involve the duke in his business and considered the other two possibilities. The Ichneumon slush fund and the separate payroll account at the Export Bank of New

Hamburg, but they seldom contained more than a few hundred thousand D-Marks.

So that was the nut of his problem, he could through embezzling the Ichneumon accounts and draining all his ready cash, raise about fifteen million of the fifty million required. His partner, Necho Allen might loan him twenty million for his half of the NH&R railroad, but even that, his last unencumbered asset, would leave him fifteen million short and with only his casino income. The Prussians had seized the Orleans Boatyard, so he couldn't sell that or access those working accounts. He'd be damned before he sold his family's last refuge, the Island Casino.

With a silent curse to that deceitful amoral emperor, he ordered a gin and tonic at the Aruba bar. Tomorrow they would arrive in Port Augusta. Maybe an inspiration would come.

The Myrtle Cotton Bank was a large operation. A three-story brick building, near the old harbor defense fort, that housed the tellers, vaults, accounting, and executives offices. The first floor of the bank had high metal ceilings, gray marble floors, and yellowish knotty pine paneled walls. Purnell preferred dark paneling, but otherwise thought the office area an agreeable workspace. Closer to the wharf area three large warehouses, with their own long docks, contained the cotton, tobacco, and other commodities that the bank traded in.

His entourage of a Prussian army colonel and four armed guards brought the manager hurrying to greet them. Purnell asked for the bank's president, Keith Woodman, a tall thin anxious man. At the time, he had wondered why the other directors had thought such an apprehensive person would be a good choice for leading their vast trading operation that was often skirting some law. Family connections, he had decided, though the fact that Herr Woodman was an easy person to sway had been his reason for supporting him as president.

"Keith, I need to know the balances in these accounts."

The president's greeting was polite, but unenthusiastic. The presence of the Prussian army in the bank's lobby might account for that.

Keith, without looking at the list, gestured for an elderly white haired man standing at a small desk besides several wooden file cabinets in corner of the spacious office. He handed over the list to the clerk and added, "Harland will have them for you in a moment. Would you care for some refreshments, coffee perhaps?"

"Thank you, no. Are the abolitionists winning here?" Purnell asked, figuring there was no need to be subtle. "My manager at Pine Hill wrote me that the army inspected the plantation for slaves. He believes he convinced the lieutenant the workers were indentured labors. Do you believe the lieutenant was that stupid?"

"I don't know. I do know that since the Mongol attack Berlin has recalled those soldiers. In fact they leave on the Aruba tomorrow."

"Why are those Prussian soldiers with you?" Keith added, after taken a moment to glance at the list handed him. Satisfied, he passed it to his visitor.

"I hired them to guard the gold I'm withdrawing." He answered, rereading the numbers. One of the accounts had a thirty-five million balance. The other Ichneumon account had ten million. He almost blurted out, "Can these numbers be right?" But caught himself, and instead coolly said. "Everything appears as I expected. I'll be closing these two accounts and the Orleans Boatyard account. The bullion needs moved to the Aruba. Have your men coordinate with the colonel."

"You can't be serious. That is not your gold," Keith said.

"It is, but first, ask your clerk to leave," he said while collecting his thoughts. The immense size of the account indicated Ratakonda had decided to finance the cotton growers' insurrection. For a moment, he thought about telling Hansen, and then realized the spy chief would demand to an explanation on how he knew that. By then the clerk had left the office and he added.

"I know it's Ratakonda's gold and you know I'm his agent and that I'm the one who setup those accounts. I'm on a secret mission for the emperor that requires those accounts."

The banker interrupted, "Harj Bhojwani delivered that gold two weeks ago and I'm to use it to pay the mercenaries. He didn't say anything about you or secret missions."

"Of course he didn't," he said. "You have no need to know."

Benjamin knew Harj would have difficulty finding and hiring reliable, treasonous, thugs willing to work for an Ichneumon, and added. "You have to have realized it's a dozen times what is required to pay the salaries of a couple of hundred men for a year and the various enticements to local sheriffs."

That point had Keith nodding and he added.

"The IRS is searching for these odd accounts, so they need closed. Open a new account in Highland Plantation name, and put three million from one of the closed accounts in the new account. Use it for the special payroll and Harj's expenses. Inform Julian Penton of the new account. She will know what to do."

Prussian army officers made up the majority of the passengers on the Aruba. The war with the Ichneumon Empire for control of the Erie River along with the recent Mongol incursion had resulted in Prussian General Staff reassigning many officers.

Young handsome ones flocked about Jenny and generally ignored Indira except for one large lieutenant that asked about her scar.

Indira wasn't in a good mood to start with. A bit jealous of Jenny who could chat with anyone, and the thought that the one thing about her that interested the young attractive lieutenant was her scar made her irritable.

"What scar?" Indira asked.

"It's an impressive scar," the lieutenant said, unfazed by her frosty tone. "Was it from a knife or a sword slash?"

What kind of question is that Indira thought? At home and even in Roanoke no one ever asked. The officer had to be a recent graduate. He looked about twenty and in no way ugly. The lieutenant was a half dozen centimeters taller that her and outweighed her by fifty kilograms, all muscle. Her standoffish demeanor hadn't bothered him. If anything, he seemed intrigued, sort of like a professor that had stumbled onto an interesting creature that had hissed at him.

"I don't remember. I was busy staying alive at the time."

"Undoubtedly, part of the Donnelly troubles?" The lieutenant asked. She nodded. "What is your name? I'm Victor Ludendorff, a lieutenant in the 88th Mountain brigade."

"I'm Indira Hopkins."

"I gather you're part of the group of Roanoke University medical students going to Berlin, aren't you young for a doctor?"

"I'm in my first year and have four more to go. I'll be an old woman by the time I finish. What about you, are you one of the prisoners rescued at Hickory Ridge?"

"No, I missed that. I'm a mechanical engineer and was in Port Augusta with Customs assigned to the anti-slavery task force."

"Ha, I'll bet that was a farce," Indira said. "Those Myrtle plantation owners will never, without a fight, abandon slavery."

"I suspect you're correct," he said as his attention moved toward Jenny who was talking to two Prussian colonels on Indira's left.

Wanting to keep the lieutenant's interest, Indira said, "If the slaves want free, they'll have to start killing their owners."

"That's a terrible thing to say," Victor said. Her remark had captured the lieutenant's full attention. He studied her a moment and then added, "It'd unleash anarchy, and get the slaves slaughtered and the plantations destroyed."

The Aruba's rolling was intensifying and Indira felt a bit queasy. To keep her balance, she spread her feet farther apart. The lieutenant didn't seem to least concerned with the pitching.

"It's reality," Indira snapped, irritated at his rebuke. "Until we started shooting back, Donnelly's men treated us like animals. And your emperor didn't help with that firearms embargo. If they want free, the Zamians need to start fighting back."

Victor had never met a Wapiti before; though he was aware that they existed. His instructors at Plön Academy had opinions about the tribe. Several of his professors thought the Wapiti artless rustics that needed Prussian protection to avoid exploitation. His structure design instructor thought them murderous savages not to be trusted. All agree the Wapiti were a comely people. The Wapiti girl Victor was talking with was attractive and appeared capable of fending for herself.

"That's unfair," he said. "The Wapiti are literate and have a hunter, warrior mentality, the Myrtle slaves have neither. I doubt any of the ones I met could read, or knew anything about firearms, other than what they might have gleamed from watching their guards."

"I'd heard the bastards keep them ignorant," Indira said. "Have you ever seen one of those camps?"

Victor told her about the Opossum Creek slave pen. The plight of the plantation slaves had her sympathy, but the slink had her asking questions. She was dubious of his assertion the slavers disciplined the children by feeding the rowdy ones to a terror bird.

"Then the Aruba arrived and had new orders for me and all of the 88th men. Berlin wanted us."

"Myrtle territory seems an evil place. Do you think the eastern truce has broken?"

"I hope it nothing more than a raid. The Empire doesn't need two wars. How long will you be in Berlin?"

"Four weeks," she said. "Who is that man in the suit?"

He looked and saw that ass, Colonel Palitzsch talking with the Orleans businessman and Colonel Essen.

"Benjamin Purnell, he's building a railroad into your country."

Indira had heard plenty about the Orleans businessman in the last year. Larry Hopkins had told her and Jenny about Rex's successful return from Delta and Orleans, the prisoner rescue, and the murder of Amy Caroom's family in retaliation over her testimony concerning Cinnabar's cocaine operation. Indira had never met Uncle Rex's friend, Amy. She had wanted to make her acquaintance during her fall break, but they never managed to connect.

Herr Purnell didn't look like the ogre Indira had expected after hearing Larry's news. The man looked more like a well-fed titan of industry, than a butcher of innocents.

The gold gave Purnell hope he might yet manage to survive the Prussians. The forty-five million D-Marks of gold bars in the

Aruba's secure lower center storage compartment ought to convince the emperor that he was serious. The gold had sure persuaded his minder, Colonel Essen. What he'd tell Harj he didn't know. The respectful greeting from two medical students startled him.

"Good evening Herr Purnell, I'm Indira Hopkins and this is Jennifer Jarrell. First, I wanted to thank you for the planned rail line to River Point. It will be a tremendous help to the area."

They were Wapiti girls. The scarred one speaking was taller than he was and very young. Her quiet friend was shorter, slightly older, maybe by a couple of years he thought, but definitely the more beautiful of the two. The dove gray Jesuit student uniforms of a short dress, pants, and black boots showed their willowy physique to advantage. They were attractive young women.

"You should thank the emperor. He's the one demanding the Erie River line. I'm but his humble servant."

"The railroad was the emperor's idea, well that explains it," Indira said. "I couldn't reconcile that enlightened act with a cowardly murderer who had an innocent mother and child hung."

Speechless, he couldn't believe the gall of the bitch. He didn't want a scene and glanced toward the colonel, beckoning him. Colonel Essen walked over.

"Is this student bothering you?" The colonel asked.

The insolent Wapiti was the same height as the colonel and returned glare for glare, unimpressed with the officer's attempted to loom in a threatening manner.

"No, but I'm not interested in their silly nonsense. Perhaps you could ask their proctor, Father Jenkin, to deal with them."

The tall Wapiti student seemed amused at his effort to avoid a confrontation. She then addressed the colonel, "No need to bother the good father." Then she turned back to him, and added, "Good evening, wimp."

A startled Colonel Essen and he watched the two students walk over to Father Jenkin and say something before exiting the lounge.

The luxurious Royal Bismarck Hotel charmed Indira and she knew Jenny felt the same, and suspected all the other Roanoke University students did too. The plush beds, endless hot water for the large tubs, fluffy towels, and wonderful soaps gave the two Wapiti girls a new appreciation for opulence.

"I could get use to this life," Indira said. She was laying on the smooth bottom bed sheet in her favorite worn nightgown. "I need to find a rich husband."

"Berlin is nice, but I fear I'd miss the valley. I wouldn't mind having a bed like this, it'll be hard going back to corn husks and rope hammocks," Jenny said, putting down her notes on the use of ether.

"Or candles instead of the gas mantle lights," Indira said. "Are you going to the gardens?" Jenny shook her head and instead drew a hot bath.

The hotel had a park landscaped with flowerbeds, trimmed hedges and groves of trees. Several tame red deer lived in the large, ten-hectare rectangular shaped park that bordered the river. The hotel had enclosed the area using the rear of the hotel and three-meter high walls of stone that ran from the hotel to the river.

The park animal that had caught Indira's interest was a tame silver fox. The hotel's kitchen workers fed the sleek creature meat scraps and it in turned allowed people to approach and pet its gorgeous fur. There were no silver foxes back home, but Indira wondered if she caught a gray fox pup, could it be tame.

The following morning the Roanoke medical students assembled in front of the hotel for roll call, before heading to their daily lecture at the palace medical center.

The prior day the class had examined a sick young man. The method of the examination had seemed odd to Indira. Instead of the more typical method of the class gathering around the patient, while the attending doctor explained the case, one of the center's professors had taken each student one by one into the room and quizzed them on the patient's symptoms.

Most of the class, including Jenny and Indira, had accurately diagnosed the patient's illness as appendicitis. Today the class would watch surgeons remove the young man's appendix.

Two seniors, doubtless hung over, Indira uncharitably thought, delayed their departure. She decided to satisfy her curiosity.

"Father Jenkin, why are we in such luxurious accommodations?" Indira asked, gesturing toward the hotel. "Couldn't the money be put to better use? Maybe use the funds for medicine . . . like providing ether to rural clinics."

Sid Moyer, the second son of an apple plantation owner and one of the affable seniors, answered her.

"Indi, for a smart creature, you can sure act provincial. The emperor, because of your scholastic achievements, is providing you a brief taste of the comfortable life the empire offers successful people."

"Herr Moyer is somewhat correct," Father Jenkin said. "Not to brag, but it's no secret that Emperor Schnabel admires the Jesuit's Roanoke University. He decided the hidebound professors of Berlin Medical College needed to meet you folks after comparing your test scores to the equivalent Berlin medical student's scores. He wants them to realize that territorial educated doctors, male and female, are equal to Berlin educated doctors. He also wants more women allowed in the Berlin classes."

"They'll never allow or admit that," Sid muttered. Indira had to agree, remembering the gargoyle that had quizzed her.

By then the two late students had arrived and Father Jenkin marched the class, at doubled time, to the Berlin Medical Center, four kilometers east of the hotel. The two late seniors were red faced and dripping sweat at the end of the jog.

Chapter 13

General Emwazi was saddle sore, but in a cheerful mood. By evening, he would be the new commander at Hickory Ridge. The journey from being the son of a cane cutter foreman to a general in the Ichneumon army hadn't been an easy one. Until his promotion, all Ichneumon general rank officers had some claim to nobility or the landed gentry.

A willingness to be as merciless as the situation demanded had brought him to Emperor Ratakonda's attention. Ending the gold miners' strike and theft of gold had made him a colonel. General Meringa's loss of River Point and General Mehta's failure to stop the Wapiti convey had sent the emperor looking for a man who knew how to control savages. His emperor had called him to the palace.

Emwazi had received his general star for promising to eliminate the savages along the Southern River and River Point as a military threat and accomplish it before the Prussians made them allies. He felt sorry for General Mehta, General Paget's selfish act of bringing his family into a war zone had put Mehta in an impossible position. But life could be unfair.

The blow to his chest almost unseated General Emwazi. A moment later, a wave of gunfire engulfed him and the Ichneumon column of mounted troopers. The general's last thought was who had ambushed them?

Matt Brewer had stopped at Smithtown for supplies and to visit. He told everyone about the successful Prussian ambush of an Ichneumon relief force.

"Then we were very fortunate in the timing of our attack," Rex said. "If that Ichneumon force had arrived a day sooner, during our attack, it could have followed us into the fort and trapped us against Mehta's soldiers still holding the upper fort."

Rex had a new problem for Matt. General Paget's daughter, Aziza, who had escaped during the confusion of the attack, needed a safe place to stay. He now knew her brother had died trying to explode the fort's main magazine.

"I don't think the Prussians know of her existence," Rex said to the surprised Matt. "General Paget will figure she died, like her brother, during the Prussian attack. Aziza wants to see Captain Malik."

The captain was a friend of Rex and Matt, an Ichneumon who had deflected to the Wapiti cause. He knew Aziza and she wanted to see him before deciding what she'd do.

Ichneumon females led a cloistered life, though the emperor permitted a few high-ranking officers to take their family with them on foreign assignments. The reason was due to a lopsided skew in birth gender among the Ichneumons. One out of five live births was a female. Teamed with a fourteen-month gestation period, and a low fertility rate, the Ichneumon population was in slow decline. Rex wished the race god's speed to extinction, still he felt sorry for Aziza.

Matt was agreeable. Amy and Aziza returned to the kitchen a few minutes later and Rex said. "Aziza, Matt will take you to the captain."

The Ichneumon loss of Hickory Ridge had consolidated the Prussian army control of the upper Erie River valley and removed the fear of an Ichneumon occupation of the Wapiti homeland, at least for this spring. Amy and Rex now felt secure enough to leave their two steamboats docked at Smithtown and the machine shop equipment under Tom Jarrell's supervision while Amy went to Berlin and Rex to Augusta.

Amy and Tara Smith waved from the steamship Sanibel second deck rail, thought they were hard to see through the early morning drizzle and fog. The steamship was embarking from New Hamburg for Port Baltic. Rex knew he was fortunate to have her as his partner and said a prayer for their safe journey.

Amy's lawyer, Tara Smith, he had rescued along with Indira's sister, Lilly, from Donnelly's men. They were friends. He was pleased the two gifted women had developed a close and confiding friendship. The Berlin bureaucrats were about to meet their match. The ladies had multiple missions in Berlin, defend Amy's patents on the new explosive, dynamite, his patent on an electric blasting cap, and negotiate an agreement with one of the large Prussian chemical companies to manufacture the dynamite. Aram Chemical, if Rex remembered correctly.

Tara would also work with Felix Cohen, Bill Jacobs' father-in-law, to file an appeal asking the Royal High Court for a stay on Berlin Commerce and Commodity Bank efforts to force Leslie Wire Company into bankruptcy. The Jacobs family thought that legal maneuver would delay the BCCB for a month or two and allow time to learn their partner's fate. Herr Cohen needed Al Leslie, or at least to learn what had happen to him, to have any hope of success with salvaging their investments.

Goodbyes done, Rex and Larry Hopkins, a Wapiti police investigator, went to find William "Bill" Jacobs at his new brick warehouse near the main New Hamburg docks. The merchant had hired a Berlin based investigator to locate their missing partner and Rex wanted to learn what the man had discovered.

"Did those lovely ladies embark?" Bill said in greetings.

Rex nodded. The storeowner was a cheerful, energetic man about Rex's age and a third of a meter shorter. He was Leslie's main partner in the wire company. Rex, Amy, and Herr Simpson, a distiller, held the rest of the stock, about twenty-five percent among the three of them.

The warehouse loading dock was a busy place with the arrival of the day shift employees, a mixture of Prussian, Clovis, and Zamians. The twenty some men and women seemed in good spirits as they greeted their boss and his visitors. Two of the Clovis men knew Larry. After greetings and comments on the dreary weather, they went into Bill's office for privacy while the workers disappeared into the large warehouse stacked with barrels of cottonseed oil and tobacco, sawed timber, and wooden railroad ties.

"I learned a bit," Bill said. He waved several sheets of brownish paper he had removed from his middle desk drawer. "Leslie left Port Baltic eight weeks ago on a steamship that had scheduled stops here, Augusta, and Orleans. His ticket was to Augusta, but there's no proof he arrived. If he'd disembarked here, I believe he would have contacted me, so I think he went straight to Augusta to meet with the Myrtle Cotton Bank. That's what my father-in-law thought Leslie had planned, though the bank said he never showed for the meeting."

"And still no word from the man?" Rex asked looking about Bill's office. The padded leather chair he was sitting in was very comfortable. It was one of six similar chairs about the conference table in the large high ceiling office. He noticed several cobwebs in the corner of the ceiling and then the steaming coffee pot and cups on a table near the window.

"Nothing," Bill said, "Other than the notice of the bond default."

Kit Jacobs joined them. After a brief greeting, he said, "I have some news. I just received Hans Melas report."

The name sounded familiar to Rex and he asked who that was, before remembering, he had met him during the Donnelly troubles.

"He's our representative in Augusta, manages our tobacco and cottonseed oil warehouse. He reports Leslie spent three days in town four weeks ago before heading inland."

"Well that's good news, so the man's alive."

"He was a month ago," Kit cautioned. "Hans says during that period, Duke Soltzendorff visited the warehouse to verify his plantation had delivered the cotton seed and several barrels of tobacco. Leslie was there and left with the duke that day, but stopped in briefly the following day to ask Hans the best place to hire a horse. That's the last he saw or talked with him. Anyone want coffee?"

"Did Hans say if duke's crop exceeded last year's four hundred tons?" Bill asked, interrupting.

He flipped through the yellow papers, "Three hundred thirty seven tons."

While the three of them served themselves coffee, Rex remembered reading cottonseed oil was toxic, unless processed. He asked, "What's the oil used for?"

"Candles, soap, and lamp oil," Bill said. "Some people mix it with lard, but it's kind of poisonous."

"I read there's a way to remove the toxic part and make a good substitute for expensive olive oil," Kit said. "I need to follow up on that, those candle makers pay so little it's hard to justify the oil press."

"Did Hans say if the duke knew Leslie?" Rex asked, getting them back on topic. Kit shook his head.

"Hans also checked with the Augusta hospitals, sheriff, and police. None of them have arrested or treated an unidentified middle age white man. Doesn't mean he wasn't knocked in the head and dropped in a swamp or the bay."

"Would he have any reason to travel inland?" Rex asked.

"Some of the plantation owners are wealthy, and he could have decided to visit one of them," Bill said. "Though without an introduction, I can't see that working. Those folks are leery of strangers, and you know Al. Can you picture him convincing some backwoods slave owner to part with his money?"

"No, I can't. But if someone like that duke suggested it, Al might try," Rex said.

"I'll write Duke Soltzendorff. He's back in Berlin and a response will take several weeks, assuming the man even bothers to answer."

"Chances are, other than that brief meeting at the warehouse, duke never saw Al again. They move in different societies," Kit said. "We need to go to Augusta and ask questions."

"Myrtle Territory is a prison outside of the port area and Augusta," Bill said. "Every county has a sheriff and guardian posses that patrols the land looking for escaped slaves. Strangers encountered on the roads are interrogation and they had better have a suitable reason for being there. The countryside lives in fear of a slave rebellion. If the sheriff thinks you're one of those abolitionist agitators, well you might just disappear. I hope that's not what happened to our partner."

"One way to find out," Rex said.

The Island Belle was an old grungy ketch that had seen better days. The gray sails had streaks and splotches of dirt and mildew, but otherwise appeared in good repair, same for the rigging. The ship hauled passengers and light cargo along the coast between New Hamburg and Port Augusta. And livestock, Rex realized from the odor. The front hole held dozens of small pigs.

The ship's normal schedule called for stops at several of the larger settlements along the Myrtle coast. Bill had chartered the Island Belle to haul Slim, Kit, Larry, Rex, and a large shipment of chain link steel fence and rolls of concertina barbwire nonstop to Augusta.

The rawboned ketch captain was of Zamian and Prussian ancestry and appeared to be in his late thirties. The man's rough appearance, stubble beard, wiry uncombed brown hair, and dirty broken fingernails, did not suggest a man concerned with maintenance. Nor did Captain Putnam's uniform of faded stained coveralls, grungy Prussian navy seaman's jacket, scuffed up brown suede leather knee-boots, and an officer's hat with brass trim that had corroded green inspire Rex's confidence. His sharp intelligent dark eyes did encourage a hope that the man was a competence captain despite his shabby appearance.

Rex and his men joined the captain at the mess table that first evening out of New Hamburg.

"That cargo of wire you have, is that for slave pens?" The captain asked, while deftly lifting a section of his fish clear of the rib-spine bones.

"I suppose it could be used for that."

The captain's inquisitiveness about their cargo was probably normal curiosity, but not knowing Putnam's stance on slavery, Rex was cautious.

All the Jacobs that Rex had met agreed slavery was evil and owned no slaves, but the family didn't let that belief interfere with business. Holier-than-thou abolitionists and bureaucrats might consider their laissez-faire mindset shameful, but their flexible interpretation of laws had allowed Rex to purchase hundreds of rifles for the Wapiti when such sales were illegal.

"Do you have a need?" Rex asked, as he examined the small charred fish on his plate. He wasn't sure what it was, though it looked a bit like a large sardine.

"Slavery is no longer legal in the Prussian territories," Captain Putnam said passing the breadbasket. "I was just wondering who else uses that expensive fencing, slavery being illegal."

"I'm sure there are many needs in Myrtle Territory for secure storage yards," Rex said, and set about freeing a piece of the fish from its skin and rib bones. Tasting the extracted piece of bone free fish, he decided it was okay, reminded him of a bluegill.

"Ah, secure storage lots, you're right. You should call on the cotton plantations, I'm sure the owners would be interested in your fencing. It would be excellent for securing their homes during a slave revolt."

"They have that concern?"

Rex loathed slavery, but maintaining his cover as an amoral opportunist was essential to surviving in the Myrtle Territory interior and having any hope of finding Leslie. A slave uprising would complicate and endanger their rescue mission. Authorities would crush any hint of a rebellion and intensify their monitoring of strangers.

"I doubt there's a slave holder in the territory that hasn't heard of Donnelly's fate," the captain said with a meaningful glance toward Slim and Larry. "You might want to consider leaving those two behind."

Rex asked Putnam why.

"The territory is hiring a lot of Ichneumons, and they have little love for Wapitis."

"How's that possible with the Ichneumon and Prussians at war?"

"Beats me, maybe mercenaries don't count," the captain said. "Regardless you'll find most of the guardians are now Ichneumons and on the territory's payroll."

"Ah, whatever," Rex said and proceeded to prevaricate. "I have no interest in politics. My job is delivering the fence and serving our customers so my boss keeps me employed."

"My apology, I didn't mean to suggest otherwise we must all do as our employer directs, or of course find other work."

"I thought this was your ship," Rex said, wondering if the local mercenaries knew of the reward.

"Levi Ottoman owns this relic."

A massive gray stone fort, rivaling the one that once existed at Port Delta, guarded the entrance into Augusta's port. A huge Iron Cross Prussian flag flew from the high central tower. Construction activity at the forward east wall appeared to involve the installation of a large platform. Rex wondered if the Prussians were installing one of those large caliber breech-loading rifled guns, similar to the ones that the Ichneumons had used to sink their battleship at Delta.

Augusta's waterfront area started several kilometers inland from the seaward fort. Several wharfs and docks with low wood warehouses lined the wide flat land on the south side of the Myrtle estuary and beautiful sandy beaches. Larger two and three stories buildings constructed of red bricks were visible on the low ridges behind the south shore. On a higher ridge a couple kilometers inland from the waterfront, Rex could see several large buildings made of cut grey stone and wondered if those were government facilities.

The wooden wharf from the ramshackle barn with the large Jacobs & Sons sign was a modest affair compared to the several wharfs passed. Captain Putnam and his crew had slipped the ketch into a berth along the wharf with no fuss. Contrary to the ship and its captain's woebegone appearance, the crew proved to be proficient. Hans Melas helped secure the lines and then greeted Rex and the captain when they disembarked.

Captain Putnam was impatient to find Levi Ottoman's Augusta factor and learn his ship's next cargo and port of call. Hans was able to provide the man's address, and after instructing his crew to unload Rex's cargo, the captain hurried off.

"I have a possible location for our man," Hans said, "Though I have no way to verify its accuracy."

Rex had fought beside Hans and considered him dependable. The stout bald man was a retired Prussian feldwebel trained as a sniper. He used an open loft attached to the inside rear wall of the warehouse for his office. Wood barrels were stacked three high over much of the main floor. The place was primarily a warehouse for the cottonseed oil and tobacco, though several wood crates with iron plow parts were stacked near the door. The actual seed pressing operation was located elsewhere and Rex hoped he'd get an opportunity to see that operation.

"Is Leslie alive?" Rex asked while reflecting on the agreeable warehouse odor. Tobacco he reckoned.

"That's what I was told, at least several weeks ago he was. He is a prisoner at the Opossum Creek slave pen."

Rex asked how he knew this and Hans held up his hand, went and checked to see if anyone in the warehouse was close enough to eavesdrop. The three warehouse laborers were busy rolling barrels of oil out to the Island Belle. Satisfied, Hans returned and said.

"Uma first alerted me that the Penton plantation had a Prussian prisoner." To Rex's question on who Uma was, Hans said,

"She's a free slave who works as a messenger for the Cohen law firm."

"Is that Cohen any relation of Bill's?"

Hans nodded and said, "Some uncle," and then added, "My boss helps escaped slaves find passage on ships. Uma is our Zamian connection, though very few slaves ever make it to here. The guardians and sheriffs capture most of the escapees and hang them as a warning to others. Anyways, she told me about the prisoner and I checked with Colonel Jagger."

To Rex's question, Hans explained the colonel ran the Augusta customs department and for a short time, he had a lieutenant making an inventory of slave breeding camps.

"According to the colonel, the prisoner was a horse thief that Opossum Creek was holding for the sheriff. Odds are that's correct and not the man you're looking for, but it's the only lead I have."

"How far away is the place?"

"About three, four days, couple of hundred kilometers, but you can't just ride out there. The sheriffs and their henchmen, the guardians, will stop and arrest you unless you have a reason for being there. Harlem Penton would have you arrested for trespassing. That's assuming you did make it past the multiple check points."

"Can you get me a wagon and three horses with saddles?"

Chapter 14

The smoke alerted them. As Rex and his crew emerged from the last switchback on the narrow gravel road, a checkpoint barred them. Three armed men in black uniforms lounged near a large wood fire off to the right of the barricade. Two Myrtle deputies were examining the papers of a middle age couple stopped at the barrier.

Rex thought the deputies' uniforms had an eerie resemblance to the color and style of the Nazi Brown Shirts. They even had a red band on their left arm, except instead of a swastika, it featured a silver cross.

The man and woman stopped at the checkpoint each wore gray denim coveralls, lace up leather boots, heavy dark red plaid woolen jackets, and large round brim dark felt hats. Rex had seen similar outfits around the Augusta waterfront's open market. They were most likely a local farm couple and the three bare foot Zamians with them in gray coveralls, were their slaves. Brought along to carry back whatever they planned to buy.

The wagon that Rex had rented came with two large chestnut draft horses and a teamster, Elon. He was a burly old taciturn Zamian who, without any instructions, pulled to a stop across from the fire. Hans had assured Rex the man's papers were in order and there should be no trouble, should they encounter a checkpoint. Rex figured Elon knew the drill and he also dismounted between the wagon and the fire, tying his horse to a wagon wheel spoke.

"Gentlemen, I'm a visitor. What's the checkpoint for?" Rex asked, walking to the group in by the fire.

"We're looking for some fugitives," the man said. "What's in the wagon?"

His shoulder patch had a silver colored cross on a dark red background and surrounded by the word 'Guardian'. Other than that patch, the uniform matched the Ichneumon army uniform, including the black leather knee boots and holster with a revolver. The man and his two partners were clean shaved, robust, middle age, and probably former Prussian feldwebels. Though with those mirror sunglasses, they could be some of those rumored Ichneumons mercenaries hired by the Cotton Grower Association. Regardless they appeared to be serious men.

"Special fencing," Rex answered, helping Elon fold the tarp back. "I work for Jacobs and Sons. We think the plantations will want our new concertina barbwire. Say my name is Burgdorf, what's your?"

"I'm Captain Pauli, and who are they?" He asked, pointing at Slim and Kit still on their horses.

"They work for the same outfit, except they are taking orders for next year's cottonseed and buying tobacco. The kid beside them is my helper."

"A group of strangers tend to make folks around here nervous," the captain said, not appearing the least worried.

"Well, we thought traveling as a group, since we work for the same company and need to see the same people, made sense."

"So you're just business men. Show me your passes and gun permits," the guardian said, gesturing for the other two mercenaries to check Slim, Larry, and Kit's passes.

"So what's special about that barb wire?" Pauli asked after inspecting the cargo and their papers.

Bill and Kit Jacobs had given considerable thought to the best way to gain entry into the Penton plantation. Rex would need a reason to inspect the breeding operation and holding pens in order to search for Leslie. Most plantations used log stockades to hold the slaves when not in chains or under armed guards. A few of the larger breeding operations had started using galvanized iron chain link fencing to build pens.

It was common knowledge that Harlem Penton had recently constructed a chain link fenced pen for their slave breeding operation. Bill thought they would be interested in the army's new razor concertina wire. Rex thought showing the bastards better imprisonment methods repugnant, but leaving Leslie to perish in a cage was unacceptable.

His crew had a loose folded four-meter section of the concertina wire ready for quick demonstrations. Larry and Slim stretched out the concertina loops into a gleaming one-meter diameter tube with a length of four meters bristling with razor sharp barbs. Pauli and his men were impressed, even the deputies walked over to look and poke at the concertina wire barbs with their truncheons.

"Damn, that makes a mean barrier, the animals will think twice before trying to cross that stuff," the potbelly deputy said. He had cut the tip of his finger on one of the barbs.

A small donkey pulled cart loaded with burlap sacks and driven by an older Prussian man wearing a hat fashioned from a coonskin, tail still attached, stopped at the barrier and yelled for the deputy to raise the barrier.

"Is that Peppelman?" one of the guardians asked the deputy with the pricked figure who nodded. Pauli and the other deputy glanced toward the barrier.

"I'll be damn, it is. Tell that bastard to wait," Pauli told the guardian and deputy. He then asked Rex, "Where are you headed?"

"We're going to start with the Rupprecht Plantation and then visit several of the other large plantations."

"Well you best be on your way," Pauli said, before walking down to greet Peppelman who was engaged in a vociferous argument with the deputies over his delay.

The stop the following day at the Rupprecht plantation offered them a chance to tryout their sale pitches before Penton. The concertina wire had generated considerable interest, but Kit's idea of buying the cottonseed was a flop. Herr Rupprecht in his blue denim bib overalls, battered straw, rough leather knee boots, and full gray beard looked like a provincial uneducated farmer. He wasn't.

"I'm not interested in shipping seeds to Augusta," Herr Rupprecht said. "The freight cost would eat up any profit, but I'd like a price on that fancy wire."

They were all standing in the large gravel driveway loop in front of the mansion with half dozen slaves and two foremen holding double barrel shotguns. Rex finished helping Slim folded up the wire demo to put it back in the wagon while Kit figured a price for fencing to enclose the lot.

Kit didn't want to abandon his idea and after providing a quote for supplying the razor wire, asked the plantation owner what he had planned for the seed from the cotton gin.

"My grandson is studying engineering at Plön Academy and he's building me a seed press. So sonny, if you're interested in supplying the barrels and paying a fair price for the oil, maybe we can do a deal."

Kit had assured the man he would be interested in such a deal. Herr Rupprecht invited them into his office, and over coffee, their discussion centered on the cost and delivery of an order for one kilometer of concertina wire.

The following night they stayed at the boarding house-inn in the small mining camp near the Ramos Clay mine. Rex and Kit, both curious, went to the mine office the following morning while Larry worked with the camp's blacksmith to repair the rear wagon wheel hub that had split. Elon, their hired teamster, knew the mine manager and went with them.

The mine owner was a stout middle-aged Prussian man dressed in stained bib coveralls. He had a new looking yellow straw hat with a wide round brim crammed on his head, smoking a cigar while standing at the edge of the mine pit. Herr Hasler had a cheerful air and appeared happy to see them and their laconic teamster, Elon, who introduced Rex, calling him Herr Burgdorf.

The clay mine operation wasn't much, a muddy hole about a third the size of a football field and a couple of meters deep. A dozen Zamian men were busy. Most were shoveling brown shale into wheelbarrows and dumping the shale off to the side of the excavation. The laborers were uncovering a half-meter thick layer of grayish orange colored clay.

Two Zamian women were using small shovels to cut and then shape the clay into grapefruit size cubes. A narrow gage set of iron mine rails ran from where two women were working to a simple wooden tipple off to the side of the pit. After cutting and shaping, the women stacked the clay cubes in a mule drawn mine cart parked on the rails.

The mule looked old and weary standing between the rails, an occasional switch of its tail the only sign of life. Another man was waiting at the tipple beside a wagon partway stacked with the clay cubes. Rex wondered why he didn't help the women, but it wasn't his concern and said nothing.

"You have the right man to get your cargo across these sorry roads," Herr Hasler said, nodding toward Elon. "I'm a bit surprised he's working for you after hearing you're selling fencing for slave pens."

The mine owner's smile didn't reach his eyes as the teamster shrugged his shoulder and walked off to inspect the wagon loading operation.

"There're lots of uses for fencing besides that. With all your slaves, perhaps you could use the fencing," Rex said, not sure what to make of the mine owner's attitude.

"I don't use slaves. Those workers are free men that I pay. Ask your teamster if you doubt that." The man had a quick temper.

"Please, gentlemen, let's not talk of territorial politics," Kit said. "What's the ball clay used for?"

"The primary use is for dinnerware, cups, and those kind of items. Several kiln operations in Augusta like my clay. It fires into a very durable lightweight cream color ceramic. The inn you stayed at uses dinnerware made from Ramos clay."

"I noted the quality of the Inn's dinnerware. It had a very pleasing color and texture, glass smooth," Kit said. "If my uncle wanted to buy your clay, who should he contact?"

"I'm selling all I can produce. Until the slavery and road issues are resolved, I'm not making any new investment."

"I thought the slavery issue was resolved. It's illegal," Rex said.

"You're a fool if you believe that." Herr Hasler said, shaking his head. "The emperor had better wake up, before Myrtle revolts."

Rex exchanged looks with Kim and then asked the mine owner to explain.

"There's nothing to explain, I'm just trying to survive, same as all those plantation owners. When some fool decides to take your property and destroy your way of life, what do you expect? Have you encountered any guardians on your trip?"

Rex nodded.

"Well someone is replacing our local bums who use to make up the guardian posses with mercenaries. The bums are going to work as part time deputies."

"I know. The guardians I've met are wearing outfits similar to Ichneumon army uniforms," Rex said.

"That's right," the miner owner said, "Most of them are Ichneumon soldiers. The mirror sunglasses hide their vertical slit pupils."

That was unwelcomed news. The perils had soared for Rex if those mercenaries entering Myrtle knew about the reward. They needed to find Leslie and get out of Myrtle territory.

The decayed picked over skeletons of two bodies hung from a large red oak tree a dozen meters off the Highland Plantation gravel drive. Their ancestry and sex not clear, though one body was smaller and could have been a woman or a child. The sight put an exclamation point to Rex's opinion that in spite of fertile bountiful farms, Myrtle Territory was an evil place.

Along both sides of the several kilometer long gravel drive to Harlem Penton's mansion were well-tended fenced pastures with a number of horses and goats. Vast level fields of rich dark soil were visible in the distance. Spring planting didn't appear to have started.

Three large buildings sat off to Rex's left, two high wall warehouses and one a more conventional barn like structure. The mansion was a two story white wood structure with a long wrap around covered porch facing the driveway circle. The roof had the patina that came from copper, no cheap lead coated iron roofing for Penton. The attractive home, white stone drive, and surrounding well-tended yard with enormous pecan trees scattered across it contributed an estate ambience to the place.

Rex and Kit weren't sure what reception to expect after Slim's report. The Wapiti hunter had made a reconnaissance of the Opossum Creek camp while they had toured the clay mine. He hadn't encountered any armed guards, but had spied what appeared to be a small jail, a shed with barred windows. It was besides a large stable with a corral on one side and a cage on the rear side.

Before Slim could approach the shed to check for a prisoner, he saw a slink venture out into the cage. If the creature should happen to spotted him, it would raise an alarm. While trying to decide whether to risk approaching the jail to verify if Leslie was a prisoner, someone released the slink.

"After dumping a steaming pile, the monster made a looping run around the camp," Slim said. "I figured it would return to its cage, instead, it stopped and returned to inspect where I had crossed the creek and study the ridge I was on. Its behavior gave me the willies. It was as if the bird could sense me. I was about to bolt, but the guard called it. Luckily, it was the monster's meal time and I left."

"You made the right choice," Rex said. "I don't know much about slinks, other than the rumor they have excellent night vision. I'm glad you didn't try sneaking around the Opossum creek area at night."

"I've heard they're ferocious eaters," Kit said. "We wouldn't want our hunter to become a steaming pile of crap."

"Thanks for your concern," Slim said. "The place is wide open to the guard towers. The only way we're going to check that jail is ride up to it as welcomed guests and have a look."

Rex agreed.

The plantation residents had noted their arrival. An older, but muscular man of Prussian ancestry, dressed in a riding outfit of brown knee boots, burgundy riding breeches, and a tan colored leather vest, waited at the bottom of the front steps. The mud bespattered outfit suggested their arrival had caught the man returning home from a hard ride. Three rougher looking men in blue denim paints and gray sweatshirts emerged from the nearest barn. All carried revolvers in belt holsters. Two had double barrel shotguns. A loud whistle from the man caused the three to jog toward him.

Herr Penton greeted Rex and Kit amiably. The plantation owner was curious as to their visit's purpose.

"I have a product that improves on barb wire," Rex said, motioning to Larry and Jimmy to unfold the concertina wire.

"I already know about chain link fencing."

"Yes sir, I'm aware of your fine Opossum Creek facility. That is why I believe you will want to consider concertina wire. It will make the enclosure escape proof."

"Yeah, right, I've heard that pitch before," the plantation owner said in a weary non-censorious voice.

Since he was the man that could grant them a daytime visit to the site, Rex needed to gain his respect. Smiling, he said, "No doubt, guilty myself of over promising, but this is different."

By then, his crew had the concertina loops unfolded into the cylinder and the older guard with a crippled right hand walked over to inspect the wire tube. His boss joined him and together, they rolled the cylinder across the drive trying to collapse it. One of the shotgun guards tried stomping on the wire and received several cuts on his leg.

"What will they think of next," Herr Penton said. "Grover, find Max." After the guard with the bum hand left, he asked, "How do you use it? Stack the rolls on top of each other to make a wall?"

"That one method, but with a chain link fence you attached the tube along the top of the fence. It prevents anyone from climbing the fence."

"By gad, it would, but how difficult is the attachment?"

"Every fence is different. I need to see what you have." Rex said.

A younger version of Herr Penton hurried down the steps buttoning his dark leather coat, the old guard following. He was Penton's son, Max and the old guard, Rex learned, was Grover Zagat.

"Max, take Herr Burgdorf and his men out to the pen and show it to them," Herr Penton said. "They might know how to make your fancy fence escape proof. I can't go, but gentlemen, plan on staying over and we'll visit."

The narrow road to the pen wound through a low scrub pine forest on gently rolling terrain. The well-maintained gravel road surface was in better condition than the main toll road out of Augusta. About three kilometers from where they had left Herr Penton the road entered a large shallow valley. A new chain link fence enclosed a significant part of the valley floor, an area of a dozen hectares and a number of buildings.

The camp construction was wood and red brick with shake roofs, except for an old cut stone two-story building that housed the main gate. None of the buildings appeared of recent construction, several had the slagging rooflines and sideward tilt of deteriorated wood buildings. The facility reminded Rex of the Nazi concentration camps for slave labor he had seen on the History channel. The breeze carried an off-odor similar to that of a poorly serviced porta john.

"That's quite an impressive operation you have," Rex said as Max rode up. He hoped his disgust didn't show.

"It's a business," Max answered. "Can't harvest cotton without slaves, yet those fools in Berlin want to outlaw it, makes no sense."

Rex wasn't in the mood for a lecture on the wonderful benefits of slavery and asked, "How long is the main pen?"

"It's about eight hundred meters by five hundred meters."

"Is the fence effective? It looks kind of low."

"It's a two meter fence. A three meter fence would have been better, but . . ., Well father didn't like the cost."

As they rode by the main gate, Rex could see the guard towers had no guards, though two elderly guards maned the gate. A dozen very pregnant Zamian women, along with a quiet group of small children, watched from inside the enclosed yard. Everyone looked thin, but healthy.

Max, instead of entering the compound, turned toward the stable that Slim had said housed the slink. Rex had only seen a dead terror bird, the one that Amy had shot in Panther Creek. He would like to see a live one, safely caged of course. Beside the stable, he saw the jail and off to the rear of the jail and barn, a four rope gallows.

"How many live here?" Rex asked. The camp seemed uncrowded.

"About seven hundred slaves, most of them are over in the east swamp camp working on a new drainage ditch."

So far, Rex had only seen the two guards at the gate and asked, "Do you have to employ many guards?"

"Not all that many, perhaps twenty full time guards, but every work crew has a foreman who keeps order," Max said. "Grover is our hunter who works with Snapper, our slink. They help the sheriff and his men track down the runaways. Between the guards, foremen, Grover, and the gallows, the animals know better than to act up."

The bounty hunter had a crippled right hand, but he still worried Rex. He might release the slink and Slim was out there somewhere waiting and watching. Max stopped at the barn and dismounted.

"Come with me, I want to show you Grover's pet."

The building with the barred windows was only twenty meters to Rex's right and after securing the horse, he walked over to it.

"Hey pal, stay away from there," Grover yelled.

Max, looking back, added, "Wrong way, we're going in the barn."

"Is it a jail?" Rex asked as he ignored them and covered the last couple of steps to where he could see in the room. "Who do you keep in it?" He asked pretending not to hear Grover.

A whiff of putrid odor and loud hiss caused Rex to look behind the barn. A fully enclosed chain-link-fence cage, about ten meters on a side and maybe six meters high contained a large terror bird. Snapper, he presumed. The cage floor was hard packed dirt, littered with numerous pieces of leg bones, along with rib cages, and split skulls that appeared to be of human origin. The creature was watching him.

A woebegone unshaven Leslie looked out the window as Grover grabbed Rex's arm. He shook the bounty hunter's hand off and said. "Max! I know this man, why is he locked up?"

My God, you're Rex . . ., help me," Leslie cried. "Don't leave me. I told them to ask Duke Soltzendorff, he'd vouch I didn't steal the damn horse. That bastard wouldn't listen." He pointed at Grover.

"You know this man?" Max asked, joining them by the window.

"Hell yes, he's Al Leslie, an inventor who disappeared a month ago from Augusta. Why is he a prisoner?" Rex asked after a worried glance toward the slink that had started a loud hissing.

Max didn't seem to know and looked to Grover for the answer.

"He called you Rex. I thought you said your name was Burgdorf," Grover said, watching him.

"It's a nickname," he answered dismissingly, and repeated his question.

"Your aunt told me to hold him," Grover said.

"Why would she tell you to lock up one of the duke's friends?" Max asked.

Rex wondered the same thing.

Grover shrugged, "I didn't asked. Maybe because of the way he acted over the hanging."

"Was he with Duke Soltzendorff?"

Max nodded and then said, “Herr Burgdorf, let’s check the fence and then return to the house and find out why your friend is here.”

The hell with questions and fencing, Rex was reaching for his revolver when he heard horses arriving. Instead, he eased the revolver back in the holster and stepped over where he could see the hitching rail by the stables. Two guardians were dismounting. Max knew them and greeted them.

A narrow escape, a moment later and the guardians would have caught him threatening Max and Grover with a gun. Worse, one of the riders was Captain Pauli. More greetings as Kit, Larry, and he join the gathering.

“Herr Burgdorf, sell any fence?”

“Not yet, but I’m hopeful Max will place an order,” Rex said, trying to summon a cheerful face.

“Max, we’re in a hurry. Our order is to return your prisoner to Augusta,” the guardian captain said.

“Herr Burgdorf knows the prisoner,” Max said. “We’re wondering why my aunt told Grover to hold him. There has to be some misunderstanding. I thought he had left for Augusta.”

The captain was instantly suspicious and asked Rex how he knew Leslie.

“I met the man in New Hamburg when he visited Herr Jacobs trying to raise funds for one of his inventions.”

Kit jumped in and added, “I’m as surprised as Burgdorf to find the poor man here. He looks terrible and I can’t imagine what he could have done to desire such shoddy treatment. Where are you taking him, I’ll arrange an attorney for him.”

“Don’t let those animals take me,” Leslie listening from the jail window cried.

"Everyone, just get back," the captain said, abandoning any pretense of amiability. "I have my orders. Grover, help my corporal secure the prisoner on the extra horse."

"Where are you taking him?" Kit asked.

"If you have any questions, talk to the Myrtle AG in Augusta, now out of the way."

Chapter 15

Leslie hadn't gone without a fight. He had hit Grover in the face with his head when the bounty hunter was attempting to handcuff him. The blow broke the man's nose and enraged the corporal who had been helping Grover. Pauli's man struck the prisoner a brutal blow with his baton.

"Stop you brute, don't kill him," a shocked Max cried. "He's not dangerous. No one even knows why he's a prisoner."

Rex jerked the corporal off Leslie and threw him hard against the cell wall. The guardian managed to hold on to his baton. With a wild swing, he attacked Rex who wrenched the club away and used it to jab the man's belly.

"Everyone, behave," Rex shouted as the corporal rolled on the floor gasping and the captain pulled his revolver. "Leslie, go with the guardians. They're just doing their job. We'll get you a lawyer."

"No shooting Captain Pauli," Max commanded, "These men are Penton guests. Your man overreacted."

What a mess, Rex thought as the corporal, radiating bitterness, struggled to his feet and Grover, dripping blood, shoved Leslie out of the jail to the waiting captain.

One wrong move and they'd have to fight their way back to Augusta. Kit and Larry's presence with their rifles had kept the captain from escalating the scuffle into a gun battle. Rex had no illusion this fight was over. He had made a deadly enemy in Captain

Pauli by interfering. Blue blood oozed from the corporal's broken lip, verified he was an Ichneumon, as Rex had suspected. The rumor they were infiltrating the ranks of the Myrtle guardians was apparently true.

"Can you handled the prisoner or should I have Grover go with you?" Max asked, trying to be helpful, but further angering the captain.

"I have it under control," the captain growled as Grover finished tying the pleading Leslie on a horse while the corporal struggled to mount his horse.

"Good, Herr Burgdorf and I need to meet my father."

Rex and Kit had accepted Max's invite to meet with his father and learn why Leslie had been imprisoned. Before leaving with Max to meet Herr Penton, Rex called Larry off to the side and instructed him to find Slim.

"Follow them close, without alerting the bastards. I don't trust them. They may have orders to not deliver our friend alive."

"Should we ambush them?"

"Try to avoid a confrontation until we join you. Who knows how many of those Ichneumon bastards are wandering about the countryside and might hear your gunfire? We don't need them hunting us."

"What if they are assassins and they decide to kill Leslie as soon as they're out of sight?"

"Use your judgement. I won't be long, but I need to better understand why the Pentons detained Leslie and why the duke had lied. Was it something personal, or to do with the Wire Company bankruptcy?"

Herr Penton was with Julian Penton, his sister, in her office. Max asked his aunt about Leslie after his father claimed not to be involved.

"I did it as a favor for Duke Soltzendorff," Julian said with no hesitation. "That man was a strange character, claimed to be an inventor. He made me uneasy even before he cursed the duke and Harlem over the way we punish runaway slaves. You should have heard the jerk. I'm sick of those liberals who love their fine soft cotton, but distain those who have to do the hard work to grow the crop. When the duke asked us to detain the man, I told Grover to hold him for the sheriff."

"You're right the man can rub people the wrong way," Rex said.

Leslie could be tactless, and Rex could believe he would have clashed with these heartless bigots. What normal human wouldn't be appalled at the treatment Harlem imposed on runaways, but he was after information and without emotion asked, "Do you know why the duke wanted him held?"

"Probably didn't want to listen to his querulousness on the trip back to Augusta," Harlem said.

"Some business deal," Julian said. "The duke never elaborated. Leslie did ask Harlem to invest in some crazy idea for sending messages using sparks. We figured he was a fraud and ignored him."

"My sister thinks Soltzendorff is a gentleman, but he's just as quirky as that inventor."

"You don't have any proof it was the same girl," his sister said, her voice rising.

"Julian is referring to the girl whose parents we hung for running away," Harlem said. "I don't like to own slaves that have a history of running off. They give the rest of those animals the wrong ideas. But, instead of hanging her, I sold her to the duke. Two days later her body was found near the Ramos Clay mine all sliced up and partly skinned."

"You're certain it was the same girl?" Max, who appeared shocked by the news, even looked nauseous, asked in a stressed voice. Julian started to answer and Harlem held up his hand to silence her.

"Damn right it was her. The skull had that same broken front tooth," Harlem said. "I don't have any choice, but to do business with Soltzendorff and the Myrtle Cotton Bank. Just know that man is sick in the head and your friend might be in danger."

"Bah, my brother is wrong about the duke. If that was the girl, she probably escaped and a slink or bear got her. Duke Soltzendorff is a gentleman, next in line, after Rudolf Habsburg to be the Prussian emperor, if Wolfgang Schnabel doesn't have an heir. However . . ." She smiled and added, "Since Archduke Habsburg was hung for treason, Rudolf's family maybe in disfavor, meaning the Soltzendorff family could supply our next emperor."

The sun was low in the western sky when Rex and Kit left Highland Plantation. Elon would follow in the morning with the wagon. They reached the inn at Ramos Clay mine around 3am, and after verifying Leslie and the guardians weren't there, roused the stable manager and cook.

They learned two guardians and a prisoner had passed through late last evening, but no one else. Rex hoped that was because Slim hadn't wanted anyone to see them.

Among the stable's collection of nags, mules, and draft horses that Kit inspected, he considered one of the riding horses worth purchasing. Rex bought it for Al. Provisioned with bacon and egg sandwiches and coffee, they rode on. Their goal was to slip by the checkpoint east of Rupprecht Plantation, before sunrise when the night shift guards, with any luck, might be weary.

One unknown was whether Captain Pauli would even stop, since Ichneumons had good night vision. Still they got tired and hungry like everyone, and Rupprecht Plantation was a logical place to stop and refresh, since they had no reason to suspect anyone was pursuing them. Slim and Larry had to be near and Rex figured they would find each other before sunrise.

If they could get ahead of the Ichneumons without alerting them, Rex had in mind a good place to set an ambush. He had noticed it on the trip west, a narrow road cut through a dense scrub pine covered ridge about a dozen kilometers east of Rupprecht. Leaving his partner's fate to the Myrtle Territory legal system was an unacceptable ending.

Larry and Slim, both tense, hoped Rex found them before sunrise. The east horizon was turning reddish and the sun's edge would break the horizon in a few minutes. The two guardians had met a third guardian on the road after Ramos. The Ichneumons had rode on for another few hours, before they stopped on the east face of a grass-covered ridge and started a fire.

"Now that they have stopped, should one of us backtrack and warn Rex before he stumbles across them," Slim said.

Then the guardians dragged their prisoner off the horse and they were now trying to tie the struggling man across a flat rock.

"Ah crap, I know what those bastards have planned," Larry said.

Rex wondered, as they rode along the dark trail, if the Rupprecht Plantation had pigeons trained to home on guardian garrisons. Captain Pauli might order the plantation to release pigeons with warnings and requests for their arrest. Two distant rifle shots broke the still night, then a moment later a third shot.

"Shots, is that a concern?" Kit asked. "They did sound far away," he added in a hopeful voice.

The accountant did not like traveling at night. Kit had kept his mount as close to Rex's horse as the animals would tolerate.

"They weren't that far. As to whether we should be concerned, I'd say that depends on who shot what," Rex said, not liking that third shot.

Larry and Slim were skilled warriors and survivors of several ambushes. He couldn't picture Pauli or that sorry corporal ambushing those two. Still, we all make mistakes. Rex urged the horses from a trot to a canter.

The sun had cleared the horizon when the trail they had been following crossed a ridge into a large cleared pasture. About hundred meters off to Rex's right near the ridge's summit several horses milled about and Slim was waving to attract their attention.

Three guardians were sprawled in the grass beside a large flat rock. A fetid odor assaulted them as they approached the rock where Leslie was kicking Pauli's head.

"Those maniacs were going to cut my heart out," Leslie shouted. With his disheveled appearance and glaring eyes, the ex-prisoner had a demented look. "To ensure the sunrise, the fool said. Surely, even these cretins can't believe such nonsense."

"They're Ichneumons," Rex answered, endeavoring to calm the man. "Now stop that. The bodies need to disappear. If the guardians learn of this, we'll have everyone hunting us."

Slim pointed to a spot in the woods below the rock and said, "Check that out. That odor is coming from there."

A small pit held about a dozen bodies in various states of decomposition. Most were Zamians, likely escaped slaves, but one was that farmer Rex had seen at the checkpoint the first day out of Augusta. Herr Peppelman if he remembered correctly. The killers had tossed the coonskin hat in the gore of his gapping chest.

More guardians could arrive at any moment, but Rex decided to chance that and take enough time to conceal what had occurred. They stripped the corpses of their uniforms to make identification more difficult. Rex tossed their blood stained garments on the fire to burn while Slim and Larry dragged the bodies a couple hundred meters into the forest and hid them. He told Leslie to clean himself enough to avoid an escaped fugitive appearance. Kit loaned him scissors to trim his facial hair and found him a fresh shirt.

The Ichneumons' horses were quality stock, but had the guardian cross brands that would attract unwanted attention at a checkpoint. Those horses, after removing and burying their saddles and reins, Rex turned loose. They divided the rifles and revolvers among themselves and then rode for Augusta.

Chapter 16

Necho Allen, the owner of several anthracite coalmines in Erie Territory and his partner in the Guderian territory railroad, had accepted Benjamin Purnell's invitation for dinner at the Royal Bismarck Hotel. They were both stout middle-aged men. His partner's heft was from slabs of muscles.

Despite Allen's considerable wealth, the man wore the same outfit every day, a black homburg hat, a black wool coat and pants suit, a plain white shirt with a modest size collar, a narrow black tie, and black knee boots. It didn't matter whether he was inspecting a coal tipple or meeting an emperor.

"You look like a damn preacher," Benjamin said in greeting, a bit relieved his partner's drab outfit was clean. He nodded toward the center of the room where a dozen vivacious Jesuit medical students were dining. "You'll cast a pale over the revelry."

"Aren't you in a delightful mood," Necho said, pausing to check out the group of students, before taking a seat at the table. "In a moment of weakness I actual said a prayer for you when I heard the emperor had arrested you, and then I learned you made some fool promise to build a three hundred kilometer spur into the wilderness."

"Schnabel can be quite persuasive," Benjamin said, shaking his head, "And allowed me little choice, but to agree."

"I imagine the rack can sway anyone."

"Let's drop that distasteful topic and focus on now. I need your help with Gruppo Iron on the rail order. The engineers tell me the spur requires a thousand kilometers of steel rails."

"Ninety-kilogram per meter rail," Necho asked. Benjamin nodded. "Ninety thousand tons, that's a huge order, they should be thrilled."

"They weren't," Benjamin said. "Try the wine; it reminds me of the purple swill you serve."

"You're right," Necho said, draining his small long stem wine glass. "A decent wine, not the pale vinegar piss you serve. So, what's Gruppo's problem, payment?"

"No, a capacity constraint, the navy wants steel plates for those new battleships and the emperor wants both the ships and the railroad completed this year. Gruppo needs to increase production, which requires overtime. No surprise, they want compensated. Their price is already high, over four hundred D-Mark per ton."

"So agree to the higher price and bill the extra cost to the army."

"Gruppo won't commit to a delivery date this year."

"Well, maybe I can help. They need my coking coal and have been after a long-term contract. Coke's spot price is double the normal because of the navy's foolishness in demanding two battleships at the same time. If I explain the new spur opens my Southern River coal property and that mine would allow me to sign their contract, do you think the iron-men might agree to put the rail order ahead of the plates?"

"They will if the emperor gives a nod. I'll tell Hansen what's needed."

Several more of the medical students joined their friends causing Necho to look over and said, "Who are those girls, they're beautiful."

"Wapiti witches," Benjamin said, "Bad news."

"Is that so," he said, smiling. "I've been trying to talk my oldest son into managing that Southern property. Is that where those girls are from?"

"And their fathers, uncles, and brothers, if you value your son, tell him to stay clear of those knife brandishing bitches."

Sanita Chopra wondered if Emperor Ratakonda knew how pathetic a group he was backing. Colonel Palitzsch was a pimp. Captain Peiper was a butcher of prisoners. Both were untrustworthy scoundrels. Rudolf Habsburg was an alcoholic dupe. The one intelligent plotter was Duke Soltzendorff, though something wasn't quite right with the man. They were the principles in the ad hoc conspiracy by proslavery Prussian aristocrats to topple the Schnabel regime. Emperor Ratakonda wanted them to succeed. To that end, he had committed considerable Ichneumon gold and sent him to assist the plotters any way he could.

Tonight, Chopra had sent Friedrich Burgdorf ahead to check the meeting wasn't a trap. The mercenary had answered his knock on the rear kitchen door of Rudolf Habsburg's large three story dark stone residency. It was one of several imposing mansions located in an attractive gated community southwest of Berlin.

Burgdorf told him everything appeared in order. Two other large men dressed in the Soltzendorff black livery waited in the hallway. They moved to search Chopra for weapons. A gesture from the mercenary moved them out of the way.

The conspirators waited in a smoky room, a library, judging from the number of shelves holding hundreds of books. A rumpled Rudolf had remained seated, offering a careless wave as a greeting. His hand held an unlit cigar.

"I wondered if you'd show," he said. "I hope you were careful coming here. I heard Hansen's agents are looking for you."

"They always are," Chopra answered, while wondering if Rudolf was already inebriated.

The man proposed by the conspirators to be next emperor of the Prussian Empire sprawled before him in the leather chair, wearing a wrinkled, part way untucked white shirt with several small reddish stains down the front. He had carelessly tossed his dark gray suit coat on the floor by the couch. A shot glass and a half empty bottle of vodka waited on the small walnut table beside the chair. The spectacle suggested a frightened man seeking courage. Whatever the reason, the man's appearance didn't inspire any confidence.

Not Duke Soltzendorff, he was his usual dapper self, and stood to cordially greeted him. "Your efforts in the east were successful."

"What's the latest on the Mongol advance?" He asked the duke who gestured for the uniformed army captain waiting by the window to answer, not the colonel by the fireplace.

"The bastards are advancing," Captain Peiper said. "Two of their armies crossed the Volga and established a breach head of a hundred kilometers. Our army seems to have forgotten how to fight."

"Well they're still a long way from Berlin," Chopra said, please to learn the Mongol army had advanced far enough to alarm

Berlin, but still not a serious enough threat to cause the emperor to end his inspection trips about the country.

"No one likes the empire involved in two wars," the duke answered. "We're not worried about losing the wars. It's the loss of treasure and sons that concern us."

Peiper had noticed the disheveled nobleman shrugging to reach the bottle and assisted him in filling the empty shot glass with vodka.

"Damn right," Rudolf said, after tossing back the shot of alcohol and adding, "Another hit captain. When I'm Emperor, I'll turn the army loose and put an end to those Mongol raids. We'll take no prisoners. And you tell Ratakonda not to be silly enough to think he can keep the Prussians out of the Erie, though we do appreciate him helping us."

"Please excuse my friend," the duke said. "He's had a bit too much to drink this evening."

Chopra took the slight with equanimity. Why anyone thought Rudolf Habsburg could function as the Prussian emperor escaped him. The duke must have sensed his thoughts.

"The loss of our battleship Schlesien and Port Delta has a number of influential people concerned about the emperor's fitness to manage the empire. Those same people are going to be rebellious when they learn that Prince Morihiro has offered to end hostilities in the east, if the emperor drops his unpopular opposition to slavery. The people who count know Rudolf is proslavery and that is their primary concern."

"Most Prussian aristocrats are pampered lap dogs with loud barks and weak bites. Will your influential people help that sot?" Copra asked, nodding toward the proposed emperor.

That remark earned a scowl from Rudolf, but no comment.

"There a few wolfs among them. They will accept him as Schnabel's replacement. Since the emperor hasn't yet married, there's no heir. In the event our emperor should die without providing an heir, the archduke had been the next ranking candidate. You know his fate. Rudolf is his son and by right, the next in line."

"Remember that, heathen, I'm the legitimate heir to the throne," the man who would be emperor said, reaching for the bottle.

"I know what you're thinking," the duke said. "After his father's disgrace, why would the council of peers consider Rudolf?"

That wasn't quite what he was thinking, watching the fool pouring himself another shot of vodka. Instead, he was recalling that the duke had a legitimate claim to the throne should the drunkard become emperor and then die. Rudolf's reign might prove brief.

"Because my spineless cousin didn't hang that puffed up merchant," Rudolf answered the duke, after tossing back the shot of alcohol. "Purnell framed my father for those false navy orders. Everyone knows he's an Ichneumon collaborator." With that remark, the man struggled to his feet.

Chopra wondered if Rudolf comprehended, he was that very thing.

"The archduke was very well liked," the duke said, after a pause to check his partner didn't need assistance. "That travesty of justice and the emperor's antislavery campaign has soured many on the high council with Schnabel's reign. There will be few tears over his passing."

"So how is this, ah, passing on to be accomplished?"

"Our emperor has, of late, become a very hands on manager. He now visits arsenals and munition factories to verify he's receiving accurate information. A tragic mishap will occur during one of those visits."

"That would be good, if his demise appeared accidental, not an assassination. When is this accident scheduled?" Chopra asked.

"Very soon," the duke said as an amused Rudolf nodded from the bathroom doorway.

"Then Ichneumon assistance isn't required?"

"Not for that, but I have a minor problem I'd like discuss with you in my coach," the duke said after glancing toward the bathroom where Rudolf had gone. "And you two," he said to the officers.

Duke Soltzendorff large landau coach had very comfortable red leather cushioned seats, Chopra decided as he waited with Colonel Palitzsch and Captain Peiper. He had Burgdorf wait down the lane from the coach with their horses. The duke joined them in the coach, after a delay of a few minutes. Chopra hoped he was satisfying himself that his two guards were in position to assure no one could approach the coach stealthily and overhear their conversation.

"Rudolf is not a detail person and I didn't want to burden him," the duke said.

More likely, he feared the drunk might speak out of turn, and alert the authorities, Chopra thought.

"The date depends on the emperor's schedule. If nothing changes, Thursday is the day, which leaves you three days to put in place your parts. Chopra, are those two cases of special Venite champagne ready for Burgdorf to pick up and deliver?"

The Ichneumon nodded.

"Colonel, make sure none of your Spirit employees decides to sample one of those bottles."

"Best it is icy cold for the celebration," Chopra added.

"Captain, how many of the Imperial guards will be at the Wednesday night meeting?"

"Since the emperor won't board the train to Aram Chemical until early Thursday morning, I expect most of them not on duty to attend, say around thirty. There will also be a number of officers from the Berlin police and the General Staff there. Best plan on serving fifty people."

"Great, Colonel is your operation ready to entertain that size group? Elmira and her girls ready?"

"Yes sir, they do it every other month. It will go smooth. What I'd love to see is that bastard Purnell's face when he learns he's the owner of Spirits."

The group all had a laugh over that clever idea of the duke's for a fall guy. After all, one never knew when something might go amiss.

"Chopra, have you reviewed the captain's plan for Aram?"

"I have, and I believe it will work. Even better, investigators will conclude a tragic accident occurred."

"Colonel a moment," the duke said after dismissing the others. "Arrange a girl for me Tuesday evening. If you can manage to make her one of those Wapiti students, there's an extra six thousand for you. Can I count on you for an entertaining night?"

Palitzsch, smiling, nodded.

Indira absconded with a small piece of the dinner bratwurst for the pet fox. The animal wasn't around its usual spot near the rear dock of the hotel, so she wandered out into the dark park looking for it. The whimpering of an animal in pain caught her attention.

The moonless night didn't help, but the sound seemed to originate from the hedgerow by the river. Indira walked along the hedges trying to locate the animal in pain. The sound's source was close, in the large boxwoods. Was it the silver fox? Had someone hurt it? She parted the thick, but blissfully thorn less bushes, searching for the animal that had gone silent. The whiff of ether she had detected puzzled her. How could there be ether in the park.

Powerful arms grabbing her and an ether dripping rag over her face answered the question. She fought, but her assailant's grip was unyielding, worst there were two of them.

Indira felt her awareness growing as the ether wore off. A large man had her slung over his shoulder with her hands and legs tightly bond. Nausea threatened and with the tight gag, she worried her own vomit might drown her. Her blindfold prevented her from determining where she was or why the man had stopped. He was breathing hard, like a man out of shape.

The place smelled odd, like flowers, body odor, and cigars. Two men, not the one carrying her, were talking. One of them must have asked a question, for the other one told him to mind his own business and leave. There was a grunt, and a woman's voice scolded someone not to hurt the doctor.

More talking, they discussed an examination, then the man carrying her started walking. After dozens of stairs and steps, a door opened, and the man carrying Indira dumped her on a bed.

"That's the best you could do," a woman said. She sounded spiteful to Indira. "She's an ugly stick of a thing. The duke said she was pretty."

"Her friend is, but she didn't come out," the man who had dumped her said. "At least she's a Wapiti, so he should be happy. I don't know why he cares what their looks are. Their prettiness never lasts long after he starts with the razor. Anyway, get your ass busy and get her ready for the doctor to check her for pox."

"The duke must plan to rape her first," the nasty female voice said, "I hate that skinning business. What mess I'll have to cleanup."

The woman can't be serious. Or she was still confused from that dreadful ether. Rape was always a danger for a woman, but skinning . . . No, it couldn't mean that. She tested her bonds. They were unyielding. Fear and nausea threatened her resolve to resist.

"Let's have a cigar first," the man said. "Got any of those thin Myrtle sweets?"

The unexpected invasion by the Mongol armies had thrown the remaining events scheduled for the Roanoke University students' Berlin tour in doubt. Father Jenkin had earlier assembled the students in the hotel lobby. His message, the class would head home as soon as space became available on a steamer headed to New Hamburg. There was a steamship with extra room for the students waiting at Port Baltic for the new Erie spur steam locomotive. The NH&R railroad expected their locomotive in the next few days, after that delivery occurred, the class would board and head home.

Sid Moyer, an affable, stout, twenty-year old, was a large intelligent man who had enjoyed the Berlin tour and was disappointed to learn it might end short. The lectures on methods to induce anesthesia in patients had convinced him to remain in Roanoke's surgeon program. Until that lecture, Sid had doubts he could tolerate the screaming and threshing of patients undergoing surgery.

Sid had met Lieutenant Victor Ludendorff on the Aruba, and become friends. Prior orders had spared him an assignment at the eastern front. Instead, Victor was waiting on equipment and supplies for the new NH&R Erie spur. He was leaving in two days to supervise the loading of those items at Port Baltic. The lieutenant would then travel with the supplies and equipment to New Hamburg. His follow-up assignment would be to instruct the territorial NH&R crews on steam safety and the proper maintenance of the complicate, expensive, and powerful locomotives.

Yesterday, Victor had invited Sid to join him and several lieutenants for an adieu party on Tuesday evening. It was at Spirits, a Berlin nightclub. The other officers were leaving to replace dead or wounded lieutenants in the army units currently engaging the Mongol forces. Their odds of returning to Berlin from that eastern abattoir were not good. As a result, they were in the mood for a final get-together bash before heading east.

Chapter 17

The nightclub, Spirits, was in a four story square brick building, located six blocks north of the Royal Bismarck Hotel. The weather was warm, and though rain threatened, Sid and Victor, both in their respected uniforms, walked to the nightclub. They met Victor's friends in front of the main entrance where there was a jam of horses and various sizes and types of coaches clogging the street. Dozens of gaslights illuminated the milling crowd.

"Gentlemen, be nice to Sid, he studying to be a doctor and men in our profession never know when they might need his services," Victor said in way of introduction.

The lieutenants merrily welcomed Sid into their group. He fast fathomed that Lieutenant Kluck, a tall muscular man who didn't look old enough to be in the army, was the leader of the group. The lieutenant was the eldest son of a general.

"I want that far corner round table, five pilsners, a bowl of toasted winter sole nuts, and a parade of your available lovely doves." The handsome officer instructed the beautiful Zamian woman wearing a near-transparent red strapless silk dress at the main dining room's entrance. He added, "Start a tab on the table."

Kluck then stopped at several tables to greet other army officers and men in black eveningwear. Best Sid could determine there were no wives among the customers.

"We're lucky, men," the lieutenant said. "I just found out the Imperial guards monthly dinner is here tomorrow and my father often tries to attend. I'd been in a world of hurt if he had been here to see us. So, tonight enjoy, tomorrow we head east."

Several of the older men in eveningwear yelled at the hostess that they'd pay the lieutenants' drink tabs. Other customers shouted orders to be sure to teach those Mongol barbarians a lesson they won't forget.

Sid didn't know if Victor's pals would teach the barbarians an unforgettable lesson, but he knew he was about to have a memorable evening thanks to them. He had never been in such a place as Spirits. The clubs and bars that he visited in Roanoke and western Guderian Territory were drinking, dancing, and eating establishments. No doubt, there were prostitutes about, but he had never encounter one. The homegrown fallen women didn't flaunt their trade. Not like Spirits, the club displayed their comfort women like the merchandise they were. The doves sat on stools arranged along a narrow stage behind the long bar. All the sparsely dressed women lacked were price tags.

"Gentlemen, the hostess will bring the ladies by for your inspection. We get a special rate, since we're off to protect the homeland, two-hundred D-Marks," Lieutenant Kluck said. The offer got a rowdy cheer from the group.

"How long with the lady does that buy?" One of the lieutenants asked the question that had entered Sid's mind.

"Does it matter, Stan? You'll be done in two minutes," Kluck said to general laughter. "Also be sure to use a lambskin, none of us need the pox."

The group laughed, teased, and lied about theirs and each other's stamina with women. Then the hostess brought the women to their table for their inspection and they got quiet. Sid would never have had the nerve to ask for a procession of whores. He downed the pilsner and said a pray that Father Jenkin and Lou Ann never learn of this party. She was the daughter of a neighboring apple grower that Sid's mother mistakenly thought he would one day marry.

The Spirits' women were beautiful, especially the Mongol girl, not at all as Sid had imagined whores to look. They were all young and smiling, not a despondent look in the group. When would he ever have another chance to discover if Mongol women were the same where it counts?

Before the emperor outlawed slavery in the territories, an occasional Mongol woman would be among the other slaves his father had hired to help harvest the apple crop. Their presence would prompt some of the older foremen to reminisce about the old days when they had a free hand with slaves. Those foremen still thought the slaves little better than livestock, but his father had always been a stickler for prohibiting any sexual abuse of the Moyer slaves. Herr Moyer might despise Emperor Schnabel and the antislavery laws, but he obeyed the new laws. Sid was proud that the Moyer plantation no longer used slaves.

During one of those lunch breaks several years prior, two of the foremen claimed Mongol women had different, as in better, plumbing from the local women. Sid, already knowledgeable about human anatomy, wasn't sure whether the braggarts had meant the arrangement of woman's vagina and clitoris, or their response during intercourse. He wasn't about to make a fool of himself by asking them for an explanation. Sid figured the older men were just spinning nonsense, but his curiosity concerning Mongol women had remained.

Would there ever be a better opportunity to verify the old windbags' claims. The other members of the group weren't hesitating and making their choices. Still he vacillated. In the end, the Mongol girl lost patience, and made Sid's choice for him.

“I’m Wren,” the small pale woman said. She wore a green sarongs made of translucent material and a yellow silk neck scarf, “Come with me, before that Zamian bitch notices.”

Sid was, by then, the only one remaining at the table. Victor and Kluck were dancing with Zamian women. The other lieutenants hadn’t messed around. They had picked and rushed upstairs with women.

“I thought the customer made the choice,” Sid said, not sure as to proper protocol in a bordello and managing to feel a fool.

“You looked like you needed help,” she said smiling. “Or did you want a boy?”

“They have boys?” A startled Sid asked.

He glanced toward the now empty stage. The earlier procession of women, and knowing they were there for sex, had effected Sid. Embarrassment over an erection that tented his pants had been the main reason for his hesitation in choosing a woman because that would have required him to standing up in front of the other officers. Wren’s cheekiness had ended his concern about embarrassment.

“You’ll do,” he said and jumped up, pausing to adjust his pants.

“Well, well, I know how to fix that,” the saucy girl said.

Wren led Sid upstairs to a small room with a bed, sink, and toilet. All business, as soon as she closed the door, off came the cloth wrapping, revealing a delightful body. All Sid’s doubts vanished and in moments, he was as unclothed as she was.

Wren knew her trade and appeared to be a willing partner. Afterward Sid figured the actual act from start to finish didn’t require much more than a few minutes. And her plumbing was identical to Lou Ann’s.

"Are you an army officer?" Wren asked as they lounged afterwards in the cozy warm bed.

"No, I'm a medical student, but I'll be a doctor by summer," Sid said. "How'd you end up here?" She sat up and unwounded the yellow scarf from her neck. "Are those scars from a slave collar?"

Wren nodded.

"You're a slave?" Sid asked. "There are slaves in Berlin?"

"Do you think I'm willingly screwing half a dozen men a night?" Wren asked. "I thought all doctors were smart," she added with disgust, while studying him.

Sid knew she was wrong on that point about doctors' intelligence, but her slavery claim stunned him.

"I swear, after all the uproar in Guderian Territory," Sid said, "How is it possible for slavery to exist a couple of kilometer from the royal palace? Berlin is supposed to be the enlightened society and the standards for the world?"

"You're wrong, Prussians are no better than anyone else. They're just better at hiding their savagery."

Sid rolled out of bed, and standing, started dressing, and said, "Damn I thought you were just a working girl. My neighbor, a worthless piece of shit, was recently arrest for kidnapping and attempted rape of Wapiti girls. And you want to hear a shocker? One of those Wapiti girls is now in our medical class, Jenny Jerrell. And now I've just screw a slave, I'm no better than Heinz."

"Hold down your voice," Wren said, glancing fearfully at the room door. She looked alarmed and ready to cry.

"Who owns this place?" Sid asked. Calming, he realized that what went on in a bordello was not necessarily representative of the society. Spirits was clearly a criminal enterprise and he had honestly never thought the girls were slaves.

"No one seems to know, though I've heard army officers," she said in a worried quiet voice as she cleaned herself.

"Does anyone ever escape?" Sid asked.

"The older ones disappear. Our guards claim rich clients buy them to be their mistresses."

"You'd think they'd want the young ones like you," Sid said.

"Exactly, the other rumor is that there's a snuff room on the fourth floor and that's where the older women go."

Sid knew the meaning of that slang term, and thinking of the clean classy club and obvious upper class clientele, found her claim difficult to believe. Suddenly he wondered if Wren was a whore looking for a way out and was playing on his sympathy. Other than the neck scar what proof was there her tale was true. He knew prostitution was a dangerous occupation, but had difficulty accepting there existed perverts that would actually pay to murder a prostitute.

"I need a beer," Sid said and headed for the main floor.

"Wait, I have to escort you," Wren said. She had finished cleaning herself. "I have to straighten the bed first."

Sid ignored her, he wanted privacy to think, and closed the bedroom door and walked away from the stairs they had used. He turned a corner and discovered another stair well and two men, one carrying a squirming bundle over his shoulder.

Suddenly Wren's allegation of murder occurring on Spirits' fourth floor seemed possible as Sid realized the thug was carrying a girl. A girl dressed in the Jesuit Roanoke University uniform, a discovery that left Sid aghast and at a loss how to respond.

"No one is allowed back here," the thug's wiry partner said.

Both men were smaller than Sid was, but he was soft and out of shape, and no match for those hard tough brutes. Both had knives on their belts.

"I'm looking for the bar," Sid said. "What's the deal with the girl?" The bonded up girl started violently wiggling at the sound of his voice.

"The bar is down the other stairs, pal," the wiry partner said. He blocked Sid's approach to get a better look at the girl whose struggles had forced the heavy brute to readjust his grip on her.

"Hell, she's awful skinny, who'd want her?" Sid asked shoving by the unencumbered thug for a better look. The girl's gag and blindfold obscured her face, but not the scar. All of a sudden, Sid couldn't breathe, the bastard had sucker punched him in the gut, the solar plexus his medical mind corrected.

"What are you doing, Hedrick? Stop, that's the doctor," Wren yelled. She hurried to Sid and helped him to his feet. "He's to check her for the pox."

Sid's mind cleared with as his breathing returned to normal. Why was the whore helping him? Hedrick was telling Wren about Sid's claim he was after a beer and not identifying himself as the house doctor.

"Well, he's a damn alcoholic like the rest of the help. It no excuse for beating him up," Wren said.

"I'm sorry Doc, you should have said something," Hedrick said. The thug didn't look or sound the least bit repentant as he added with a knowing smirk, "Follow us up to the top floor and you can check her out all you want, the colonel and duke won't be here for at least a half-hour."

"Yeah, yeah, you asses are too quick with your fists," Sid said. "I need a beer first." Hedrick had looked doubtful about

Wren's claim he was a doctor, but Sid's remarks seemed to settle the issue of his identity. "Show me where the bar is, woman."

The thugs went on up the stairs, while Sid grabbed Wren's arm and fast walked her back the hall to her room.

"What were you thinking, interfering," she whispered, shaking off his hold. "You'll get me killed."

"We're all in serious trouble," he said, "That bundle was Indi, one of my classmates. Can you locate Victor?"

"He's the big lieutenant that was with you?" Wren asked. He nodded. "He's in Lucy's room, two door down on the left."

"Wait here, I'll be right back."

Sid knocked and told Victor the captain wanted him at the bar. Since Prussian officers weren't supposed to be in bordellos, and there was no captain in their group, he figured worry and curiosity would motivate Victor to be quick. He was, and Sid had him in Wren's room before Lucy could check where he went.

"The bastards have kidnapped Indi and taken her upstairs to murder her," Sid said. He explained what had just occurred down the side hall. Wren verified his story.

Victor, feeling relief there wasn't a captain after him, remembered the Wapiti girl that Sid said was in danger. The feisty student had intrigued him and he wanted to help rescue her.

"There are two armed guards at the main door, and those bouncers working at the bar are armed," Victor said. "None of us are. I need to find Kluck."

"I can do that, wait here," Wren said. After she left, he asked Sid if he trusted her.

"I'm not sure, but she saved my ass with those thugs that had Indi. Wren told them I was the house doctor.

"When they realized what she did, she'll be in danger."

Sid nodded in agreement. A moment later, Kluck burst into Wren's room and stopped.

"Who's choking?" Kluck asked. Wren and a Zamian woman crowded into the small room behind the senior lieutenant. Sid explained.

"Why are we interested in risking our careers and necks for her?" Kluck asked. "Not to be hard hearted Sid, but you know Spirits is rumored to be owned by connected people who will not respond well to being exposed as enablers for murderous perverts."

"When your uncle, General Markel, learns you saved a Wapiti princess from rape and mutilation, even death, he'll appreciate your effort because it'll make his job easier," Victor said, realizing his friend had no answer.

Sid wondered since when did the Wapiti have royalty, but then realized Victor was puffing up Indi's importance for Kluck's benefit. He should have thought of that. His brain seemed slow this evening.

"Alright, if this blows up, that's our excuse. We thought it would help the western campaign. Besides, as gentlemen," Kluck said. Both lieutenants laughed at the gentlemen tag, "We have a duty to rescue maidens in destress."

"Sid, think she's awake enough that she can move on her own?" Kluck asked all business. Sid nodded.

"The ether worries me. Let's go get her before they dope her again. Put on your shoes, we'll not be back."

"What about guns?" Sid asked. He knew those thugs had knives and probably guns he hadn't seen. The two lieutenants shrugged.

"Ah, we'll work something out," Kluck said, not seeming the least concerned over the lack of a weapon. "Does one of you ladies have a knife I can borrow?"

The women looked at each other. Then Wren whipped a sharp lethal looking dagger from under the mattress, startling Sid. She handed it to Kluck who felt the edge and smiled. Victor found a heavy wood cane some past customer had forgotten.

The lieutenants went before them up the stairs with a nervous Sid and the ladies following, everyone endeavoring to be quiet. Kluck stopped before the fourth floor door.

"Doc, since they know you," the senior lieutenant whispered, "I want you to go first, in case the thugs are waiting in the hallway. If they are, just greet them, so we know they're there. Victor, check out that other stairway."

Sid didn't consider himself a brave man, but knew if he didn't try to save Indi, he'd never forgive himself, and besides the lieutenants confidence bolstered his courage. He opened the door, entered the fourth floor, and found Hedrick leaning against an open door halfway down the hallway.

"The Doc is here, wait before you dope her," Hedrick told someone in the room. The one that carried Indira stuck his ugly head out the door to see to whom his partner was talking.

"Hey, did you two get her delivered?" Sid said, surprised his voice sounded normal.

"Yeah, the bitch is waiting on you. Do your thing so we can finish tying her to the bed."

Sid noticed that Hedrick, occupied lighting a cigar, did have a revolver stuck in his pants waist. Sid wondered if he'd leave the room alive as he crowded by the ugly brute who had carried Indi and was blocking the door. Then he spotted a gray hair thin ugly woman, *she'd make a good witch in a play* Sid thought. She was standing beside the examination table where the wrapped up bundle that was Indi laid.

The three criminals were watching him and he knew if he was to survive, he best act like a man in charge. "What's that filthy hag doing in here?"

Startled, the old woman muttered, "I'm to clean the sacrifice."

Sid noticed Indira was struggling and turning blue. He ripped off the gag and vomit spewed out.

"Damn, what a mess, now I'll have to clean the table," the hag said.

"You stupid fool," Sid said. "She could have died. Don't you know ether makes people sick? God, if she died, the man would fire all of us."

Hedrick with his cigar lite approached the table for a better look.

"Unfasten her arms and legs so you can clean her proper," Sid said. He hoped his father was right about if you act as if you're in charge, most men will assume you are.

"Hedrick, she needs a bath," the witch said, looking disgusted. "Smell the bitch. Do you think the duke wants a filthy thing like her? There'll be no bonus for us if he's smells that. I need my extra bit."

Hedrick looked mulish, so Sid added, "Surely you two brutes aren't afraid she'll over power you and escape. Put her in the tub, and then untie her so the hag can clean her."

Sid was starting to smell himself. His armpits were dipping. The big thug was now looking in the room, adding to Sid's nervousness. He feared giving away the lieutenants. What were they waiting for? What was Indira thinking, by now she had to have recognized his voice and now the witch had taken off her blindfold.

Indira looked wildly around the room, ignored Sid, and asked Hedrick where she was.

"Be a good girl, and you won't get hurt," the thug said as he with ease picked her up after casting a bucket of water on her to wash off the vomit. He sliced her leg bindings and holding her up by a tight one-hand grip on her shirt, he used his right hand to strip off her boots and pants.

"Now stand up," he added placing her in a large copper tub. The hag was over getting another bucket of water from a large sink. "Now turn around so I can cut the rope."

Indira rubbed her wrists. For the first time since Sid had known her, the Wapiti girl kept quiet, even looked meekly at the thug. Sid realized Hedrick's partner had disappeared, as had Hedrick, for he turned his head toward the door after cutting Indira's bindings, and yelled, "Clem."

The muffled gunshot startled Sid. The hag's mouth was hanging open as Hedrick slowly collapsed by the tub.

"Are you one of them?" Indira asked in a quiet voice as she stood in the tube and pointed the thug's smoking revolver at him.

"Lord no, I was trying to save you." She looked dubious. He accepted the Wapiti girls were still a bit reserved toward him because of his neighbor's son attempted rape of Jenny and her sister. "Indi, please be careful with that gun, there's friends in the hallway," he added.

"Where is the bastard's partner?" She asked while awkwardly climbing out of the tub and alternating her attention between the door and old woman.

"Sid, is it safe?" Lieutenant Kluck asked from outside the room.

"Who was that?" She asked, pointing the revolver toward the door.

"Indi, don't shoot, they're here to help." She nodded, not taking her eye off the door. "Lieutenant, I think it's safe."

The Prussian officer looked warily into the room from the door. He had a revolver, which he pointed toward Hedrick on the floor.

"Did the idiot shoot himself?"

Sid shook his head and pointed to Indira, which caused the lieutenant to look around the doorframe to see the rest of the room. He saw a half-naked Wapiti girl with a revolver pointed at him. "I'll be damn," and smiled.

"Is he dead?" He asked her.

"They were going to skin me," She said, lowering the gun a tad. "What is this place?"

"It's supposed to be a bordello," Kluck said. "We were here acting like fools before leaving on our assignments in the east. Sid was our guest, lucky for you he saw those thugs bring you upstairs and asked for our help. But now we need to leave without attracting attention. Sid, hand her the pants, it's distracting." He went to check on Victor.

Indira had grabbed her pants and boots from the embarrassed Sid and had them on before Wren and Matias cautiously entered the room. The two prostitutes stopped on seeing Hedrick on the floor in a spreading pool of blood and a girl with a revolver.

"She grabbed his revolver," Sid explained to Wren, nodding toward Hedrick's body. "Indi, do you have any hidden injuries?" he then asked, finally thinking like a doctor. She shook her head.

"I had no choice."

"I know," Sid said. "I'm thankful you did, now let me have the revolver."

Shaking her head, she ignored him and said, "They were going to do terrible things." Pointing the revolver at the trembling gray hair woman squatted in the corner away from the door, she added in a rising voice, “That creature complained because she would have to clean the mess they would make skinning me alive.”

“Woman, please, no shouting or shooting,” Kluck said, as he entered the room with Victor. “You saved us a great deal of trouble, but more gunshots will bring the guards. We need gone. Can I have the revolver? Victor needs it.” After a long pause, she handed it to him and he passed it to his partner in the hallway.

Victor grabbed the hag who had been slithering towards the door. “Where’s the ether?” he asked her, holding her by the arm.

“The guards will kill all of us,” the hag said. “Let me go, I won’t say a thing.”

“Where’s the ether?” Victor asked again. She pointed to the wall cabinet behind the copper tub. A half of liter of ether was in a glass flask with a ground glass stopper.

They all heard the sound of people rushing up the stairs. The two lieutenants reached the room entrance just as a man outside the room asked who shot. Five rapid shots rang out as the lieutenants disappeared into the hallway.

A couple of heartbeats later Victor stuck his head through the door and motioned for Sid and the women to come. The hag gabbed the bottle of ether and hurled it at Victor who caught it. The glass stopper popped out of the bottle and ether splashed the hallway. He flung the open bottle down the stairs. Indira punched the hag, knocking her flat as more gunshots rang out. The sudden flare of light and a loud whoosh, followed by screams told them the ether had ignited.

“Move it folks,” Victor shouted, motioning for everyone to ignore the licks of flames and dense smoke blocking the rear hallway.

“The front stairs are still clear.” Kluck added.

The lieutenants had the dead guards' rifles and an extra revolver. After a nod from his partner, Victor handed the revolver to Indira as the party hurried to the front stairs. Finding the stairs unguarded, the lieutenants dumped the rifles in the empty room to the left of the stairway.

"Keep the revolvers, but out of slight," Kluck said."

The party then rushed down the stairs to the third floor where they met two guards coming up from the second floor.

"Hurry, the top room is on fire. Hedrick and Clem need your help. They told us to get the women out of here and warn the others," Kluck said.

The younger guard looked suspicious, but the older guard said, "We need to help Hendrick. He'll have our heads if the roof burns."

As the guards went toward the smoky end of the hallway, the group ran down to the second floor, where they split up and started yelling fire. In moments, the hallways were a madhouse of men trying to dress and run and women screaming. Smoke was already collecting along the ceiling adding to the panic. The lieutenants ditched their stolen revolvers. Indira didn't want to, but Sid insisted. They all joined the human tide pouring into the main dining room and out onto the street.

"What about us," Wren asked Sid. Matias and Wren hadn't joined the group of prostitutes gathering by the Zamian hostess in the street. "The witch saw us."

Kluck was busy verifying all the other lieutenants in their original party had safely escaped the burning building.

"Victor, come here," Indira yelled.

Sid realized his friend had recovered her bossy ways as the Prussian lieutenant jogged over.

"You said your aunt lives in Berlin, can she hid Wren and Matias until we figure out a way to protect them?"

"Are you joking? They're slaves."

"They know our names," Indira said.

The police were arriving and would soon have order established. They knew the window to slip off unnoticed would soon close. Indira and he didn't need Father Jenkin learning of their involvement, especially the killing of one of her adductors, justified as it was. Kluck and three lieutenants jogged over to join them.

"We have to go," Klick said. "Someone will call the MP's and none of us can afford to be caught. I know a way out, follow me."

"What about them," Victor motioned for the whores to join them. "They can identify us."

"Cut their throats if that's your worry."

"What, you'd murder them," Indira said. "You can't be serious."

Chapter 18

Duke Soltzendorff, wearing unadorned gray-green army coveralls, had dressed down for the planned messy evening entertainment. The ringing of bells was his first indication there was a problem. Then his coach stopped. Looking out the window, he could see the front of Spirits a block away. People were pouring out the club's front door and police were setting up a blockade on the boulevard to control traffic. The lick of flames from one of the club's top floor windows explained the scene in front of him, a fire.

In a fury that his fun would not occur due to some fool's carelessness, he opened the coach door to go find the colonel. The sight of firemen and police establishing order in the milling shouting mass of people in the street stopped him from exiting the coach. He didn't need to attract more attention than his large coach already was with its four horses and liveried driver and footmen. Instead, he told the driver to take him home after sending off a footman with a message.

When Sid and Indira arrived back at the Royal Bismarck Hotel, they found a number of their classmates outside watching the flames from the burning Spirits building light up the Berlin night sky, including Father Jenkin.

"How'd you get so dirty? Where were you two?" Father Jenkin asked. "Curfew was half hour age."

"It's my fault," Sid said. "We jogged over to see what was burning. The smoke and ashes were bad. I forgot the time."

"What is burning?" The father asked. Sid told him some nightclub.

"Bunch of drunken fools set themselves ablaze," the Jesuit said. "Well, I hope no one got hurt. You missed the announcement. There has been a delay in delivery of the locomotive for several days. Since the steamer contracted to deliver the steam engine is the only west bound ship to New Hamburg with extra room for us, we can't leave until that machine is loaded aboard."

Father Jenkin acceptance of Sid's tale that they were just watching Spirits' fire had allowed Indira to maintain her composure. Had he challenged Sid's account, she might have blurted out that she had killed a man. Instead, Indira waited until she was secure in the bedroom with Jenny, before spilling out her tale of thugs kidnapping her so some duke could skin her.

"Indi, you're right, we must not go outside the hotel, unless we're together or with other students," Jenny said after listening and offering reassurances that her action was self-defense, not murder. "Now try to sleep and in the morning you'll feel better."

"Where did you put Larry's derringer?"

Colonel Palitzsch was impatient to have the next couple of days behind him and collect his two million D-marks. For several years, he had owned what was the classiest gentlemen's club in Berlin, and managed that feat without the army discovering his involvement. Discovery would have cost him his rank, pension, and even perhaps his freedom.

The Hedricks had made his clandestine ownership possible. They proved to be surprisingly effective managers. Elmira, a freed slave, served as the hostess and handled the girls and bar-kitchen. Her husband, a cashiered feldwebel, supervised procuring the girls, gaming rooms, and housekeeping staff, along with any enforcement needed. A trusted clerk, Herr Mortimore, helped Palitzsch handled the drugs, money, banking, and payrolls from the clerk's office in the warehouse across the alley behind Spirits.

This evening he had come in early to the warehouse to verify Burgdorf had delivered the Venite champagne. The fancy sparkling wine was a favorite of the Imperial Guards at their annual meeting for toasts. He also checked that Elmira had it on ice and safely locked away in the storage room.

Palitzsch now understood why a peer of the realm, Duke Soltzendorff, had purchased Spirits and established a paper trail that showed the club owner was his enemy, Benjamin Purnell. Even better, he knew his club employees, especially the Hendricks, always join in the toast-salutes to the emperor. He got cold chills thinking about it.

"She killed my son," the Hag, screamed, slamming open the warehouse door, startling him. "They started a fire, do something they're escaping."

Then fire bells started ringing to usher in the worst night of his life and it wasn't over. Now, with the sun not even up, he was standing in the duke's home office waiting. At least a servant had brought a tray in with coffee and small sandwiches.

"You do appreciate the fire has wrecked our plan to decapitate the emperor's imperial guard force?" Duke Soltzendorff asked his normal élan absent.

"Yes, and that's not all that was wrecked," he answered sharply. Resentment that efforts to satisfy the man's depravities had triggered the fire, along with fatigue made his ire surface.

"What have you lost, Colonel? You're walking away with two million."

So the pervert says, but I still haven't received the promised gold for my sham transfer of the club to Purnell. Now I don't even have a club, he thought. But Palitzsch knew this wasn't the moment to point out those facts. Not to a man, who had planned to murder ninety percent of the emperor's guards.

"I have to decide whether to proceed with the plan or abandon it after spending millions because you couldn't control a few carousing army lieutenants and a couple of students."

"That wasn't my fault. It was that damn Hendrick. He's the one who failed. Who would have believed he couldn't handle a couple of drunk lieutenants."

"Well since your man didn't, I want you to make sure those Jesuit medical students don't start tales. Talk of slaves could attract unwanted attention from the law."

"What about the fire marshal? There're four bodies in the debris. That discovery will cause a lot questions and alert Purnell that he is Spirits owner. He'll refute that, which will cause more questions that none of us want asked."

"No one will believe him. They'll figure it was drug related. I'll handle the fire marshal. What about the girls?"

"They know the drill. They won't be trouble. Elmira will keep them stoned and out of the way. There is a potential problem. One of the Mongol girls is missing, maybe another one too. With any luck the fire killed them."

"I damn well hope they're dead. Any more good news," the duke asked. The colonel shook his head.

"You need to report to the General Staff office in case one of those lieutenants did report on the fire. I want you assigned as the lead investigator on the Spirits fire. Don't worry about those lieutenants. They will be too busy staying live on the eastern front fighting the Mongols to worry about a girl and fire. Everyone else who knows what occurred is dead, except those Wapiti students."

That wasn't correct, Elmira, Hendrick's mother, and maybe those missing whores knew.

Jenny's news worried Indira. Father Jenkin had requested her presence in the lobby within an hour to answer police questions about last night. They were in the lobby thirty minutes later. A friendly Berlin policeman directed her to the manager's office and told Jenny to wait in the lobby. Indira found Father Jenkin, a worried Sid Moyer, another Berlin policeman, and Colonel Palitzsch who she remembered from the Aruba, seated around the hotel manager's conference table. The manager wasn't there.

"Indira, witnesses' claim Herr Moyer was in an establishment of ill repute," Father Jenkin said, "The same club that burned last night. He was with several army lieutenants and during their drunken fooling around set the building ablaze and several people died."

The colonel interrupted.

"I'm not interested in prosecuting students, the university can deal with you two," the colonel said. "I want the name of those army officers."

"Let me finish colonel," the father said. Indira could tell he was mad, at who was her worry. "Herr Moyer says he wasn't in Spirits and his only involvement was watching the fire for a while with you. So is that true, Indira?"

"Yes, father," Indira said. "And Sid wasn't drinking either, we just watched the fire for a while, then returned to the hotel." A sweaty Sid shrugged his shoulders, apparently having told the same story earlier.

"Colonel, I'm sad to learn people died, but I can't help you," Sid said.

"I agree. I smelled no alcohol last night," Father Jenkin said. "Colonel you're wasting time here, I'd suggest you start interviewing the Spirit employees and find the owners. The newspaper claims the building was a house of prostitution. What a disgrace that such a sleazy establishment could operate in the palace's backyard. The police should be ashamed. Who knows what other illegal activities were occurring."

The embarrassed Berlin policeman assured Father Jenkin the authorities are fully investigating that matter.

The look from the colonel sent a shiver through Indira. Their eyes had locked for a moment and Indira sensed he knew of their involvement. His malevolence toward her had her wondering if he was involved in the club. Then she remembered the hag's reference to a colonel and a duke, could Colonel Palitzsch be the person behind her abduction last night. Until that thought, she had assumed only Benjamin Purnell was involved.

"Some of the people watching the fire said they saw women slaves. Isn't slavery illegal here?" Indira asked the policeman to test that thought, while glancing toward the colonel. He broke eye contact to look toward the policeman, but otherwise had no reaction.

"We have received similar reports and are checking their veracity," the policeman said. "Thank you Father Jenkin, students, for your assistance, we're done here."

As the duke had expected, Colonel Palitzsch had received a message from General von Moltke to report to the Prussian General Staff headquarters. He expected the general's summon to concern the fire at Spirits, but first he wanted to witness the police interview of the students. One of the duke's footman had earlier advised him of that meeting.

The demeanor of the skinny Wapiti had surprised him to the point he decided the Hag was mistaken. The girl wasn't the person who had shot Hedrick. Thanks to Elmira and that witch, he had names of who had freed the Wapiti girl and murdered Hedrick and Clem. The ringleader had been General Kluck's oldest son.

Normally the colonel might have used that information for extracting future favors from the general involved by offering to cover up his son's involvement. Not in this case. The general was a respected field commander, who would demand an explanation of how Palitzsch knew his son was involved. Those questions might then lead to an interrogation of him and the Spirits employees by the emperor's spymaster, Hansen.

The Wapiti girl had responded as he and the duke had hoped, denying any knowledge or involvement to protect her friends. She'd have no credibility if she later tried to claim Spirits employees had abducted her. Such a story might have prompted the Royal Prussian Church and Jesuit investigators to look into Spirits' operation. Her denial of knowledge aborted that worry.

"Emperor Schnabel wants to know if that burned nightclub was using slaves." General von Moltke said. "I want you to investigate. I need an answer for the emperor."

"Yes sir, I will start at once on the investigation," the colonel said.

"Good," the general said, not bothering to return his salute. "Oh, here is an anonymous message. It seems the club used slaves and one of them is hiding at this address. Have someone check it."

The involvement of the emperor worried the colonel. If Schnabel took a real interest in Spirits, he'd would involve Hansen, and a cover up of the club's slave use would be impossible.

The presence of General Kluck in von Moltke's office had given him a start. The general was on his way east to assume command of the 9th Division blocking the Mongol invaders north thrust. He was there for final orders, but remained to hear their discussion of the fire. If the lieutenant had spoken with his father, the man would not have remained silent. That realization helped Palitzsch relax a bit.

Though exhausted, he returned to the smoldering site and talked with the firemen. Four bodies had been recovered, all males. Elmira had since verified two female slaves, a Zamian bitch and a Mongol were missing. They were new, not yet hooked on opium. Hedrick had arranged their purchase over his wife's objection. Elmira had thought they were too perceptive and apt to cause dissension among the club's other working girls. He had foolishly sided with Hedrick and bought them.

Now he worried the lieutenants had helped his slaves escape. But he had checked. The lieutenants were on their way to the eastern front. The troop train had left two hours ago and he couldn't imagine those whores successfully hiding aboard that train. He had also checked earlier with the police. They hadn't gone there, so where could they be hiding? Could those two medical students be hiding them? The Jesuits and church having those bitches to interrogate was too awful to contemplate. Maybe the prudent course was to kill the girl and that blundering apple grower's son, along with Hedrick's wife.

The address General Motke had passed on proved to be a false lead. The elderly couple clearly had no knowledge of slaves. Colonel Palitzsch considered his next move while walking out the cul-de-sac where the couple's modest house was located. At the intersection with the main street, he hailed a hackney carriage.

The colonel needed sleep, but decided to again visit Elmira at the warehouse located down the alley behind Spirits' burned out shell. The sight of the charred rubble made him ill. He had plowed the bulk of the club's earning into paying off the mortgage with the plan of selling the business next year and buying a north Baltic estate.

Then the duke, playing some long game he hadn't understood at the time, had made him an offer he could never hope for in a straight sale. One of the duke's requirements was the documentation show Benjamin Purnell had started Spirits and was the current owner. That bit of friction had required the help of Berlin Commerce and Commodity Bank in eliminating any tract of his original mortgage and property tax payments over the last several years. The duke handled the bank along with arranging the files in the proper Berlin bureaucrat's office to show Orleans Boatyard had been paying Spirits license fees and taxes.

The why Colonel Palitzsch now understood, the duke was organizing a coup d'état and had wanted the imperial guards out of the way and Rudolf Habsburg as emperor.

Hedrick, the cursed and now dead fool, and Elmira lived in the warehouse's rear loft. The survivors from the half dozen slaves that had worked as prostitutes in the former club had moved into the place after the club fire. Four female slaves were still there with her, dependent on his opium, which he could no longer afford, unless Elmira put them back to work.

"Any word on those bitches you let slip away?" he asked Elmira in greeting.

They were in the kitchen area of the open warehouse. Colorful curtains screened off areas around the open space and served as sleeping areas for the residents. The room was in effect one large jail cell. The exits were the two stout double locked doors, one into the kitchen area, and the other to the loading dock.

"Don't be blaming me," Elmira said, looking unusually disconcerted. "I told you those two weren't ready."

One of the slaves, a thin Prussian girl was washing the morning dishes in a dilatory fashion. Elmira had been criticizing her cleaning job when he arrived. The other whores were lazing in their beds. The girl at the sink started to walk away.

"Where do you think you're going, Daisy? You're not done. I want those plates rewashed, in hot water."

The barefoot girl, wearing only tattered cut off pants, meekly nodded, and went to the stove where a large iron pot used to heat water was steaming.

"We'd be having the shits again, if not dead from rotten food, if I didn't make them follow basic sanitary practices," she complained.

"Where's the hag?" He asked. Something was wrong. It wasn't like Elmira to be jumpy and worried about housecleaning.

"I sent her to buy me a liter of schnapps. She'll be awhile. She's going to ask around about those two missing bitches."

Elmira must be hungover, Palitzsch thought. Her last comment, though, reminded him that his career, even his life, was in the hands of those escaped whores. If one of them turned up in the wrong place and started talking, that might put the authorities on this location. Even motivate the duke to terminate him. Right now, only two people could tie him to the missing slaves and she was standing unarmed in front of him. Besides, the chances of him restarting another Spirits in Berlin were slim to none. He lacked the necessary capital along with the drive. He reached for his revolver.

"Before you do anything regrettable," the suddenly alert Zamian woman said, "Be aware, I visited a lawyer and left two letters for him to mail. On my death, he'll send one to Herr Hansen, the head of empire's secret service, the other to Bishop von Bingen."

"That's the oldest ploy around," the colonel said.

He desperately wanted the threat of exposure that he owned slaves removed. Killing Elmira and the hag would do that. Surely, the bitch had just made that story up. He drew his revolver.

"It was a barter deal," the tense woman hastily added. "The elderly attorney enjoys the monthly special massages I provide. So much, I know he'll take umbrage over the loss of my service and want to see the person responsible suffer."

The story was plausible. Her greatest asset was her body. Allowing the lawyer occasional gratis visits to her pudenda would assure the man's interest in her well-being far more effectivity than a one-time payment of D-Marks. The deal just verified what he already knew. She wasn't dumb. He dropped the revolver back in its holster to her clear relief.

"I'm not worried about letters, without you to testify, they're useless. I'm mad you let them escape, but help me find them and then we'll partner equally in a new club."

"I'd like that. And let's avoid slaves," Elmira said. "We don't need the hassle and danger. Drugs are a better control. Get the girls addicted and they'll behave." She pointed to the whores lying in bed not paying attention to them.

"Rent us a new building and I'll make you a lot of money," she said.

"First, find those missing bitches. Their testimony is a threat to both of us." Elmira nodded.

"I'll not rest until I do."

The colonel left the warehouse conflicted. Had that bitch just maneuvered him? If she was dead, he was safe, but broke if the duke reneged on their deal. But with her expertise and a decent place to work out of, she was right. They could make good money.

He headed back to his office, unaware the Duke had called on Elmira earlier today to learn the truth behind the cause of the Spirits fire, among other things.

Duke Soltzendorff had expressed no comment or concern about the involvement of the lieutenants and Jesuit students, other than to express amazement that the guards and her husband couldn't control them. Then he had shocked her. He asked that she amend her letters.

"Whatever are you referring to?" She had asked, eyeing the two large footmen who had arrived with the duke.

"Please, you're a smart woman," the duke said, "No way you don't have insurance against the colonel turning on you. If I had to guess, some lawyer has an exposé letter to mail in event of your untimely death." She shrugged her shoulders, not sure what to admit.

"You know too many of my secrets. Normally one of my trusted men," he nodded toward the fearsome men by the door, "Would attend to you, but you can do me a favor and in return I'll allow you a chance to escape."

The man was terrifying in a quiet cultured way.

"I want the name of your lawyer."

She considered lying, but in the end told him the lawyer's name. The duke motioned over the smaller footman and told him to go get the letters. Elmira felt a moment of pity for the old man. He didn't desire to die.

"Now get your paper. I want a new letter with all the nasty details of the Spirits operation, the use of slaves, allowing the murder of girls for large sums of money, everything with names.

You know because your husband supervised the business. Add Benjamin Purnell's name as his boss and owner of Spirit. In return for a sworn signed copy of the revised letter, I will pay you two thousand D-Marks and being a sport, give you one week to vanish. Is it a deal?"

Elmira looked toward the two footmen, no chance getting by them. She feared the duke would renege and have her murdered after signing the letter. Prussian dukes had powerful friends and connections. She had no doubt that the disappearance of a Zamian whore would require little effort on their part. The man was insane, but having no other option, she decided to trust him.

"Okay, I'll do it, she said, and started writing. Her writing wasn't her best. Her hand wanted to shake and she made a few ink blotches. Thirty minutes later, a middle-aged solemn man in a black suit arrived and spoke with the duke. They shook hands.

The duke read her two-page letter and made a few changes that she rewrote. Satisfied he handed the letter to the somber man who asked her if she was Elmira Hedrick. She nodded and the man notarized, stamped, and had her sign at several places on the document.

"Thank you Elmira," the duke said getting up. He handed her four gold five-hundred D-Mark coins. "You have seven days. Get out of Prussian. We won't look too hard for you elsewhere."

Seven days. Elmira hadn't reached the ripe old age of twenty-three by ignoring warnings. With her savings, Elmira had eighteen thousand D-Marks to start a new life. Fifteen minutes later, before she could pack, the colonel had walked in.

The duke's earlier visit and now her boss's visit had her in a near panic. By chance, the duke and the colonel hadn't encountered each other this morning. Otherwise, she and the colonel would be dead.

One important fact Colonel Palitzsch didn't appear to appreciate was that Duke Soltzendorff had to view him as a serious threat. The colonel, along with her and the hag knew of the Duke's perverted tastes, and that he had murdered six women in the last two years. She knew the Duke wasn't overly concerned about them, their word would mean nothing in court, unlike the colonel's testimony.

She was packing her second and last bag when Hedrick's mother returned with the liter of schnapps.

"If you value your life," Elmira said, "Pack a bag and come with me."

"Should I change first?" the slatternly woman asked, after checking none of the whores were paying attention to them, except the thin girl who was eyeing the bottle.

Her mother-in-law was referring to her disguise as a poor, but respectable elder Prussian lady. Elmira would act as her maid-companion.

"Yes. You need to hurry. Give that bottle to me."

A tenth of the liter was missing and she didn't need her mother-in-law drunk. Instead, she put it in her bag for later. She had noticed the girls had been eyeing the bottle and acting restless. They hadn't had their fix today, which reminded her the beat cop would be by at midday for his weekly payment. She planned to be long gone before then. Since she wouldn't be here, she figured some free fancy wine should satisfy the grubby bastard. She set three bottles of the Venite champagne on the kitchen table and considered taking one with her for later.

"Don't touch these bottles, they're for the police," she said, figuring that was a forlorn hope. "If I'm not back, Daisy, hand them to the man who knocks at the rear window."

Chapter 19

Felix Cohen, a small white haired man dressed in a fine dark gray suit and vest with a matching gray top hat, greeted Rex, Larry, Kit, and Al Leslie at the main Port Baltic passenger wharf. Bill Jacobs' uncle looked the part of a successful financier. The four well-dressed and armed burly assistants with Felix, at a nod from him, surrounded Rex's group and whisked them off with their baggage. They went to the central rail terminal where a private rail car waited to take them to Berlin.

The steam age was a recent development on Erden, thought one wouldn't know that from the scene before Rex. He was waiting on the third floor open deck of the rail terminal for Felix to complete his business at the telegraph counter. In every direction, Rex could see steam powered cranes, buildings with numerous smokestacks, steam locomotives of one, two, and three sets of drive wheels moving rail cars about on the vast rail yard along the waterfront. Off to his right, several kilometers away, a large iron ship hull was under construction and surrounded by more steam powder cranes. Despite the ubiquitous black soot on every exposed surface and the pervasive odor of manure and sulfur dioxide, he could have spent a week touring this example of a flourishing industrial port prior to electricity.

"Von Siemen who schedules appeals before Emperor Schnabel was very clear both sides will have a ten minute period to present their case," Felix said, joining Rex. "I'm not sure Leslie is the man to do that."

Having been with the inventor for the past two weeks, Rex had to agree. Leslie was a linear thinking man, slow to arrive at his point, and oblivious of the listener's body language.

"Tara Smith is who we need," he answered while thinking of the incongruity of using an indigenous woman as their advocate before the emperor of this misogynistic society.

"The Wapiti lawyer," Felix, dubious of his suggestion, asked. Rex nodded. The banker scrutinized him for a moment, before adding. "Well, we have a few days to decide. The hearing is in ten days."

"Good, I need to meet Amy and Tara in Aram. We should be back in Berlin in a few days."

Turned out that Felix wasn't the only one to send a telegram, Larry Hopkins had sent one to Jenny Jarrell, who with Indira Hopkins greeted them at the main Berlin Railroad station. The girls had become beautiful young ladies since Rex had last seen them over a year ago. His friend was now as tall as Larry was.

Indira had seemed concerned about something, but she assured him all was fine and her grades were good. Rex figured a boy. He thought about teasing her and Jenny, though standing on the rail station platform surrounded by strangers wasn't the place for that. Instead he hailed a four wheel enclosed carriage to take them and their luggage to the hotel. Jenny and Larry held hands while Indira set across from Rex in the hired coach taking them to the Royal Bismarck Hotel.

Out of the blue Larry remarked, "You're serious." Looking at Indira, he said, "Okay cousin, what's this story about you shooting a man?"

Rex's drowsiness vanished as his niece told the details of her kidnapping and the fire at the club.

"My god, you were so lucky Sid Moyer recognized you," Rex said. "You would have vanished without a trace. More amazing are those Prussian lieutenants risking their career to help rescue a foreigner."

"Sid told me that Lieutenant Ludendorff said I was a Wapiti princess. By saving me, it would aid General Markel's Erie campaign," Indira said, smiling for the first time while shaking her head. "It's a hoot that anyone would think we had royalty. It makes me worry about those lieutenants."

Indira needed no persuasion to get her to direct them to the site of the burned out Spirits building. The club's outer brick walls had survived and now formed a rough bin containing the remains of the collapsed roof trusses, slate roof, and a still smoldering jumble of charred beams, furniture, and flooring. Someone had roped the area off and several uniformed men were busy searching the rubble. A policeman standing with two gentlemen yelled at the coach driver to keep moving. Rex recognized the fat man and told the driver to hold up.

"Herr Hansen, what brings you out on a cold snowy evening?" Rex asked the startled man.

Larry and the girls had also jumped out of the coach to inspect the site and followed Rex.

"Oh lord, the Wapiti are in town," Joe said to his man, Inspector Bailey, before exchanging greetings with Rex and the gang, even the policeman was included. "We're trying to determine what happen here, by any chance were you two in town yesterday?"

"No, Larry and I just arrive from Port Baltic. The girls were. They're medical students here for seminars."

"No kidding, they're part of the Jesuit class," Joe said, switching his attention to the girls. "The inspector was just telling me the most amazing story. There's a rumor that a Jesuit student was about to be raped and some lieutenants in a gallant effort to rescue her set the place afire." He looked at Jenny and then added, "Something similar happened to you, as I recall."

Rex started to put a stop to the interrogation, but realized Jenny and Indira didn't need his help.

"I hope they were as successful as Colonel Caprivi was for my sister and me," Jenny said.

She appeared calm and collect, and unembarrassed by this reminder of the horror slaves had to endure. Indira wasn't as calm as her friend was.

"Caprivi of the general staff," Inspector Bailey asked Joe who nodded.

"No one knows," Joe said, pointing to ruined club. "I was hoping you folks might know."

"Father Jenkin can verify I was at the Royal Bismarck Hotel yesterday all evening."

"And were you," Joe asked Indira.

"Not until later."

The two observed each other. Rex figured she wanted to tell Joe, but was worried word might get back to Father Jenkin or cause the lieutenants problems. So he said.

"Larry and I need to check in. Stop by latter and we'll have a drink."

Benjamin, after the dinner meeting the other night with Necho, was confident the steel rail issue was on its way to being resolved. Still, he best make sure, and returned to his Royal Bismarck hotel room with plans to pack a bag and notify Colonel

Essen they were going to Gruppo Steel in the morning. An uninvited guest, who lounged in his room's one plush leather chair, made those plans suspect.

"Herr Chopra, since I'm not dead, you must be here on other business."

"A guilty conscience troubling you . . . relax, I'm aware of your Prussian minders in the hall," the wiry Ichneumon assassin said. Motioning to the sofa he added, "Have a seat."

"I prefer to stand."

"Suit yourself. Their presence begs the question, are they protection for an ally, or guarding a prisoner . . . No, don't tell me, it's not important. I wouldn't know if it was the truth. However, whether you still have the forty million in gold is."

How did the thug even know about the gold?

"Who are you working for?" Benjamin asked, stalling.

The fact that a person with the correct code could access the Myrtle account most likely explained why he was still alive. Chopra wasn't certain if the emperor had issued new orders regarding the gold. He had to know his emperor had honored Benjamin for his help in the recovery of fort at Delta. Without his false navy orders, the Ichneumons would never have dislodged the Prussians from Delta.

"I deposited 600 kilograms of Emperor Ratakonda's gold in the Myrtle Cotton Bank about a month ago," his visitor said, answering the unasked question. "My partner sent a message that you had withdrawn the gold."

"I did. The Prussians demanded I build a railroad to the Erie. Emperor Ratakonda wants me to indulge them. The gold will be used to purchase the steel rail."

"You've taken leave of your senses, if you expect me to believe my emperor told you to spend his gold to build a railroad, so the Prussian army can more easily send troops to defend the Erie."

"Railroads run in both directions, my friend." Benjamin figured the emperor had intended the gold to finance the revolt the cotton growers dreamed of and added, "Ichneumon troops can disembark at River Point and use the railroad to travel into Guderian and Myrtle territory. Admittedly, those fools losing Hickory Ridge was a setback, but General Paget will retake the fort and River Point in the spring. And the railroad will take a year to build. So try to think ahead, like your emperor who is willing to help Schnabel tie up Prussian troops and gold in that god forsaken place."

"I don't believe you. If the hair brain scheme only involved the expenditure of yours and Prussian gold, the emperor might give his nod, but you're planning to used Ichneumon gold."

Benjamin could sense sweat forming in his forehead as the silence dragged on. Chopra just studied him while the barrel of assassin's revolver never wavered from pointing at his face. At last, shaking his head, the Ichneumon lowered the revolver.

"I doubt Ratakonda knows about this. I figure instead, Joe Hansen is holding those false naval orders over you in order to force you to build the spur. The Prussians expected you to use your gold, but you, being a thief, decided to raid those funds Ratakonda entrusted to you."

Chopra paused and sounding worried, added, "Or Hansen is using you to discover where those funds are and who our territory agents are."

"Hansen knew I had dealing with the Myrtle Cotton Bank. He knows nothing about those other accounts," Benjamin hastened to claim. He hadn't considered the possibility that the Prussians wanted him to expose the Ichneumon agent network.

"The gold is currently at BCCB," he added, realizing deceit was pointless. The Ichneumon had figured out his scheme. "I'm using it to buy ninety thousand tons of steel rails."

He shrugged his shoulder. "I'll inform the emperor, he can decide your fate. The war may delay that decision, but until the emperor decides, do not withdrawn from the other accounts."

Waiting for Purnell to return had cut into the time Chopra had to make his meeting with Duke Soltzendorff. He knew the fire at Spirits had voided the plan to poison the imperial guards and figured the meeting concerned that matter.

"The favor I need is for two of those Roanoke Jesuit medical students to vanish," the duke said as he worked to get his pipe right. The pipe tobacco smelled spicy, almost pleasant.

"As in dead," Chopra asked while wondering why a powerful duke with all his connections would need him.

"No, I mean as in gone, no trace, a mystery. One is a young Wapiti female. The other is the son of a Guderian plantation owner. Both were involved in that Spirit Club fire and Colonel Palitzsch is concerned the police may interrogate them."

"Why should you or I care?" Ichneumon agent asked. "Doesn't Purnell own the place?"

He wished the interior of the coach wasn't so dark, he like to see the duke's face. See if he was lying, though to what purpose he couldn't imagine.

"The colonel was involved and he is a key player in arranging the emperor's accident," the duke said. "I don't want him distracted."

The information surprised him. The circumspect officer hadn't struck him as the anarchistic type, in particular one involved in a coup d'état, a business that carried a death penalty, if discovered.

"He fears those students might connect him to Purnell's illegal operation and wants me to arrange their silence. Since I have to sell Rudolf to the council, I need clean hands, no blemishes on my reputation, since our candidate has plenty."

Answering the loud knock on Rex's hotel room door revealed an agitated Joe Hanson. Inspector Baily was with him and two policeman. Something had occurred to irk the normally calm bureaucrat.

"An hour ago, six more bodies, four young women and two patrolmen, were discovered in a warehouse across the alley from Spirits," Joe said. "I need your niece to talk."

"I believe her only hesitation is from a desire to protect those who helped her." Rex said, wanting to help, but remembering this wasn't the twenty-first century Berlin on Earth with laws assuring a citizen's rights to a fair hearing. They needed to be cautious.

"Go find Indira and tell her to come here." After Larry had rushed off, he asked Joe, "What killed the women, smoke?"

"Poison," Inspector Baily answered. "They had been drinking champagne."

Rex thought that amazing and asked how it happened.

"That's a damn good question, how do you put poison in champagne without causing it to lose the pop on opening and its bubbles?" Joe asked. "Each group had an open bottle of Venite champagne. The lab is trying to determine what the poison is. That's not my concern Bailey will handled that. My concern is learning what the other twenty-two bottles were intended for and who made them."

"You can't be suggesting she had anything to do with that?"

"If the place hadn't burned, right now the Association of Imperial Guards would be setting down to their annual dinner. The meeting always starts with several champagne toasts to the emperor. You get the point," Joe asked.

Rex nodded in understanding, but he couldn't help wondering at the group's choice of location, a damn bordello.

"You need to arrest the club's owners, not a visiting Wapiti teenager."

"We're not here to arrest her. I just need to learn what she might have heard. I already know who the owner is, since the property taxes were paid by Orleans Boatyard."

Friedrich Burgdorf knew the Ichneumon was in Berlin to support the coup against the current Prussian emperor whom he felt no loyalty. He just wanted to survive, collect the promise payment, and head to the western gold fields.

"I'm not clear on the target," he repeated to the Ichneumon who had met him in the dingy bar near the railyard. "The names mean nothing to me. Hell they all look alike."

"I know. I have the same problem. Could you kill all of them?" The agent asked.

Disconcerted by that rash suggestion, he paused to reconsider if he should simply bolt and chance escaping Prussia and the Ichneumons. Still, Chopra, who was wearing a dirty hoodie and dark glasses to help concealment his identity, had a reputation of being rational. And murderous, so Burgdorf decided to treat the suggestion straight, and said.

"The way that group jogs down the street to the hospital each morning, a couple of us probably could, but I trust you're not serious. The church and Jesuits would lock down Berlin to find who massacred the students. I thought the two were to vanish, with no uproar."

"Your right, forget that idea. Colonel Palitzsch and I will meet you in the morning, across from the Royal Bismarck hotel. He can point them out to you."

The colonel, dressed as a day laborer, seemed nervous standing on the brick sidewalk beside him and one of those fancy iron trash receptacles common throughout Berlin. They were watching the students assemble on the opposite sidewalk. Chopra had stayed behind in the alley used to approach the front of the massive hotel. The two Jesuits proctors were busy with the roll call and paid no attention to the two of them as they lined up their charges.

"Indira Hopkin is the tall Wapiti girl. Sid Moyer is the chubby man in the back row," the colonel said, pointing.

"You fool, don't point," Burgdorf said. It was too late for both Wapiti girls had noticed them. "Does the girl have a scar on her face?"

"Yes, do you know her?" The colonel asked as he turned to hide his face and pretend interest in the contents of the trash can. The girls alerted, had watching them until the proctors had ordered their class to jog off toward the hospital.

His memory flashed back to that brutal last day at Donnelly's fort. There's no way that Wapiti mother and her daughter escaped the locked burning jail, and after a moment, he answered. "No, the scar will help confirm I got the right student."

Sleep had been brief, but Larry and he made the Aram train morning departure. They had been up most of the evening listening in on the interrogation of Indira and Sid Moyer by Joe and the police inspector. Her narrative corroborated Rex's opinion that his niece, never one to mess with, had grown into an accomplished young woman. How or who shot Hendrick remained unsettled, though Rex had no doubt. Inspector Bailey wrote death was accidental self-inflicted in his report.

The Moyer lad came across as a decent person who was on a lark that exploded into a lethal confrontation. After the questioning was over, Rex thanked Sid for saving his friend. News that Purnell was involved in the club surprised no one. He hoped the Prussians hung the bastard.

The peaceful rural countryside the train traveled through to reach Aram captivated Rex and helped him relax. Between the dense towering blocks of forest were prosperous appearing farms and neat fenced fields ready for spring planting. He even saw several herds of long horn shaggy brown cattle, the first he'd seen on this world. Maybe there was hope that he'd yet one day enjoy a delicious porterhouse steak. He hadn't had beef since that mysterious event snatched him off Earth.

The steam locomotive pulling the train to Aram reminded him of the engine used in the television show, "Hell on Wheels", he had watched back on Earth. The machine's huffing and puffing sounded the same, as the train raced along the tracks. After a couple of hours of the same scenery, Rex decided to visit the locomotive. Several of his fellow riders informed him that railroad rules didn't allow passengers to visit the engine.

He waited until the conductor had left the front passenger car, and then went forward to reach the locomotive. Larry had reminded seated in an effort to get some sleep.

"How fast are we going," Rex asked the surprised fireman and engineer, while dusting himself off. Reaching the engine had required a trip across the coal stacked in the tender car.

"You're not allowed here," the stout middle-aged engineer said. He looked the part, dressed in a set of dirty gray coveralls, laced knee boots, long leather gloves that reach his elbows, a brimless grimy gray cap, and sprouting a mop like gray beard.

The man had kept his left hand on the steam throttle lever while examining his visitor between glances out the cab's right windshield. He had to be the man in charge. Rex was happy to see that he didn't appear the least concerned by the presence of a stranger in his cab.

The cab was a noisy environment. The rapid clicking from the engine's wheels crossing over the bolted steel rail joints, the deep cyclic reverberation of the heavy moving pistons and linkage driving the wheels, and the constant puffing of the steam exhaust were all reassuring sounds to Rex. The engine was performing well.

A dirty environment, black dust coated all the cab surfaces. Outside, a stream of dense black smoke and soot swirled above the cab and trialed back down the train cars. The coal appeared of poor quality to him and that along with the clinker forming on the firebox grate would account for the dark exhaust. The cab air was clear.

"Maybe forty kilometers per hour," the engineer answered, "Though, on the grade coming up, the old girl's speed drops to about half that. So who are you? I'm Dutch and he's Cedrick."

He nodded towards the fireman, who had on the same gray bib coveralls as the engineer, but was shirtless with a grimy red bandanna wrapped around his forehead. The powerful built man smiled in acknowledgement.

"I'm Rex, run a couple of river steamboats, and wanted to see your operation."

"This is one of the original 2-4-2 Focke-Wulf locomotives," Dutch said. "You should see the new 4-6-4 pulling the emperor's train, it's a beauty."

The engineer was referring to one of the ways companies classified steam locomotives. The first number was the number of leading wheels, the middle number the power-driven wheels, and the last number the trailing wheels.

"I'd like to see that locomotive."

"It'll be at Aram. I heard there's going to be a demonstration of some super explosive. I want to see that. Hey, don't be slacking off, keep Betsy fed, her pressure is not staying up."

"This crappy coal is forming clinkers, blocking the draft," the fireman said. "I have to take time to break them off the grate."

"Let me help," Rex said and grabbed one of the iron pokers. He had already gotten his clothes dirty and was familiar with clinkers from burning coal in his steamboat. The firebox draft help limit the heat radiating into the cab from the intense bed of glowing hot coals and clinker visible through the open firebox door. In a couple of minutes, they had chipped enough of the fused ash off the grate to allow a hotter fire and a happier engineer.

About ten kilometers out of Aram was a control tower and switch where the single pair of rails jointed a second set of rails. The trackman waved down the locomotive.

"Dutch, something bad just happened. I think one of the munition trains exploded in the yard," the trackman said, pointing to the vast dark columns of smoke ahead. "Did you hear the boom, feel the ground move."

Dutch shook his head and said, "Hardly with all the shaking and racket Betsy makes. Switch us to the left track and we'll go see what's what."

"Lord, I pray nothing happened to our emperor," an alarmed Dutch added.

The industrial area of Aram was sandwiched between a multiple track railyard that stretched for a couple of kilometers up the river valley along the eastern ridge and a fast flowing river to the west. Several large warehouse type structures with numerous brick chimneys protruding through their roofs sprawled across the lower section of Aram. Scattered between the buildings were elevated wooden water tanks, racks of barrels, and riveted iron storage tanks on the ground. The southern, upper part, of the valley appeared to be the residential and business area of the town.

The twin rail tracks approached the town along the eastern ridge before dropping in the last couple of kilometers into the shallow river valley. There they had a clear view of the devastation. The wreckage of two trains burned intensely in the rail yard, generating vast clouds of dark smoke. Several cart size craters extended in a line up the west side of the rail yard. Rex figured that line of craters marked the location of the munition train cars that had exploded. The loading docks beside the craters had sustained serious damage. The blast had toppled two of the yellow brick chimneys that in turn had smashed several iron tanks. The leaked content from one the crushed tanks burned with a dense black smoke. Gray dust coated everything. The scene reminded Rex of that Iraq market he had helped clean up after a massive truck bomb had exploded. Finding Amy was his first priority.

Duke Soltzendorff had always loathed having to wait on news. Had Captain Peiper's plan been successful? Was the emperor dead, or had the assassination attempt failed, and an enraged Schnabel was urging his minions to find the assassin? He wouldn't know until the Aram train arrived in Berlin, which reminded him someone needed to proceed with that eccentric man's idea of sending messages over a wire.

The Berlin Commerce and Commodity Bank had put the Leslie Wire Company into bankruptcy over missed interest payments. He had an offer pending for the company and needed to check on its status with Herr Kolmar. Felix Cohen had made some inquiries into settling Leslie's past due debt, but without the man to testify, the lawyers believed the bank could sell the company to whomever they wished to recover their money. Soltzendorff intended to be the successful buyer.

The Ichneumon agent had assured him that his man in Myrtle territory, Captain Pauli, had used Leslie for a Sun God sacrifice and buried the remains. So, while he waited for news, he might as well go light a fire under Kolmar to close the sale of the telegraph company to Soltzendorff Industries.

Two hours later Rex knew the emperor had survived what some were calling an assassination attempt, others, a tragic accident. Aram Chemical Company's offer to demonstrate a new electric detonator, Amy's he had wondered, had caused the emperor to disembark from the train. It had been a fortunate decision. The company representative assured him that Frau Caroom and the Wapiti attorney involved with the device demonstration had gone with the emperor's party. The Sixth Dragoons were escorting their coaches back to Berlin.

Figuring his sweetheart was safe, Rex returned to the railyard to help Dutch's crew. They worked to repair sufficient track to allow reversal of the one operational steam locomotive at Aram so a train of injured could be taken to Berlin. The railroad police and army had swiftly established order and taken charge of the blast site. The injured numbered in the hundreds. Fifty of the victims with the most serious wounds and burns required transport to Berlin hospitals.

Captain Peiper of the Imperial Guards had taken command of the hospital train and restricted the passengers allowed to board to members of the guard troop and those with wounds and burns that required treatment at a Berlin hospital. Dutch told the captain that Rex and Larry were members of the crew, firemen.

The Berlin Commerce and Commodity Bank office was located in a modest two story red brick building on tree lined residential street about a dozen blocks east of the palace complex. Duke Soltzendorff had never asked, but he'd bet the little bank executed more substantial transactions than the massive Royal Bank across from the palace did with a staff five times the size of BCCB's office. A liveried guard opened the bank's door for him and the manger rushed forward to inquire how they might be of service.

"I'm meeting Herr Habsburg, and please inform Herr Kolmar I need a moment, when he's free."

Rudolf's office was in the rear of the main lobby with a large glass window that allowed the occupant to watch the lobby traffic. Today heavy wool curtains blocked the view. The duke was surprised to find his coconspirator sober.

"Was Peiper successful?" Rudolf asked, jumping up to greet him.

"Too early for news," the duke said, adding, "I have a man at the station who will bring word here. That's the reason I'm here. I want to settle that Leslie business and build those wires."

"You're referring to the telegraph?"

"Is that what it's called?

"That's what they call it. Felix Cohen and Leslie are in with Kolmar now bring the account current."

"Leslie is here?" Taken aback by the unexpected news, he attempted to clarify his surprise. "I'd heard he was dead."

His partner had a shrewd look as he said, "The man is making some wild accusations about you hiring Ichneumons to kill him in Myrtle territory. Is there any truth to that? Not that I care."

As long as Julian Penton kept quiet, Leslie could make all the claims he wanted, but could prove nothing. "No, there's nothing to it." Best to go on the offence he decided and added, "Let's go see the traveler and Felix."

The duke went straight to the president's office to the left of the main lobby entrance and barged in. Kolmar appeared irritated at his interruption, old man Cohen appeared intrigued, and Leslie outraged. The inventor leaped to his feet.

"You tried to have me killed in Myrtle to steal my ideas and company. The emperor will hear of your scheme. I'm going to sue you. My lawyer will be contacting you."

"Oh shut up, you sound like some numskull that got drunk and now are blaming imaginary monsters for your actions."

"By God I have witnesses to confirm my story," Leslie sputtered. He grabbed the duke's coat lapel and an instant later laying sprawled on his back on the conference table.

The spilled pitcher of water and scattered cups of coffee and tea splashed the two men and proceeded to soaked Leslie as he whimpered on the table. Blood seeped from his nose.

"Let's conduct ourselves as gentlemen, not a bunch of stevedores," the duke said, adjusting his cuffs. Were there no capable assassins, he wondered, thinking of that Ichneumon agent's glowing praise of Captain Pauli's ruthlessness, before adding, "I figure his antislavery yapping irritated some of those Myrtle guardians and deputies. Those folks don't tolerate abolitionists.

Herr Cohen, tell the board I'm prepared to invest ten million in the venture."

"Never, you are lying, a sneak. I'll never agree to that," Leslie said, reviving enough to set up on the table.

"Relax pal, I don't care if you remain the president. I figure Felix will keep you under control and employed. After all, it is your invention. I want fifty-one percent of the company and the wire installed along the railways."

"I have to agree with my partner," Herr Cohen said. "We're not interested in your investment."

"Kolmar, I don't want the BCCB agreeing to anything. It's only fair to let the courts settle the bankruptcy."

While the duke had been talking, a messenger had given Rudolf a note. The duke told them to think over his offer and follow his coconspirator back to his office.

"The emperor is alive, unhurt, and racing back to Berlin. What will happen?" His frighten partner asked. "You want one?"

The man was flush in the face and worried. He had a bottle out, ready to pour himself a drink, vodka from its clear appearance.

"No. They'll treat it as an accident and start an investigation. You stay clearheaded. I'll find Peiper and learn why they failed."

The lecture on proper disinfection procedures was ending when Indira remembered where she had seen that man outside the hotel. Burgdorf was his name. The pitiless mercenary who had taken her mother and her to Donnelly's fort where they were to have been part of the group of female slaves promised to Cinnabar's warriors. Rex and his men had saved them from burning alive after Donnelly's men set fire to the jail.

Indira had recognized the other man with Burgdorf was the colonel who had questioned Sid. At the time, she had wondered what the army officer was doing. Not now, the one reason for him to be pointing her out to a known killer was he knew she was the escaped victim and feared her testimony. She figured those two violent men subscribed to the old maxim that dead men, or in this case, girls, tell no tales. They were too late, Sid and she had told their tale and the police had her signed statements.

Sid brushed off her warning that one of Donnelly's mercenary and that creepy colonel had watched them at the morning roll call and he should be careful.

Chapter 20

Indira hadn't been the only one to recognize Burgdorf was in Berlin. Disembarking from the hospital train, Rex had seem the mercenary deliver a message to Captain Pieper. His original plan was to return with Larry to the hotel and wait on the women. But Amy was safe. Besides, he was curious why a captain of the Imperial guards would have business with Burgdorf whom he knew had worked for Purnell and Ichneumon interests. He decided to follow them.

"Larry, hire two horses and meet me in front of the station."

Rex trailed the two men through the busy station to the main entrance that opened on to von Bingen Boulevard. It was the main north south road in Berlin. There a large black carriage pulled by six horses waited there. It had a fancy eagle like emblem on its door, two armed livered footman waited on the rear of the coach, and an armed guard watched the station's entrance from the front bench with the driver. Both of the men he was following entered the coach, which straightway headed south on the boulevard.

Duke Soltzendorff heard the coach arrive, and having dismissed the servants, went into the hallway and unlocked the front door. He still felt confident the police couldn't connect him to the assassination attempt, but why have witnesses to his meeting with those who did have blood on their hands. He greeted Chopra, Peiper, and Burgdorf at the door, and after thrown the bolts, followed them into the library. Rudolf Habsburg, who for once was sober, greeted them from his seat at the conference table.

"Grab a chair," the duke ordered, taking the chair by Rudolf. Everyone proceeded to pick a chair and set down. The room's atmosphere was tense and silence, none of the usual joking and gossip.

"I understand the attempt was unsuccessful. Captain Peiper, please explain what occurred. Why the fool is still alive."

"The engineer on the munitions train perfectly timed the passage of the four box cars by the emperor's railroad coach. The two hundred tons of canon power in those cars exploded and destroyed the emperor's car."

"Yet the emperor is still alive. Doesn't sound perfect to me," Rudolf said.

"My lord, allow me to finish," the unruffled captain said, and after a moment with no more comments, continued. "The initial explosion setoff the remaining forty car loads of munitions, causing vast damage to the railyard. The Aram depot, several buildings, two water tanks, and those tall chimneys you could see long before entering the valley, all collapsed. The rail yard tracks are a mess, which means no new munitions trains will be loaded and sent east in the near future."

"I thought that wasn't to happen, just those four cars would explode," the duke said. "The army had been demanding additional gunpowder shipments to the east."

"So did the train engineer, but I couldn't leave them for the police to interrogate?"

"Good point, will they find anything to point to us?"

"There'll be a thorough investigation into the cause. They might find the remains of the detonators, but I had several cases of detonators placed throughout the cars to explain their presence."

"Damn, that is so against safe practices," Burgdorf said. "Those investigators won't rest until they determined who was responsible."

"They'll find him, only he won't be talking."

"Very clever, captain, I like it," the duke said and then asked, "How many dead?"

"They were still searching the rubble, but the count when I left was seventy-eight dead. The emperor wasn't one of them. Hundreds more were injured and burned. The ones with the worst injuries were hauled to Berlin, which is how I got here."

"Got away, what rotten luck," Rudolf said.

"The two badly injured guards I spoke to on the hospital train said the emperor entered his rail coach and told the conductor to start. A moment later, the conductor stopped the train to allow an official from the chemical company to convey a message. The emperor ordered the guards to come with him and they all hurried off to the Aram office. The building saved them, though the blast did collapse it. The guards didn't know any more."

"Someone warned him," Rudolf said.

"I don't know, but I doubt it. He would have warned his people to also run," Peiper said.

"We'll know soon enough," the duke said. "What the status of the bomb makers?"

"The colonel and his man are helping the army with the investigation," the captain said. "And in the process they will destroy evidence."

"I want you two to use the time to locate and eliminate the loose ends from that damn Spirits fire. Have those students been dispensed with, the missing slaves located?"

Chopra and Burgdorf shook their heads.

"I thought you asses were supposed to be super assassins," Rudolf said. "Aren't they just students? What the problem?"

"The Jesuit guards and not wanting the police involved in their disappearance," Chopra said. "However if you want, I can have them shot on the boulevard as they jog to their morning class. Of course there is always the risk some of their classmates might also get shot."

"Nothing simple anymore, we'll defer to your professional expertise," the duke said. "But Rudolf is right. Sooner is better."

Burgdorf as a rule would never volunteer an opinion, but he felt not warning them might prove fatal.

"I recognized that Wapiti girl with the scar. Her uncle is Rex Knight and I saw him get off the hospital train. He is bad news."

"Damn, I hope you're mistaken," Chopra said. The duke asked why. "He has cause the Ichneumons much trouble along the Erie River. My emperor has a fifty thousand D-Mark bounty on his head. But our main concern here is his friendship with Joe Hansen. Being on that train means he was at Amar during the explosion and if he saw Peiper and Burgdorf together he'll be quick to suspect a connection to the blast."

"I just heard that name this afternoon," Rudolf said looking towards the duke. "He's the man that Leslie said rescued him from those Ichneumons who were going to kill him."

"Then kill him along with the girl," the duke said, looking at Chopra. "I'll visit the palace in the morning and try to meet with the emperor. Find out how he survived. Until I know more, no attempt on the emperor,"

Rex wanted to pass on his information to Joe Hansen, but didn't know where to find him so he went to the main police station and asked for Detective Bailey. Skeptical of the information, Rex had explained to the investigator how Larry and he managed to return to Berlin.

"You don't know Burgdorf, but Joe Hansen does," he explained. "The mercenary was Donnelly's main man and was last working for the Ichneumons along the Erie. You think your partner wouldn't want to know that man was meeting with one of the imperial guard officers and some peer of the realm?"

The policeman would only commit to making Hansen aware of the meeting when they next met.

Duke Soltzendorff carriage returned them to the Berlin rail station where Capitan Peiper caught the train to Aram. The other two conspirators had a discussion in front of the station on dividing the tasks the duke had demanded they accomplish with haste.

"I have the room numbers where those students are staying," Burgdorf said.

"There are still a couple of hours before they'll stir. Let's hit them now. You want the girl or the boy?"

"You can have girl," the mercenary said, worried her uncle would never forgive her murderer. He didn't need that bastard with a vendetta against him. "What about Purnell?"

"I can reach him any time. We need to cleanup those students and find those missing slaves." Chopra said thinking of the note Levi Ottoman had delivered from General Paget. Emperor Ratakonda had been enraged to learn about the gold and wanted Purnell dead.

Burgdorf had earlier visited the hotel and learned the Jesuit proctors had segregated the medical students, males on the third floor, and the four females on the top, fourth floor. They used the loading dock door and rear stairs to sneak into the Royal Bismarck

Hotel. The Wapiti females were in room 413. He stopped on the third floor and entered the dark hallway to find room 314 while the Ichneumon went quietly on to the girl's floor.

One break for Burgdorf, the room where Moyer was sleeping was across from the door off the rear stairs. Escape would be easy and the door was unlocked. Three bunk beds with six snorting men in a dark room presented a recognition problem. Which hump was Moyer? They had agreed to use knifes to avoid alerting the other group. One of the students woke and asked what he wanted.

"I'm looking for Moyer."

"That's me."

"I got a message, but lets' go out in the hallway, not disturbed your friends," Burgdorf suggested, pleased with his luck.

Moyer, pulling on jockey shorts, followed him into hallway, pausing to ease closed the room door. Turning he asked, "Who's the message . . ."

The sudden deep slice across the student's throat left the young man standing and trying to stop the spurting blood with his hands. The student appeared sad as he started to fall. The mercenary caught his body and lowered it to the floor. A crash followed by a gun shot from above announced his partner had encountered trouble.

Indira, a light sleeper, woke to the faint sounds of someone trying to slide their room door bolt. On guard since recognizing Burgdorf the other day, she had taken procession the derringer Larry had given Jenny who didn't like guns. The little pistol fired the lethal 9x19mm cartridge. Its single shot left no leeway for error if the person trying to enter intended them harm. She nudged Jenny awake.

“There’s someone at the door,” Indira whispered, “Get your knife.”

Both girls were on their feet when the wooden door busted open with a load crack and fragments of wood flew into the room. A thin man rushed in with a short sword. Indira’s shot hit the man in his face causing him to spin to his left and drop the sword. Jenny plunged her knife deep into the small of his back. The assailant staggered into the hallway and collapsed as Indira reloaded.

A large man exited rear stair doorway and looked down the hallway toward where they standing over the dead man. Indira recognized the mercenary and bought the derringer up to fire. The man jumped back in the shelter of the stairwell before she could fire.

Rex and Larry had stopped at the front desk to check for messages when they heard a faint pop that might have been a gunshot.

“They’re on the fourth floor, you check that,” Rex said. “I’ll block the rear exit, just in case this is some insane repeat adduction.”

Larry ran up the main stairs while Rex headed for the rear stairs and exit. Both men had revolvers out. He reached the exit door just as a large man dressed in black came rushing down the stairs.

“Halt,” he yelled, recognizing Burgdorf.

The mercenary didn’t and he shot him in the left leg. The man missed the last two steps and crashed into the closed exit door, knocking Rex aside. A moment later his niece, in pink pajamas shorts, eruption out of the stairs exit, holding a tiny pistol.

“Good, you got the creep,” she said.

A couple of male students arrived, moments later, along with Father Jenkin who demanded an explanation.

"I'm not sure," Rex said, "But I know this guy is somehow involved in the Aram explosion."

"Explosion . . .," the proctor asked, noticing Indira woeful lack of dress, sputtered, "I can't believe you. Go get some clothes on, now!"

Rex seeing the blue blood on her leg, asked. "Where did that come from?"

"His Ichneumon partner kicked in our door and . . ., He's in the hallway by our room."

"Who is?" Father Jenkin and Rex both asked.

A student rushed out of the stairwell, yelling, "Father Jenkin, Sid Moyer has been murdered."

His niece ran up the stairs. Rex told proctor to summon the police and Inspector Bailey as he finished securely tying up Burgdorf. He then headed up to find the girls and Larry, stopping on the third floor to check on Sid. A half a dozen students were trying to save the young man, but everyone there on seeing the extent of his wound and amount of blood on the floor knew it was hopeless.

Indira, crying, left the group and told him to follow. They ran up the stairs to the fourth floor where they found Larry and Jenny in the hallway. A dead man and a short sword were sprawled in front of a room with a broken door.

"He kicked in their door," Larry said, answering the unasked question. The blue blood meant he was an Ichneumon.

"That Jesuit proctor and the police will be here any moment," Rex said while Indira yanked on the paints and skirt Jenny had handed her. "They'll take a harsh view of a Wapiti having a firearm."

"They murdered Sid," Indira said, slipping on her boots. "You know he intended to murder us."

"We know that. You did right, but we need a story," he said. "Is that the pistol?" Indira nodded handing over the derringer. After removing the cartridge, he added, "Quick, find the empty casing before someone shows up."

Jenny had picked up the shell case from the floor where her roommate had flung it earlier when reloading the derringer. In a moment Rex had replaced the good cartridge with spent and placed the gun on the floor by the body.

"Larry, hide his sword in one of the empty rooms. Here's the story, you heard him forcing the door. When he kicked it open, one of you stabbed him." He looked at Jenny and asked, "One of you did, right?" Jenny nodded and he continued, "While, when Indira kicked the door back in his face, he somehow managed to shoot himself when the door slammed him."

"In his left eye . . . You think the police will buy that cock and bull story," Larry asked, returning from hiding the sword.

"After what happen in Aram and him being an Ichneumon, I think the police will. They'll know it was part of belated Spirits cover up, why else would they attack these two? Whoever is behind this attempt didn't know Sid and Indi had already given their statements. The medical school, Father Jenkin, is another matter. He'll soon realized this business had something to do with that nightclub and suspect Sid and her lied, but I think it'll blow over."

In a warehouse owned by Focke-Wulf and part of the Port Baltic railyards, Lieutenant Ludendorff had just finished excepting delivery of a beautiful new 4-6-4 steam locomotive for the Erie spur. He was a busy young man, though now he was taking a break in the new engine's cab to read the latest Berlin newspaper that the accountant had loaned him. The headlines concerned the failed coup attempt. Of special interest to him was Benjamin Purnell's arrest for activities at the late nightclub, Spirits and the murder of Sid.

Victor was amazed to learn that the man building the new railroad, in a sense his boss, was a procurer who provided young girls for the nobles to abuse and murdered. That Herr Purnell might be involved in a coup d'état was believable, but running a whorehouse?

Property tax and licensing fee records were the source of the charges against the businessman. He figured Indira was celebrating her nemesis arrest. It's a shame his friend Sid had to die and miss knowing justice had occurred.

An ad on the back page of the newspaper caught his attention. Gunther & Gunther, an expensive Berlin law office, had posted a ten thousand D-Mark reward for the apprehension of Elmira Hendrick who the police wanted for questioning. He remembered that was the name of the club's beautiful hostess.

"What do you want loaded first," Feldwebel Prittwitz asked, "The kegs of rail spikes or start on the rails?"

The army had sent the captain handling the dock operation, along with half of the combat engineering company of sappers, to the eastern front. The colonel in command of the port area told Victor he was now in charge of the troops remaining and responsible for loading of the rail supplies for the Erie spur project. Several ships would be required. There were thousands of steel rails stacked in the yard, along with the locomotive and one hundred rail car trucks.

Everything needed berths on ships going to New Hamburg, even the two escaped slaves from Spirits he had agreed to help. He wasn't quite sure how Indira and Sid had managed to saddled him with the job, but after he learned of his friend's murder, was glad he had accepted the role of their protector.

The Zamian whore, Matias, and Wren, the Mongol whore, he had assigned to help the civilian cook. Victor's company of twenty troopers had Jake, a fat older man of mix ancestry, whose job was to fix three meals a day and keep the mess wagon clean. He was very happy to have two helpers and in turn did not ask any difficult questions. Victor told both women to look as ugly as they could manage and attract no attention.

"The locomotive will be loaded first," the lieutenant answered, "Go ahead and start."

He had vacated the cab, and was filing his copy of the transfer documents showing NH&R Railroad was the new owner of the 4-6-4 engine, when Wren motioned for him from the warehouse rear side door.

"I saw the hag," the Mongol woman said. "Elmira is with her at the mess tent. Those bitches are trying to get a free meal. Can you arrest her for poisoning our friends?"

Two mornings after the shooting of the Ichneumon agent, Rex was in bed with Amy listening to the baby's heartbeat. She had earlier been describing the business deals her and Tara had signed, but now he had her interested in something else. Joe Hansen banging on the room door broke the mood. Amy jumped up and said she'd take a bath while they talked.

"I need Burgdorf to talk," Joe said. "I fear another rack session will kill him."

"He's a thug. What would he know? What's that Captain Peiper have to say?"

"He was killed yesterday in an explosion while helping with the Aram cleanup. One break, an army lieutenant captured the Spirits manager in Port Baltic. She claims Duke Soltzendorff made her write that letter incriminating Purnell. According to her, the duke is a monster. He likes to skin girls."

"For god sakes, she was the enabler and every bit as evil."

"If she's telling the truth, your wife's nemesis never had any connection to the club. Colonel Palitzsch was the club's owner. And the Hedrick woman claims she knew nothing about any attempt to poison the imperial guards or that the champagne was tainted."

"That's hard to believe. Did the colonel?" Rex asked. "Has he confessed?"

"He has disappeared. Alas, I fear he's dead. The emperor needs more proof than the word of a slave and an admitted perjurer to arrest a Soltzendorff. He wants proof of involvement with the assassination attempt. Hell, some are now saying it was a tragic accident and even the emperor is wondering if there was coup d'état attempt."

"Do you think that Ichneumon who attacked the students was the third person in that group that went to the duke's home?"

"His name was Sanita Chopra, a well-known assassin and agent for Ratakonda. Those girls did the world a service killing that murderer. If he was the third member, that is powerful evidence there was a coup planned. The duke denies knowing Chopra. He thought the two men with the captain worked for him. He had no interaction with any of them, except, Captain Pieper who stopped by with news of the Aram accident."

"How does Purnell explain Orleans Boat Works paying the taxes and license fees for the club?"

"He denied it. He was the one that posted the reward that resulted in the Hendrick woman's capture. The interesting thing is the senior file clerk at the Berlin Tax office fell to her death yesterday. Even more curious, BCCB claims the payment records on the club's mortgage are missing."

"If Purnell is telling the truth, which may be a first for him, then who ever had the records altered, is your ringleader. Is that the duke?"

"Whoever he is, his plot to poison the imperial guards would have made a coup d'état easier. The complication for him was to create a believable fall guy. Purnell was a good choice, but the fire upended his plans," Hansen said.

"If you still need Burgdorf's testimony, offer him the one thing he might value. Free passage to the Erie River and escape into the western gold fields."

Three days later, Rex, Amy, and the Jesuit students were in Port Baltic waiting to board the Aruba for New Hamburg when the Berlin newspaper arrived. The headline read 'Duke Soltzendorff dead'. The accompanying paragraph referred to a tragic hunting accident.

Epilogue

The loss of Hickory Ridge halted the Ichneumon push up the Erie valley that year, but the Mongol army continued to engage the Prussian army along the eastern boundary lands. Rudolf Habsburg returned to the Armistice and Trade Commission.

In May, the Myrtle Territory government threatened to declare independence and asked the Ichneumon army for assistance.

The new rail spur to the Erie River had progressed thirty-five kilometers to the first mountain tunnel by late summer. Even the emperor acknowledged that his completion date for the project before winter might have been optimistic. The army and Purnell blamed each other for the lack of progress.

The hard-pressed tunneling crews started falling ill and dying. Indira, who had a summer job on the construction project as a nurse, suspected the silica rock dust from the drilling. But empires don't stop major projects on the opinion of a first year medical student.

Electricity had captured Amy's interest and she was using their royalty income from the dynamite, batteries, and blasting caps patents to equip a lab for exploring the mysterious force. Rex wished her success. Their machine shop was doing well, but with access to the ocean trade blocked, iron was scarce. His partner wanted him to find a new source.

Rex and Amy married in April. She delivered twins in mid-June with no complications. They were delighted with their two healthy lively daughters. The girls' arrival ended any residual desire he had for a return to Earth. Rex had found a home.

David C. Brown

DONNELLY'S WAR

Rex Knight, a native West Virginian and Afghan War vet, is mysteriously teleported from a peaceful surveying job to the semi-lawless frontier of an alternate Appalachia world of Civil War era technology, slavery, drugs, cotton, and competing colonial empires. The world straddling Prussian Empire, whose emperor claims to have descended from God, is vying with the sinister Ichneumon Empire for control of the North American continent.

Endangered by the clashing empires are the indigenous Wapitis. Rex is appalled by the oppression and murder inflicted on the Wapitis by James Donnelly, a warlord employed by the Ichneumons. Azure blood and social structure mark the Ichneumons as not quite human. The Wapitis, locked in a deadly struggle to avoid slavery and extinction, appeal to Rex, who looks like a Prussian, to help them obtain rifles and ammunition. Aware the Prussians hang people caught selling firearms to the Wapitis, Rex . . .

"A notable kickoff to an intriguing alternate-history series." – *Kirkus Reviews*

THE BOILERMAKER

BOILERMAKER is book two of Rex Knight, a native West Virginian and Afghan War vet, adventures after fate has mysteriously teleported him from a peaceful surveying job into a war along the semi-lawless frontier of an alternate Appalachian world of Civil War era technology, slavery, drugs, cotton, and competing colonial empires.

With Rex's help, the indigenous Wapitis have prevailed in their confrontation with warlord James Donnelly. Having survived the war between the Wapitis and the warlord's mercenaries, Rex faces the age-old human challenge of making a living in an alien world. He believes an opportunity exists in the new invention: river steamboats.

The Wapiti tribes' defeat of the warlord has alarmed the not-quite-human Ichneumons. Their emperor unleashes the Ichneumon army and network of agents to block the Wapitis' efforts to reach an accommodation with the Prussian empire. The renewed hostilities endanger Rex and threaten to wreck his efforts to make a life for himself in the violent world.

CAROOM'S RAID

Caroom's Raid is book three of Rex Knight's adventures. The steamboat, the Mischief, has a contract to deliver the Wapiti's valuable cargo of prized winter-sloe nuts to Port Delta on the Gulf coast, a voyage of 1000 kilometers down the pirate infested Erie River. East from the port, along the Gulf coast is Orleans where Rex's partner, Amy Caroom, an escaped slave wants to go. She intends to collect a debt owed her by Herr Purnell, her former owner and father.

Rex thinks Amy's idea reckless since her father has posted a large reward for her capture, dead or alive. Then the Ichneumons arrest Rex while he's collecting the gold payment for the cargo. He escapes, drugged by his partner, and wakes to find himself, the gold, and his boat in Orleans. Then there's the matter of the exploding war between the Ichneumons and Prussians empires closing the Erie River and the Ichneumon navy confiscating the gold and his Mischief.

www.ingramcontent.com/pod-product-compliance
Lightning Source LLC
Chambersburg PA
CBHW020550180626
46810CB00007B/2446
9780983190790